FAST-CHICK FLICK

A CLOSET COMEDY

COLWEN KIRST

CANDIRU CREEK PRODUCTIONS

Candiru Creek Productions
Chicago, Illinois

Publisher's Note: This is a work of fiction. Names, characters, places, and incidents are a product of the author's imagination. Locales and public names are sometimes used for atmospheric purposes. Any resemblance to actual people, living or dead, or to businesses, companies, events, institutions, or locales is completely coincidental.

Book Layout © 2017 BookDesignTemplates.com

Fast-Chick Flick: A Closet Comedy / Colwen Kirst. -- 1st ed.

ISBN 978-0-578-61826-5

*Sunt bona, sunt quaedam mediocria, sunt mala plura
quae legis hic: aliter non fit, amice, liber. Nu?*

— MARTIAL, TROLLOPE, SHMULY FINKELSTEIN

For:

Frank Harris, Elizabeth Cady Stanton, John Cleland, Jean De
Berg, Donatien Alphonse François de Sade, E.L. James, Ritter
von Leopold Sacher-Masoch, Gordon Grimley, "Oscar Wilde"
et al, Pauline Réage, the "Abbé du Prat" (Jean Barrin?) tr.
Robert Samber, Anais Nin, Georges Bataille, Stanislas de
Rhodes, Nicholson Baker, and Emmanuelle Arsan.

Dedicated to Robertson Davies. Quoting Wikipedia quoting
RD as regards opi similar to mine in "A Voice from the Attic":
"The dreariest of literature, most second hand and fusty of
experience!"

Sounds like a cover blurb to me...

PREFACE

The obvious. Why a sex comedy, and in dramatic form to boot? Well, I was about to say that it's because some A-hole got to *King Lear* before me, but...why the hell not a sex comedy? and, that in the overcrowded waters of erotic fiction it's not such an odd duck after all, it has serious provenance: the string of Renaissance and Enlightenment era "Whore Dialogues," wherein a sexual ingénue is regaled and instructed by a lady of wide and startling sophistication (*Luisa Sigea*, *Ragionamenti*, various randy nuns in sundry nunneries). Nevertheless, isn't there more than enough erotica, many centuries' worth? I agree, and I add that the right response to this sorry state of affairs can only be satire. This is satire. So, blow me.

What else. Porn is unremittingly navel-gazing, the action scenes are of a piece, and lacking in variety? I've called on each of my scenes to mock an exemplar in the field. Now the interludes are diverse, and to the extent that navels are being gazed into, I'm gazing into other people's. (Fun fact: The Marquis de Sade's was an "outie.") The urge to flip through to get to the salty parts is nigh irresistible, rendering a good chunk of the book a waste of cash? Repartee scans quickly and resists skimming, which is why I've borrowed the dialogue approach to spur the narrative. Writers of erotica walk the knife's edge of possible ridicule, resulting in work that leans toward the po-faced, the deadly earnest, the DOA? Knife's edge, phooey. I'll dance on a pin like a dissolute angel.

As for closet dramas, written to be read and not staged, these had a particular vogue during Cromwell and the Interregnum; not so much, since. Maybe I'm whimsical in penning one, I hope not, I despise whimsy. No, I despise your show of whimsy. My own whims, I'm fine with.

This collection of Whore Dialogues assumes the guise of an uncommonly gabby script for a hardcore adult production. In regulation format, the text would run to something over two hundred 8 ½ x 11 pages. By the usual calculus, one page equals one minute, a full length movie and then some. I didn't use the format, however, which like all purely functional things is fug-ugly.

I adopted the pattern of the cinematic "story porn" I've encountered: characters talk, they boink, more talk, additional boinking, talk/boink talk/boink etc, trusting readers will forgive the consequent slimness of plot, a hallmark of the genre in any case. Here and there I've repurposed lines and phrases from some of the older authors, Stanton, Sade, Barrin, and Bataille. If "sampling" can be declared a term of art, I would argue that it should be available to arts other than music. However that conversation is for another day.

The sexual passages themselves are not thoroughgoing pastiches, I think. I make no claims, am not an agile parodist. Rather, the stained specimens under my microscope are in every case those that said to me in hushed and chalky tones, *"Go and do likewise, heh-heh."* I did. And while I concede that two of the volumes were issued five years after the events of my scenario and should be disallowed, I refer complainants to Emerson's observation about foolish consistency and little minds.

And now, pintsize deity that I am, I rest. And I saith, can we not have an end to this? Enough already with the smut! If inspiration is an idea's beginning, parody is its dying breath. From first inhale to last exhale: what is left but to raze the not-so-great house of its literature and pour saltpeter on the sparking ash? Look. Trawling the category classics, we have Mysteries (elegant puzzle pieces), Science Fiction (steel-clad speculation), Horror (prehensile dreams, scuttling up the sulci*), and...Pornography? Mostly clumsy, creaky or downright clammy. Like bad sex. Or, let us troop past their respective household gods. Doyle and Simenon, Wells and Dick, Poe and Campbell. De Sade? Interesting thought, *pace* Rousseau, picked through by drearily icy-fingered atrocities.** Arsan? Sleek prose, gobshat maunderings.*** Baker is ingenious; not pukka erotica. James is...well, James.

Not all writers must walk the plank, of course. I draw a distinction between authentic erotica (scarce) and grubby fuckbooks (legion). But you know who you are, and pornographic your stuff certainly is, skull banging dewy-eyed readers with weak locutions and weaker imagery, deadening repetition, and a general air of OMIGOSH I'M DOING THIS I'M REALLY DOING THIS!

Yucky.

"But Kirst," you protest, "You abhor, you abjure, you pitch a bitch—big noise, and yet here you go adding the thickness of one more book to the top of the pile?" Um, yeah, but my onetime affection always had teeth in it, and also I suspect along the way a chill gray dawn visited me too late. I came to wonder if the action in strokers is so often much of a muchness, as they say, because the literature of arousal is unwilling to renew itself. Could it be that, as with the sex organs, its viability lies in its dogged, uncluttered utility? Sex scenes have to get the job done. The job does not vary.

I'm still glad I wrote this.

Brief historical note. John Cleland published *Fanny Hill*, swore never again to do such a thing, was duly pensioned off by a grateful John, Earl Granville and his Privy Council at £100 0s. per annum, descended in time upon Petty France, South Gloucestershire, and retired a literary gelding, fat, happy and wholesome. Donald? I'm in the book. Call me!

Sweet!

**A neat trick, libertine libertarianism—without the liberty. With respect to his mulishly celebratory, too-convenient atheism: what's to celebrate, unless a shot at free will? It's the sole upside to a godless universe. But Sade the Materialist no sooner has it than sends it packing with a gusty sigh of relief. "Since the position of Almighty is unoccupied, permit me to elevate a clockwork Nature into the role. Nature is an endless flux, She favors neither virtue nor vice, we are brick-laid by Her atom by atom, imbrued inside and out in Her and just as She made us, no better or worse. Society's warrant cannot stay us. We, Her offspring, only cede to our given selves when we ease into iniquity." (Quotation courtesy of Department of Imaginary Quotations.) Surely a sadist (the Ur-Sadist!) above everyone should see the futility of trading one brutal Master for another...

***All right, I confess. So delighted was I by Arsan's cod-philosophical yip-yappery, I wrote several equally dubious examples myself. *Bon Appétit!*

CHAPTER 1

Legend appears, white letters on a black ground:

CALIFORNIA, JANUARY 9, 2006.

Beneath it:

SAN FERNANDO VALLEY.

(Interior, Monday at Noon. To the sound of someone whistling a Cajun waltz tune, Fade In on an Office door, "Pie-Rite Pictures" stenciled on smoked glass. The door, seemingly of itself, drifts inward. Edie Gann, a petite young California [by way of Acadiana] blonde in her early twenties, with an appealing coquettish quality coupled to a frosty-verging-on-glacial presence, enters the cramped, shabby workplace. Shown from behind, she sits in a chair facing Charlie Vogel at his desk, a heavyset middle-aged man in a short-sleeved shirt and tie, with thinning hair, a Jersey accent, and a purplish mouse under his eye, lounging backward, his hands disappeared in his lap, his seedy aspect offset by a roguish charm and a room-filling personality. Throughout the dialogue to the end, we observe her from the rear; then her eyes or lips in Extreme Close Up—her face is not yet visible. After a second...)

EDIE: (warbling as she alights) *"Jolie blonde, regardez donc quoi t'as fait!"* (crosses her legs) Well?

CHARLIE: Well, Edie, I guess this is the part where I'm supposed to admit defeat and start kissing your ass.

EDIE: Yeah. This is that. (her eyes narrow) I was one of your best performers, Charlie. You fired me? (serene smile) I fired back!

CHARLIE: All right, I perchance was a smidge intemperate in my behavior. Perhaps I instigated a wee imbroglio. In truth, I'm a flawed personage, I got a negligible patch of tarnish on my otherwise sterling disposition.

EDIE: Proceed.

CHARLIE: But is that really what last week was about? Your wounded vanity? Really? I should pin a corsage on you now and hire a limo, you're such a prom queen?

EDIE: Yeah, I'm the belle of the ball.

CHARLIE: So how do I make it go away?

EDIE: I demand a dozen white roses, and a card with a love sonnet and tiny angels in the margins. (she thinks) Oh. And a ten thousand dollar signing bonus on my new contract.

CHARLIE: (stricken) L-lemme get this straight. You require I give you ten thousand extra—

EDIE: I don't require it. I just demand it. If you don't understand the difference, you don't understand women.

CHARLIE: And our long-unconsummated relationship, my high esteem for you, is of no consequence?

EDIE: Stop it, you're making my scrotum tingle.

CHARLIE: At least tell me how you did it. I already ascertained you've been romancing my girls all week. And what the hell, none of 'em will *touch* my guys anymore.

EDIE: Thus fucking you.

CHARLIE: Yeah. Fuck me. But how?

(We see her in Medium Close Up, her forehead bandaged, her stare whittling Charlie to toothpick proportions as the image Dissolves to the next scene.)

EDIE: How could I gun down your little porn studio? (beams at him) Like the detective said, it was *easy.*

(Interior, Late Morning, the Previous Monday.)

EDIE, IN VOICEOVER: You know, the thing about Viagra is, it's apropos of absolutely nothing.

(A standard Bedroom Set, tarted up as a rocket ship cabin: large fake porthole above the headboard looking out at the vasty deeps of space, futuristic bip-beep electronic music chiming in the background, multicolored lights twinkling on two bedmates.)

I mean, I call it a personal insult that I don't even need to be in the same zip code *for wood to occur.*

(A sex scene follows, involving Edie and Wülf Iliad, a macho studly type wearing a silver spray-painted bicycle helmet and attached antennae, in bed, in various positions.)

Besides which, I believe it might in fact impair one's sense of, um, propriety.

(Edie NARRATES their idyll, putting on a lunkish, surfer dude-inflected voice in blatant mockery of her partner Wülf.)

EDIE: *Sorta kinda thisaway:* I wet my lips. She was astonishing: having a fine-boned build but with large breasts, flat belly, wide hips, her legs silken, the curve of her ass perfect. The exquisite rosette of her pussy under the trim bush, blushed maidenly in my sight. She was altogether without flaw in the unforgiving iridescence. As she ambled about, all was rendered to my judgment, and I looked and looked again in boundless transport. Now she was limned in green, now in blue, in red.

I swallowed and my hand hastened of itself to the ripe sex, a flash of incomparable necessity thrilling my heart. Blind almost, I clasped her naked body, and felt her yield.

Thus encouraged, I resolved to advance my suit. Guiding her closer, my finger darted inside her; the warmth of her mouth burst upon my own; her tongue slinked in and held its secret inquests. Her arms encircled me, her sex tensed and she was mine in earnest. In an instant I had her under me, and sweeping away the bed linen we lay length to length, pulse to pulse.

Parting her knees as I mounted her, she seated my prick at her entry-way. She was ruttish I could tell, and a fire seized me too soon: lest I grow overhasty, and spirt, I thought to make a tally of her defects, scant though they were. Her eyes were a touch too big, then, her flank too narrow, her bush more shadow than substance, her cunny and dugs too rubicund and her bosom too firm to soften readily to my caresses. But all for naught. She was a pretty creature, and I could not slight her to any great degree.

Very well. I slipped in with ease, she sighed in a vexed manner, shifted, tipped herself beneath me, and drew me in to the hilt. I could have wept for joy. I thrust, she panted, the love-dew came. For a space we lay, splendidly fitted each to the other, and then I endeavored to ply my cock within her, putting it far in and back out as her legs lifted to enclose me; then, by the nicest of punctilios, I pushed farther into her; and out again, to the fleecy threshold.

Full of my desire to show her every grace, I employed brisk strokes and long luxuries in turn, and she rocked below me, submitting to all my incursions. The game played on, endless minutes. Her face shone and her breath grew ragged, the whole measure of her gripping me unrestrained. My thrill quickened. I whispered, "Bring me the bore worms!" "No, Klytus! Not the bore worms!" she moaned.

Twisting, artfully raising her delightful bottom, she seemed to want me a small way in, so in I got. But when I answered the summons, she flinched and cried out—

(Stationed behind her, Wülf adjusts his equipage.)

EDIE: (caroming sideways) Whoa, boy!

IZZY: (from Out of Shot) Cut! (the music recedes) What's the hitch?

EDIE: Where's he going with that thing?

(We see Izzy Lombardo, another transplanted New Jerseyan, athletic, dark haired, handsome except for the slaphappy expression stamped on his puss, and his four man crew, nearby in a more earthbound portion of the bedroom set: no portholes, no twinkling colors.)

IZZY: Okay, put it down to poor marksmanship. But did we not discuss the possibility?

EDIE: What're you, Wrong Way Feldman? "No" means "No!" (as the kaleidoscope effect fades and white light bathes her area of the set, she recovers her clothes and dresses. Izzy can be heard fulminating under Edie's and Wülf's byplay.)

WÜLF: Fer Chrissakes.

IZZY: *Who and what the fuck...*

EDIE: (to Wülf, facing away, over her shoulder) Shut it, you turnip-headed sad sack mope.

IZZY: *...and where does she get off...*

WÜLF: Come *on*, Edie. I could fuck a wet fart right now.

IZZY: *...and when did she become such a rare prize?*

EDIE: That's what I'm afraid of!

IZZY: (stomping toward Wülf) You mutt, you were going to surprise us with anal today? Maybe a cake next time would be better.

WÜLF: You told me!

IZZY: No you don't. In exactly what corner of Creation would I recommend *that,* with no prep-work by the girl?

WÜLF: You said before you called action, "Why not attack her other slot in the rear, with your pants-snake?"

IZZY: "With your pants-snake??" Imbecile. What I said was, "Let's try another tracking shot here, on this last take." Are you deaf as well as dumb?

WÜLF: I got the tinnitus, from the Viagra. My ears ring sometimes.

EDIE: I'll make your ears ring!

IZZY: (to Edie) Can I please handle a situation on my set?

EDIE: I don't know, can you?

IZZY: Don't you start in.

EDIE: I ask for Brad Pitt, you bring me Piltdown Man with a prophylactic!

IZZY: (pause) A moment of your precious consideration, Miss Gann. In private. (sees his cameraman tap his cell phone) You know what? Do the call.

(He and Edie leave to pursue their debate. Camera stays on Wülf. Perched on the bed, helmet in place, he finishes himself alone, muttering throughout.)

WÜLF: I'm Wülf Iliad, goddamn it... disgraceful... professional misconduct... could be home in Encino... Encino... Lompoc... uh... Anaheim... mmm... Azusa... Azusa... ahh... *Azusa*...

(Edie and Izzy reach the outskirts of the bedroom.)

IZZY: I'm telling you for the last time—

WÜLF: (from Off Screen, where they direct a couple of disinterested glances) *Cuca-monga!*

EDIE: "Poor marksmanship," Izzy? Don't even. I made a choice, everyone can deal with it.

IZZY: Did the man get a trifle boisterous? He did. It was trifling, a piffle, a fraction of one piffle, but yes. He did undoubtedly trifle with you. (speculates) Possibly halfway from a trifle to a piffle. And you're upset, and I can emphasize with you. But it was a misunderstanding, pure and simple. Nobody is laying in wait to steal the brown crown jewel you hide between your processional objects!

EDIE: Misunderstanding, yeah. One like that is one too many. The bigger issue is, I expect real men who can stand and deliver, as opposed to these broke-dick show ponies you insist on handing me.

IZZY: (to crew) Singin' her favorite song! (to Edie) How often I gotta—Viagra is a boon to the industry. Pointin' to Poughkeepsie for four hours straight? Priceless! What, we should await Your Highness's pleasure? Viagra, Levitra, Cialis, it's like we tossed some magic beans at the guys and whoosh! all of a sudden there's a monster stalk for you to climb. It's a fairy tale come true. So why can't you ever, ever lay the fuck down, bat your baby blues and think of England, and a few pops later we could be home drinking Ovaltine and watching Mister SquarePants!

EDIE: (folding her arms, stroking her chin) Let me rephrase your statement as I understood it: "Blah blah blah yack yack jibber jabber jibber."

IZZY: What the fuck? Seriously, are you too dumb to learn, or too ill to try? Which is it?

EDIE: Well, I'll tell you. In 2005 the School of Medicine at Johns Hopkins University did a six month randomized triple blind study, and they were able to determine to a two point five percent margin of error that my shit actually doesn't stink.

IZZY: (downloading the data) Remarkable. No aroma at all?

EDIE: It's delicately scented. Like a field of daffodils.

IZZY: Okay, okay.

EDIE: You could run barefoot through my feces.

IZZY: Yes. Got it. Thank you. (to the crew) Take ten! (he scratches his jaw, attempts an oleaginous smile) You know, I dunno, it's feasible you are too smart for porn.

EDIE: Is that the theory?

IZZY: Starting to be.

EDIE: That's the rumor.

IZZY: The buzz, yeah. Carries on like she's too smart for porn. Reading books during scene setups? I'm getting a contact higher education just talking to you.

EDIE: Erotica. It's a headspace thing. Helps me fuck on camera for a film crew that looks like third string rejects from "The Rocky Horror Picture Show."

IZZY: Still. Letting six years of my experience speak to you, (upraised finger) "Man cannot masturbate and cogitate at the same time," is my theory.

EDIE: (smirks) Where'd you get that? From a rhyming dictionary?

IZZY: I'm just saying. Why can't you be more like the other babes? Like, for example, Derrien? She's cute, she's ingratiating, she's...obliging, she's everything you seek in a slut!

EDIE: (sage acceptance) She's a sunbeam with sugar tits. She's a rainbow in a butt thong.

IZZY: Go ahead make fun. When this girl walks in, she lights up the room.

EDIE: (mock alarm) She's a pyromaniac?

IZZY: What? No, she's charming. She has a pleasant disposition.

EDIE: If you like her so much, why don't you marry her?

IZZY: Maybe I will.

EDIE: Maybe you should.

IZZY: Maybe I will.

EDIE: Maybe you should!

IZZY: All right, truce. (he lowers his voice) Anyway, I'd personally rail you even without Viagra.

EDIE: Wow. The ultimate compliment. (she sees someone Off Screen) And, here's Doctor Detroit.

IZZY: (looking) Hi, Boss.

(Charlie enters.)

CHARLIE: (to Edie) The fuck are you doing? Why do I have to come here, again?

EDIE: "Good morning," Charlie.

CHARLIE: (to Izzy) What happened?

IZZY: (cocks his head at Craft Services, where a denuded Wülf is tucking into a very tasty blueberry blintz) Rear guard offensive.

CHARLIE: (to Edie) Keepin' it like the Kaiser. All right, Princess, you want him gone? (to Wülf) Scram! (to Edie) You want I should consume his firstborn child? (to Wülf) Hey, set an extra place at dinner tonight, and remember I like mashed potatoes with my toddler! (Wülf skulks out) (to Edie) Satisfied? More? What? Ariel—

EDIE: Edie.

CHARLIE: (waving it off) Irrelevant. I'm a man with a broad view beneath my noble brow, I don't sit in judgment, but it seems to me your whole diva shtick is pretty tired. Not to mention you disrespect me in front of the help with that "Doctor Demento" crap.

IZZY: Uh, Doctor Detroit.

CHARLIE: Shuddup. (to Edie) This'll be a shock to your system, sweetpea: I got afflictions of my own, I don't need to double dip.

EDIE: Well aren't you The World's Forgotten Boy.

CHARLIE: (quizzical inspection) Excuse me, did you fall down the wrong rabbit hole by mistake? We do pornos here, speedy and cheap, the way our Lord and Savior "Nekron the Death God" intended.

EDIE: I—

CHARLIE: You know what most people's motto is? "Good enough is good enough." Wanna know what my motto is? "Not good enough is good enough." (indicates Izzy) This bozo gets it. You, you gotta run around and bitch and moan and piss all over my cabbage patch. For what? I don't smoke. I don't snort.

I don't gamble. If I don't shoot fuck films, what have I got left? The monastery?

EDIE: They even *have* monks in the Church of Satan?

CHARLIE: Funny. Your problem is, you think you're the hero of your own biographical saga. But when they compose your bio, honeybuns, the main character will be me. And whilst you examine the crust whereupon your bread is buttered, let's riffle through your resume from eight months ago, shall we? An outcall stripper, with ten web photosets, one amateur video, and zero prospects. I made you. And he who makes, can also break.

EDIE: (death stare)

CHARLIE: You're giving me The Look? Shake it off. Ingest a bromide. You don't get what a sugary setup you stumbled into, and where's the gratitude? You work when you wanna work, you flake when you wanna flake, you got a No List longer than Plastic Man's pecker, but I'm still waitin' for my "Thank You" card. I'm famished! Where's my box of chocolates? Where's my spray of chrysanthemums? (leaning into her ear) I WANT MY GODDAMN CHYSANTHEMUMS!

EDIE: (gruesome bloody dismemberment stare)

CHARLIE: (scowling in the direction of the departed Wülf) What's more, I've been supremely understanding about you buttoning up the back door of your PJ's. Now, I hear you won't even vaginate with the guys I hire.

EDIE: (exasperated) Pill poppers, Charlie. They're tainted meat.

CHARLIE: Yeah, and there's dolphin in my tuna salad. So we're agreed life is cruel, right? (he moves closer, *sotto voce*) Or maybe I should eliminate a world of hurt with a pair of words. What do you say?

EDIE: (mystified for a millisecond, then it registers) Fuck you. I've got a contract.

CHARLIE: (leafing through his memory book) Which you've repeatedly broken, ad infinitum, ad quod damnum. And I quote: Section Seven A, Paragraph Two.

EDIE: Next to the Morals Clause?

CHARLIE: (after an interval) It's good that we can have these intermittent chitchats. (he turns away, turns back) Oh, just occurred to me. Before I forget? You're fired! (he exits)

(She glares after him, furious.)

Botherations, botherations.

IZZY: Edie?

EDIE: Go to hell. (she storms out)

(Dissolve to Interior, Early Afternoon Monday, Edie's Place. During Narration, a Montage of Edie entering her home, a modestly dapper, stylish condo, accelerating toward the liquor cabinet, pouring a shot, pondering her options.)

Call Pat Ramsey's agency, hunt for a new studio gig? No rush. I was about to ask for a week or two off anyhow, schedule some personal appearances or whatnot. But I honestly felt at that moment that it behooved me to investigate the possibility of making you severely regret your way-over-the-top rabidly inappropriate response to my totally mature and thoroughly reasonable behavior. It had become a sort of David versus Goliath thing we were doing.

CHARLIE: (muttering) Godzilla versus Tokyo...

EDIE: You asserting an opinion?

CHARLIE: No.

EDIE: Good. Because in the civilian zone, Charlie? You know, where "face cream" is something women have on before they get into bed? An innocent young damsel such as me has to protect herself from villainous types who would do her harm.

(She leans on the cabinet, reflecting.)

She has to go on the offensive.

(Finishes her drink.)

She has to seize the initiative.

EDIE: Think so, Charlie?

She has to use somebody's balls for egg batter.

(Smacks the glass on the cabinet.)

EDIE: I think not!

Botherations, botherations. What I needed was a game plan. No, I needed a war council.

(Montage, of Edie in her bathroom showering, in her bedroom changing clothes, replacing her previous heavy makeup with lighter.)

What's a lady do, Charlie, when she's itching to slam a guy, and plot his downfall, and in general speak a lot of unholy shit about him?

(Leaving her home.)

She has a night out with the girls, of course.

(Exterior Shot, Late Afternoon, of a Neighborhood Watering Hole, "Spirits on Rox" running down a vertical sign.)

And that evening, the girl under discussion was my British stablemate and fellow contract star, Kit Wormwood (Tildy

Higginbotham, on her green card), who was holding court as
usual at the "Spirits on Rox" bar, downtown.

(Interior, Bar. Edie walks through the clubby, affable crowd,
acknowledging the regulars. Ed Tragos, a broad-beamed
boomy-baritoned ruddy-faced thatch-haired deckle-edged
stubbly barroom graybeard, falls in step beside her. The rest of
their progression is spasmodic.)

ED: Eden Gann, as I live and breathe! Eden and Ed, together
again for the first time!

EDIE: Drunk.

ED: Edie, my sis' from another Miss! My twin from another
kin!

EDIE: Quit talking.

ED: My sib' from another crib?

EDIE: Wait. You're almost sober. Cut off, huh?

ED: The cheese don't grow on trees, poopsie. (eyetooth-baring
grin) Ready to do the interview you promised me?

EDIE: I told you, have *MEH* send some questions. Done. But
from a journalist. Not a glorified professional mook.

ED: (nettled) You swipe at the Gordian knot that is my heart. I
tell you, said heart is a constant bubble rolled out of raw suet,

spackling paste, and a bagful of tenpenny nails. No, not a bubble, it's a bible, a vest pocket bible of but a single verse: (*Sprechgesang*) "Weaver of wiles, I beg you, do not crush my spirit..."

EDIE: Blow. (she strides away)

ED: (calling) "Release me from my agony..." *Rats!* (he off-loads at the opposite end of the bar)

(Edie approaches Tildy Higginbotham, an attractive middle aged brunette with a rotund British accent and a grande dame manner, slouched on a stool, tipsy, alongside a nondescript man, in the midst of being hit upon.)

TILDY: Edie, doll! Meet my new best mate. This is Rusty, Rusty Trombone.

MAN: It's Jack Fletcher. Hello. (he smiles at Edie, who is oblivious to him throughout the conversation)

TILDY: Mister Felcher.

MAN: Fletcher.

TILDY: Quite. Now, I'll have a tossed salad and a bowl of donkey punch.

MAN: I...they don't serve salads, and I've never heard of the second.

TILDY: And for my friend, a six pack and a pair of tea bags?

MAN: I don't...it's a bar.

TILDY: You see, I have my Hummer parked outside, and I left a perfectly comely pearl necklace in the back seat. So make like a flying camel and quick quick quick, get us a hot lunch.

MAN: It's a bar, it's not a bar and grill. It's not a pub.

TILDY: Not a snowball's chance, then?

MAN: I'm sorry.

TILDY: (gazing at him with some merriment, in a goo-goo voice) You're adorable, my little blumpkin. Aren't you Mummy's little blumpkin? Yes, you *are*.

(He looks at Edie.)

EDIE: Never mind. Get us two beers, please. Make hers a near beer.

MAN: Right.

EDIE: And go away.

MAN: Go?

TILDY: Scat! That's thirteen.

MAN: (to Edie) After I buy you drinks?

EDIE: Sport, any other time I'd give you a real frisky night in exchange for one free beer. But today I'm afraid I'm going through The Curse.

TILDY: The woman's curse! Our monthly mutual dividend!

MAN: The curse?

EDIE: The curse of being constantly drooled on by chuckleheads who refuse to take "Fuck you" for an answer.

(Awkward silence as he absorbs this concussion.)

TILDY: Ouch.

MAN: (pause) You ladies have a pleasant evening. (he vamooses)

TILDY: 'Night. (to Edie) Why so nasty, Sanchez?

(Edie settles on the stool next to her.)

EDIE: It's a "Dirty Sanchez," and do not start your nonsense with me, Tildy. I've had a rough day.

TILDY: No, luv. What day is it?

EDIE: Monday.

TILDY: And Monday is Tildy's day to beef, is it not?

EDIE: The "age" issue again? Excuse the expression, isn't this subject getting pretty old? (she motions "no thanks" to the Bartender's wordless offer of a libation. He retreats to Ed's end of the bar.)

TILDY: Hardly.

(Cut to Ed, corkscrewing forward, fumbling for the beer tap. He's curtailed by the Barman.)

ED: (stainless virtue, innocent curiosity) Where *is* that bowl of nuts?

BARTENDER: No shoes, no shirt, no scratch—no service. Go on talking, though, talk is cheap.

ED: Yeah, too cheap to cover a drink. (to the room at large) Why rouse myself to scintillate like a star, to coruscate like the sun, damn you, in the country of the blind? (his survey encompasses the mob)

BARTENDER: Nuts.

ED: Huh?

BARTENDER: Nuts? (slides the bowl to him)

ED: (still bloviating) Shall I sow my confidences on the low grasses, cropped by a creature satisfied to be a crook staff to the vulgar herd? Seducing drunkards into yet more drinking? How laggardly.

(A fanfare of raspberries is trumpeted by way of reply.)

ED: Unlike you, I have ambition. Call me a "Man of the Middle Distance." (they ignore him)

BARTENDER: Keep your stool until someone with an account balance gets sore feet, you're welcome, but the house won't carry you another cent.

ED: Your stool and my piles are at present engaged in a contretemps, thou lickspittle. A cordial? A tot of the good stuff? To anneal my, um, fundament?

BARTENDER: No.

ED: All right. I don't require it. I want it. They need it, my co-conspirators. (tilts his head at two adjacent inebriates, pallid quivering apparitions slamming down scotch upon scotch) You know how we obtain our living? We review videos for *Mature Entertainment Headlines*, the periodical. Can you divine how many discs *MEH* receives each twelvemonth? Eight thousand. Here's a free lesson in basic arithmetic. Subtracting weekends and holidays, vacations and the random sick day, there are about two hundred forty working days in a year. After official and unofficial downtime, six solid working hours daily, one thousand four hundred forty hours per year. Eight thousand vids divided by three wage slaves equals two thousand, six hundred and sixty six. That's one-point-eight-five pornos per hour. Round it up to allow for popping DVDs in and out, and breaking the shrink wrap with ever more arthritic fingers, and you get a different sex vid viewed each half hour for every hour on every day in every month of every year of our professional lives. Let me show you something.

(He pivots toward his workmates.)

ED: FELLATIO!

(One of the two screams. The other faints dead away.)

ED: Really, at this juncture they're more animal than man.

BARTENDER: Not you.

ED: No. I have ambitions; I can see past the scrim. And what do I see, but a trade eager for a scribe to tell its tale. Because I want in on the features department at any of the remaining men's magazines, each rosy dick to me is a pen dripping ink, and each open cooze is a page opening on my byline. However opportunity is scarce, understand?

BARTENDER: Post a blog. Everybody is a writer nowadays, if they call themselves a writer, am I wrong?

ED: Yes, on the internet everybody and his six-toed cousin is a writer, and there's the rub. When everything is condoned, nothing much counts. But print publishers are the gatekeepers, the surety, the signpost for quality *belles-lettres*. That will never change. And all I require is a story to tell them. (he casts a wormy glance at the two women at the end of the bar)

(Cut to Edie and Tildy.)

TILDY: I was exactly like you, darling. Young and innocent.

EDIE: That's definitely me.

TILDY: Innocence! But it wore off. (reflects) It was probably rubbed off.

EDIE: You're fine, Tildy.

TILDY: Did I ever tell you I used to be a legitimate actress, Ed'?

EDIE: Once or twice. Per week.

TILDY: My acting coach had a theory, he called it the theory of the "Dirty Buddy." Which is the feller in the film who follows the hero about. Less clever, less fit, less chic. For the contrast—the toadstool, next to the tulip. And through the decades, this is what I've descended to. Your Dirty Buddy.

EDIE: Tildy, you're not my Dirty Buddy, and you're not a toadstool!

TILDY: I'm a crow's foot away from doing MILF videos, dear. For a lady in porn, that's the OK Corral.

EDIE: Which videos? MILF?

TILDY: Ear to the ground, my girl. It's the latest thing. Carnal kiddies and bearded biddies.

EDIE: All right, if you–

TILDY: (theatrical moon-baying) MILF videos! Ohhh, the humanity!

EDIE: If you believe that, why not move on? Not even fucking is forever.

TILDY: (backpedaling) Well, one doesn't want to leap overboard, that is, it doubtless awaits careful study, and, um, well...

(Zzzt! A neon beer display sputters to life above Edie. Her Narration continues on top of Tildy's demurs.)

TILDY: ...because manhood... a man's... the male element... is... like to love and... the male element... held high... run riot... overpowering the feminine... manhood and womanhood... the hard... feel... in the... condition of... that man, who... will make the women... strong... long... man feeds woman... try to please... his condition... must be as near... man as possible... his... vices... strip her... she must look... accept... and make... them... all this... corruption... to desire... some business... hard, grinding... man... needed... excesses... bitterness... selfishness... need... purity, virtue, morality... action... first step toward... health, strength, and prosperity... I... wish... all men are hard... and brutal... the most beautiful... with manhood... would hold all these... a constant effort... the... heat... an extension... of the... men... better... sex alone...

And that's when it hit me, in idle conversation. Maybe that's how all the Important Ideas came about: Shoe trees. Press On Nails. Making you my prison-bitch. I thought, If it's war Charlie's waging, let it be a war of attrition. He has five contract girls left, and the year's big Adult Entertainment Expo in Vegas, where he's planning to show them off, launches in a matter of days. What I'm gonna do is, I'm gonna cut a lamb from his fold, day after day, one after another, and when he's got nothing to shoot but the breeze I'll ask him, "How you like me now, 'honeybuns'?"

I mean, Tildy didn't say she wouldn't *quit the industry. And if all she required was a tiny bit of courage, I could certainly supply the* Dutch *kind.*

EDIE: (to Bartender) Whiskey, please! (she taps the bar) And leave the bottle.

(Cut to Ed's end of the bar. He waits for the Barman's return.)

ED: What was that?

BARTENDER: That was some people enjoying a snoot full. I've come to realize over the years that every once in a great while, I am privy to such goings-on.

ED: It looks more like the short Yank getting the tall Brit drunk.

BARTENDER: Hold on. (answers imaginary telephone) Hello? (sticks it out) The Pulitzer committee is on the line.

ED: (touches his nose) Something's up. You keen to earn a fat twenty dollar tip?

BARTENDER: You mean, add twenty to your tab?

(Ed places a twenty on the bar.)

BARTENDER: Motherfucker. (he flashes a paring knife) Who do we know who's outlived his usefulness?

ED: Do this: swing your childbearing hips in the direction of our two acquaintances, bivouac there until you're a swollen hive of hearsay, sashay back, stretch wide your pillowy blowjob lips, and don't slacken them unless I'm a wiser man.

(The Bartender snags the bill and sets off on his mission.)

ED: (noticing his two cohorts, revived and recovered) DOUBLE PENETRATION!

MEN: Aaaahh!!

(Dissolve to Interior, Early Evening Monday, Charlie's Office, Charlie at his desk and Izzy seated.)

CHARLIE: (to his cell phone, on speaker) I'm *writin'* it down, Moira.

FEMALE VOICE: Ay. Tee. Arr.

CHARLIE: (not writing at all) I've got a deliberate hand, sue me.

VOICE: Oh. Pee.

CHARLIE: Don't spell it. Give me that, at least. Don't spell.

VOICE: Oh.

CHARLIE: (still not writing) Done. Done. Next Monday, twelve thirty pm. With bells on. (hangs up)

IZZY: I'm—

(The office speakerphone buzzes: Charlie hammers at a button.)

CHARLIE: Hold yer water, I'll be with ya in a minute! (makes traffic cop "Stop" signal, at the entire world. To self:) Simmer. Simmer...

IZZY: I'm here why?

CHARLIE: Because of the slow economy, Pie-Rite is hitting the market and a sale is imminent. As a result, the High Command has spoken from above. I've begun thinning the herd around here, awright? Cutting costs and severing craniums. That dim bulb three-eyed two-headed gash jockey Wülf Iliad, he's on probation. My secretary Shirl is on vacation, it might become permanent, we'll see. I'm making due. You infer where I'm going?

IZZY: (his shoulders sink) Uh-oh.

CHARLIE: Relax, your cranium is screwed on, more or less. But I'm gonna require you to commence doing extra duties from now on. In front of the camera as well as behind.

IZZY: Okay, could be. As you may be aware, I started a performer.

CHARLIE: Of this I'm aware. Izzy "The Crowbar" Lombardo. Matter of fact, you were a very reliable stickman back in the day.

IZZY: Plus I could act.

CHARLIE: Yeah? Somebody get me a paper bag, so I can demonstrate what you couldn't act your way out of.

TILDY'S VOICE, on speakerphone: Charles!

IZZY: Thanks a lot. If I'm being honest, ehh, been there, done that.

CHARLIE: Don't be such a blushing bride. You know the drill: tell your Andrew Johnson to rise and salute the flag, and soon you'll be gettin' more pussy than a pasha.

IZZY: (hopeful) I'll be a potentate?

CHARLIE: You'll be the Sultan of Bumfuck, Egypt!

TILDY'S VOICE: Hel-*lo?*

CHARLIE: Wha'd I say? Inna minute!

IZZY: (deep breath) As a charter member of the big dick club, I humbly accept.

CHARLIE: Good, good. (picks up a pencil stub, scribbles) By the by. Not for nuthin,' you're a prisoner of your fantasies, you got astigmatism, whatever. But I've seen your putz, and for a porn star, it ain't such a much.

IZZY: What!

CHARLIE: No offense, but the late John Holmes laughs from the grave at your midget penis. (illustrates by dangling the stub from his fingers) No offense.

TILDY: Holmes?

IZZY: Gee, none taken. I guess.

CHARLIE: Need a jeweler's glass to see that tiny schmekel.

IZZY: Please stop.

CHARLIE: And I'm promoting you to my PA, my adjutant. Teach you the business end.

IZZY: Great.

CHARLIE: No raise. There's your first lesson. (to phone, affecting a musical mealy-mouth manner) Pie-Rite Pictures, Charlie Vogel speaking, how might I assist?

TILDY: (drunk to the point of suspended animation) Charles, you odious lump!

CHARLIE: Whozzat?

TILDY: You squalid horrible man. You bleb. You blister. You parboiled pustule!

CHARLIE: 'Scuse me?

TILDY: You Paleolithic sausage peddler!

CHARLIE: Kit, this you?

TILDY: Steaming, liver colored loaf of elephant flop. You gorgon. You gargoyle. Which are you, a gorgon or a gargoyle? Could you possibly be so hideous you turned *yourself* into stone?

CHARLIE: You know, I'm starting to get my feelings hurt a little bit, here.

TILDY: I quit, I...I quit! I resign! Goodbye.

CHARLIE: You quit? What, is it Monday? Your weekly resignation?

TILDY: I have outgrown the life.

CHARLIE: Nah, you got a few more miles left on you before I trade you in.

TILDY: MILF! MILF! MILF!

CHARLIE: (to Izzy) I think she's speaking in tongues. (to phone) Yeah, milf-milf to you too, honey. Now find someplace to sleep it off, and I expect to see your sagging flesh on my set tomorrow morning. (hangs up) Believe that? How dare she? Doesn't she realize this is my personal fiefdom?

IZZY: Say again?

CHARLIE: Fiefdom. You're sittin' in it.

IZZY: I'm the fief?

CHARLIE: (saint-like patience) No, you're the peasant. I'm the feudal overlord.

IZZY: Why can't I be the fief?

CHARLIE: Doesn't work that way. So from tomorrow on I'm going to presuppose you to be–

IZZY: I'd...I'd still really like to be the fief...

CHARLIE: –Shut the fuck up.

(Cut to Exterior of Tildy's House, Monday Night, Camera Zooming in.)

EDIE NARRATES: *One down, four to go. At Tildy's place Monday night, I—*

CHARLIE: *Wait a minute, wait a minute. That was the second time you've repeated a conversation you weren't there to hear. How can you be describing an exchange you weren't present at?*

EDIE: *Chill, Charlie. Everybody's going to fast forward through this shit anyhow.*

CHARLIE: *Oh yeah, right.*

EDIE: *After I poured her in a cab and escorted her home, she got somewhat sentimental on me. This'll happen when your blood alcohol level is—well, by then her blood didn't have an alcohol level anymore. The alcohol in her veins had a teensy blood level.*

(Cut to Interior of Tildy's messy Living Room, a study in clash and clutter, where she lolls half-sprawled on the settee, Edie standing upwind of her, arms crossed.)

TILDY: (slurring her words) ...would do for me quite nicely, please and thank you, and, oh my dear, I'm away to sunnier climes.

EDIE: Mm-hmm.

TILDY: One more drink, Ed', and we'll piss off.

EDIE: You live here.

TILDY: Darling, I'm a mite squiffy. (peers at her) You've noticed, have you? (she struggles to sit up straight)

EDIE: Need an airlift?

TILDY: (abandons the effort) Ah, John Holmes. *Urp!* I'll bet those were the days.

EDIE: Save that thought for tomorr—

TILDY: Those *were* the days. Did you know, Edie, that a six-man team of Nepalese Sherpas once led a climbing expedition up the north face of his willy?

EDIE: That's it. I'm putting you to bed.

TILDY: Oh, punkin', I didn't know you cared. Rowf!

EDIE: Hmmm. (considers) If I fuck you?

TILDY: Wouldn't be the first time.

EDIE: Will you promise to settle down and get some sleep?

TILDY: I shall lapse into a perfect coma. No vital signs whatever. (sinks into the cushions like a quicksand victim) Come to Mumsy...

(Sex scene, Edie initiating oral. Momentarily...)

TILDY: Talk to me, luv. Sexy talk.

EDIE: Um, okay.

TILDY: Seduce me.

EDIE: Er, it's not my usual thing.

TILDY: Best shot.

(Rubbernecking around for inspiration, Edie spies a dozen bottles of wine in a miniature casier close by, their labels visible. She ululates on Tildy as she speaks, peeking now and again at the bottles.)

EDIE: I admire your big jugs?

TILDY: Do you? Tell me more.

EDIE: I'm going to kiss you all the way from your big jugs to your, uh, your tawny port.

TILDY: Mmm. My tawny port. You like?

EDIE: Oh yes. I love your tawny port. And your nappy valley.

TILDY: Lick my nappy valley, darling. Lick it.

EDIE: Mmm.

TILDY: You adore my little rose, yes?

EDIE. Yes, your petit rosé is delicious. Mmmm...

TILDY: Mmmm... This is my favorite sex talk ever!

(Edie NARRATES in a very dodgy English accent.)

EDIE: Well warmed by the dozen shots of whisky she had pressed upon me, my heart relinquished any tumult or dismay as my inamorata's lips roved about the further part of me, exploring everywhere at once. Her tongue called out my very essence below, scolding the tinder of my disposition into a heat past enduring. I lay, enchanted every way, stretched on a rack of delight, given so to her expert attentions that my whole apprehension of myself went to that fevered niche, where I lived entire, lost in joy, more mechanism than maid. Edie wrought with so winsome a skill that my loins trembled, the ecstasy reared up and searched out each fibre of my substance to the utmost; a fabulous, a superb madness! Then the gale ranged over the bow of my faculties and sent a lightning strike into my aft deck, so I vibrated in my bliss and could not move.

She embraced me and I held her desperately, my lips wandering her face in an anguish of beggary, muttering small encouragements whilst her cosseting tested the last of my resolve. I was a beast tamed by her care, a spark dancing in the blaze of her passion. My eye sought her bosom. What lush fruits hung there! And the downy fur beneath them, oh, the sweet singing glow nestled within! I was beyond bearing, beyond everything! Edie took my hand and positioned it at her castle keep, I felt the moat-bridge dampness there, and she amused herself by guiding my movements until the invasion was complete. Now my little bawd flung her body onto me and breathed in me such a kiss that her soul mingled with my own, and we were one; meantime her fingers were bold thieves, clicking the tender pin which safeguarded my modesty.

Honing her caresses, Edie struck the flint of my mortal lamina into a flame kindling us both, mindless and fierce, raging across her flesh as to devastate it. She rose to my predations, transported, and after another humid kiss she threw her arms about me and her sex met mine in an access of desire so immoderate it caused her to gasp and flash her sharp teeth, and with a spirited cry I joined her in the incandescent tabernacle which rests atop the wildest exultations, supervising all, daring the tempest to touch its steeple, and Oh! What ambrosial pleasure! What impossible, what mad revelry! The tide wholly overtook the ramparts of our senses, and together, thoroughly spent by our exertions, we succumbed to deepest sleep...

CHAPTER 2

(Dissolve to Interior, Charlie's Office, Late Tuesday Morning. Charlie at his desk. Izzy walks in.)

CHARLIE: Lom-BAR-do! "Time is the fire in which we burn," says the poet Schwartz.

IZZY: Beg pardon?

CHARLIE: Why are you here contributing to my destruction?

IZZY: I thought you'd want to hear, Kit Wormwood was a no-show today. I used Derrien in her place.

CHARLIE: (dismissive) Aah, she'll be back, no worries. (flicks at a chair by the door) Park yer farts right there, chum.

IZZY: Two days into the week, and her and Edie too? (sits)

CHARLIE: Who?

IZZY: Edie. Eden Gann. You know, "Ariel Caliban."

CHARLIE: Ariel, she's one less check I gotta write. As for Kit, that old bedspread was gettin' kinda threadbare at any rate, if you catch my drift.

IZZY: That's rough, man.

CHARLIE: She called me a gargoyle, Izzy. If I were carved out of stone, would I be weeping these tears of sadness you distinguish hereupon my kisser?

IZZY: (unimpressed) I don't see any tears.

CHARLIE: Inside, you mug. Behind my clown paint, I'm a waterworks.

IZZY: You require a minute?

CHARLIE: (giving up the act) Nah, I'll muddle through.

IZZY: Okay, uh, I also cooked up some pitches to run by you.

CHARLIE: What, now?

IZZY: Yeah.

CHARLIE: Fine, good. (gazing above Izzy, his expression lights up) Why, look: I see before me an envelope. (glances at him) Start pushin' it!

IZZY: It's a gonzo. All fisting, all the time. As much as we can get away with. It's called, "Get Yer Mitt Off My Clit!"

CHARLIE: (suspicious) Fisting?

IZZY: As much as we can get away with.

CHARLIE: Which is how much? I'm a law-abiding citizen, within reason, as you know.

IZZY: Four fingers, one and a half knuckles each.

CHARLIE: A half a knuckle? What's a half a knuckle?

IZZY: It's one half of a knuckle, one half.

CHARLIE: You're the one being fisted, it's either a knuckle or it ain't. Either p or q.

IZZY: Sure. An exclusive rather than an inclusive disjunction.

CHARLIE: Of course. What're you, an idiot?

IZZY: He goes in past the first knuckle, goes halfway to the second knuckle.

CHARLIE: That's—

IZZY: That's half a knuckle. What would you call it?

CHARLIE: That's half a knuckle.

IZZY: Certainly!

CHARLIE: Don't you reside halfway from here to Whittier? Does that make you a half-Whit?

IZZY: The idea is—

CHARLIE: Next.

IZZY: N-Next?

CHARLIE: Next.

IZZY: Um, right, um, I've got one, scene after scene of girls getting off by inserting foreign objects in themselves. I call it "Conduct Unbecoming an Orifice."

CHARLIE: Once again, we are teetering at the far edge of what is acknowledged to be legal, in word if not yet in deed.

IZZY: Huh?

CHARLIE: You're gonna get my ass arrested.

IZZY: No, no, I can work this. Think about it: if we ourselves create objects which didn't exist, they can't be foreign because we get to say what they are. *Capisce?*

CHARLIE: No.

IZZY: We manufacture 'em, we use 'em such and such way. We get to say they're sex toys. That's the function, what they're there for. We define their whole, um, identity.

CHARLIE: (arm up, model student/Hitler Youth-style) That would be Identity in the ideological, or the ontological sense?

IZZY: The, uh...

CHARLIE: Just so we're on the same fuckin' page, here.

IZZY: Whichever.

CHARLIE: But not only function is important, but form, so phallic-looking, correct? Or else a judge might throw a fit and issue a writ.

IZZY: Relax, they watch enough of our porn, everything starts looking phallic.

CHARLIE: (points down) My stapler?

IZZY: Phallic. Wasn't a stapler, it could be a dildo.

CHARLIE: Yowch. My name plate, my computer mouse?

IZZY: I'm so turned on by the contents of your desk right now.

CHARLIE: Howsoever, in the Platonic conception sex toys do exist already as Ideal Forms. It could be argued you created nothing original, in essence you produced a particular physical manifestation of an Ideal. And if Ideas and Forms exist in the mind of God, who Himself conceived of the Butt Hook, the Penis Sleeve, and the Prostate Massager, does this not reduce your creativity to mere craftsmanship?

IZZY: (blinks rapidly)

CHARLIE: And is the notion of originality rendered an empty construct? Because to define "creativity" as the channeling of Ideas which God thought up, like the Nipple Electrode or the Human Pony Harness, should be a contradiction in terms. Or how do we create at all, if the argument is valid that Ideas about Forms are recollections of inborn knowledge?

IZZY: (bubbles spout in retinas)

CHARLIE: And yet if God by definition created, and therefore is outside of, space and time, is it meaningful to say He conceived of Spiked Ball Stretchers and Inflatable Anal Plugs before you did?

IZZY: (steam whistles out of ears)

CHARLIE: For if He knows all events simultaneously in an eternal present, then you and God must have conceived of Ben Wa Balls, Anal Beads, Urethral Plugs, and Wireless Waterproof Remote Control Vibrating Love Eggs, at the same instant.

IZZY: (eyeballs dance about in sockets)

CHARLIE: Or is God, as Professor William Lane Craig of Talbot School of Theology suggests, atemporal without Creation and with probably very limited vested interest in sexual paraphernalia, and temporal since Creation? And if Aristotle's "Third Man" expostulation is on target, does not the

Theory of Forms lead to an infinite regress in any case? And, insoforasmuch as everything including ideas is dependent on God, in a hierarchical intendment, are we not returned to—

IZZY: (Fillings drip out of teeth. Braincase dissolves into magma. Fissures appear in skull.)

CHARLIE: Take a breath.

IZZY: (Shudders. Eyes regain their focus.)

CHARLIE: Welcome back. Anyways. We create them, we assign them an identity, and we say they're sex toys.

IZZY: Yup.

CHARLIE: Nope.

IZZY: Nope?

CHARLIE: Nope. (slides forward) May I coo a dove-like note of dissent?

IZZY: Yes, you may.

CHARLIE: Might I tickle your eardrum with a dainty paradiddle?

IZZY: Yes, you might.

CHARLIE: The envelope that I propose you to push does not have the name "San Quentin" in the address. It does not contain a "Go Directly to Jail" card inside.

IZZY: I have one more.

CHARLIE: Oh, good.

IZZY: (speaking magniloquently) Let my concept I'm about to say float in the ether around you, Boss. Allow it to percolate through your cerebellum. Are you ready?

CHARLIE: Ready.

IZZY: I call it "Babes in Toiletland." It's like Japanese bukkake videos, except instead of a bunch of guys cumming on the girl's face, they—

CHARLIE: Meeting adjourned!

(Cut to Interior, Entrance Door to Tildy's Home, Tuesday Noon. The Bell is Rung. Tildy, in a bathrobe, slippers, and desultory curlers, wearing no makeup, enters the Shot and cracks the door.)

TILDY: This is my lazy day, luv.

VOICE of ED TRAGOS: 'Morn...um, afternoon to you.

TILDY: Lazy day, lazy day, my darling.

ED: I happily stipulate I'll impose on your generosity for half the proverbial tick, lovely lady.

TILDY: Oh for Heaven's sake. If you've sunk to base flattery, we may as well hide your shame under my roof. (she slips the chain, he lumbers in)

ED: My name is Ed Tragos, Mister Tragos. (she offers a wan smile and a limp handclasp) I'm employed by *Mature Entertainment Headlines.*

TILDY: Yes, of course, I remember you.

(He escorts her to a humpbacked leather chesterfield. They sit.)

ED: My reputation, paltry as it is, has preceded me?

TILDY: Your aroma has preceded you. (sniffs) An ambulatory beer-battered flounder, dipped in sauce and twitching on my couch.

ED: Better a flounder than a bounder, my dear. If I were an oyster, I'd say "Shucks."

TILDY: I suppose that'll pass for wit on a slow Tuesday afternoon.

ED: Continue, Memsahib, pointillising my portrait if you please.

TILDY: If a winery and a brewery had a child?

ED: That would be your correspondent, madam, with a full body and a frothy head. Fair play. But do I not recognize a fellow disciple of the grape?

TILDY: (raises a beaker near a bottle on the end table beside her. Drinks.) Hair of the mastiff what bit me last night, Eddie boy. And Yes, I could scarcely fail to recall you from the bar we frequent, considering that on most days you open it, and close it, and undoubtedly polish the fixtures, too. Help yourself.

ED: (commandeers the bottle, takes a pull, smacks his lips, cradles it in his lap) I've also been known to pickle the eggs, when the mood strikes me.

TILDY: Are you here to pickle mine?

ED: I wouldn't presume to presume. (he fumbles in a pocket) Conjecture, the inner self, is verbalized. (fumbles) It resonates a moment. (fumbles) The winds hurry it to irrelevance. (frees a cell phone, switches on the voice recorder) You and I shall cry "Stay!" to the changeable elements.

TILDY: Oh don't record that, dear, you'll sound an awful pillock. (drinks) You want an interview for *MEH*?

ED: For *Wangler Magazine*. (confidentially) I've requested a few sick days from *MEH* this week, between you and me and the dog's breakfast.

TILDY: *Wangler!* That rag? Since when do they do anything but slag off the other studios?

ED: (digging his toe into the deep pile) Not at all, Princesa, a puff piece, I assure you. You deem *MEH* the more congenial outlet? I am a ship's swain to your merest broadside. *MEH* it shall be. (toasts) *Diphylla ecaudata!* (drinks) A certain hairy-legged vampire bat has told me you're undertaking an early retirement. You'll be sorely missed, milady; could you perhaps expound upon the reason why?

TILDY: (zero to sixty mph reaction) Early retirement, he says! (grabs the phone, holds it a centimeter from her mouth) Feast on this shriveled carcass! (she extends it at arm's length)

ED: The camera's broken.

TILDY: (phone to her mouth) This ruined tower which once was a stormy citadel of delights! (drinks) Yes, I'm out of the game, for well and for true.

ED: I'm curious, withal. What exigency might have precipitated you out of said game?

TILDY: (ignoring the question) What's next for the dowager Higgenbotham? I've squirreled away a Lincoln penny here and there, natch, but idle hands... (drinks) What do you think? A royal appointment with the King of Burgers, or a sojourn in the humble Hut wherein Pizzas are made?

ED: But tell me—

TILDY: MILF!

ED: Okay, I'll tumble. You give me the lowdown, and for my part, (drinks) I shall nock the bolt of your distemper, and fly you across a range of possibilities!

(They clink vessels.)

ED: (donnishly pedantic, in Tight Closeup) I expect you've read your Hippocrates, your Galen, who wrote that every individual is a kind of mystery-meat pie, composed chiefly of baloney, but larded and barded with each of four humors, viz.: blood, choler, phlegm, and melancholy. In varying proportions. (drinks) "Know thyself!" the Seven Sages said. Such like, know which humor one possesses in abundance, and the path is clear and fitting. Now it happens that I have crafted, as my own lowly contribution to the journalist's toolkit, a variation on the standard Myers Briggs personality test, based on those four humors and highlighting the places where the interlocutor's sea-spun depths rush onto our worldly shores, in and out, evincing the quivering jellyfishes of emotion and the garbage patch leavings of our many plastic selves—

(He's interrupted by Tildy: closed eyes, subterranean snoring.)

ED: Hrrumph.

TILDY: (unresponsive)

ED: HRRRUMMPPHH!

TILDY: (death-like torpor)

(Ed liberates her wine glass from inert fingers, waggles it under her nose like smelling salts.)

TILDY: Huh? (she rescues the glass) Mine! (drinks)

ED: Soldiering on. (drinks) One doesn't simply "do" porn. A moral compact arises, and the social order closes the deal. To the day you die, you will be, by an infection of circumstantial sputa, forever a porn star. But if character is indeed destiny, and it is possible to divine your character to the nth molecule, I contend a second destiny may be had. (drinks) We shall review a string of statements, to which you must answer "Yea" or "Nay."

TILDY: (eyes closed, snoring)

ED: (kicks her)

TILDY: H-Huh?

ED: Yea, or nay (consults his notebook):

- "I prefer solitude to the company of others."
- "I express emotions easily and without embarrassment."
- "Often I would rather go to sleep than have to drive to a party, but the ideal would be to drive while sleeping."
- "I dislike mess."
- "I make decisions based on available data and systematic analysis."

- "I like to fix people as much as I like to fix things. In either case, duct tape and a power drill are essential."
- "I enjoy being the center of attention."
- "I wonder about the nature of existence."
- "I believe an ancient civilization of mole men is stealing my radishes."
- "I call myself a 'big picture' thinker."
- "I choose to fit in and not stand out."
- "When someone I know is feeling bad, I offer sympathy, then advice. Then, heroin."
- "Deadlines encourage me to achieve my goals."
- "I react poorly to negative feedback."
- "Whenever I have dinner with my invisible friend the Right Honorable Sir Blimpy Jabbernowl, I stick him with the check."
- "I would sooner improvise than plan."
- "I hate to leave projects unfinished."
- "If a room is full, I look to the walls rather than the interior. If the walls are crowded, I look for a window or a door. If the windows and doors are crowded too, I look for my machine gun."
- "I like intuitive people more than cerebral."
- "My intestinal tapeworm, Mummenschanz, speaks through me and directs my thoughts. Which explains my habit of wriggling naked on the pavement on rainy days—" (looks up from his reading)

TILDY: (eyes, etc.)

ED: Damn it! (he seizes her shoulders and shakes her)

TILDY: (petulant moue) Owww! (she pummels him) Balaclava, my safe word is "balaclava!"

ED: You'll give me the word, all right. Why should Eden Gann care whether you're retired? Spill!

TILDY: Um, Vogel.

ED: Vogel?

TILDY: Ask Charlie! (slumps sideways)

ED: (pushing up out of the chesterfield) Charlie Vogel.

(Cut to Interior of Edie's sunny Bedroom at Midday on Tuesday, where Edie and Shelly Aguirre, a lankier, tougher redheaded variation on Edie's type, several years older and more seasoned, bask in the afterglow of recent sex as NARRATION proceeds.)

Tragos was shaping up to be a problem, although I didn't realize it yet. People think men's magazines are mostly cheerleaders for the industry, and they're not wrong. And the very slick Mature Entertainment Headlines, *like a lot of the hottest cheerleaders, is also the biggest whore. They wouldn't run a hatchet job that could damage a studio's reputation, they pretty much exist to promote the product. And a negative report from you, Charlie, wouldn't hurt my chances if I absconded to another studio, since you're rivals, and why should they trust you?*

But Wangler *not only published a magazine, they ran a studio which shot videos in direct competition with Pie-Rite Pictures. A negative story there, knocking Pie-Rite and bashing me, could cost me jobs, and they might just print it: clobbering the competition would suit them fine.*

As I said, I wasn't consciously aware of what he was doing, but you know the shivery sensation you get when you're walking across a dark street in the dead of night, and you're afraid to look around because something grisly and disturbing might be stalking you? There's a term for that creepy bog dweller stealing up behind you. It's called an Ed Tragos.

At the moment, though, Mission Control was calling. And the next duck in my personal shooting gallery was the universally renowned and acclaimed Leanna L'Amour—mailbox name, Shelly Aguirre. This was almost too easy: she and I were already in a relationship. Casual, non-exclusive, but still. See, as fiercely man-hungry as Leanna was in your DVDs, in her civilian life Shelly regarded males the way Jonas Salk regarded the polio virus. The rest was...

SHELLY: Not bad, Gannsy. Not bad.

EDIE: I had a good teacher, didn't I, Shel'?

SHELLY: True dat. (she strikes a match) How about my Izzy news? Second in command. And, performing again. If you rise in the world and fall at the same time, did you go anywhere at all?

EDIE: (granite-faced) Are you going to smoke in my bed?

SHELLY: Yes. Yes I am. Would you like to see a smoke ring?

EDIE: In my bed.

SHELLY: Rings, schmings. (conflagrates a cigarette) With this tongue, I could blow an Escher print. (puffs a gray ring at the Camera)

EDIE: (underwhelmed) Groovy.

SHELLY: Which reminds me. You haven't agreed to pose for my photo essay. C'mon, hon,' we can submit it, maybe you'll get a pictorial and some pin money. Your web site isn't exactly breaking the bank.

EDIE: Nope. Don't do photo ops for rando sites anymore.

SHELLY: Don't say "bad memories." I'll remind you, we met on a girl/girl for Penthouse-dot-com. Or was it Playboy-dot-com?

EDIE: Neither.

SHELLY: And didn't that help me get you the Pie-Rite gig? (puffs a larger, grayer ring in the Camera's direction)

EDIE: It was "Bosomy Bondagettes."

SHELLY: Dot-com!

EDIE: And I doubt they want me back.

SHELLY: (coughing) That's right, you clocked their photographer! Why, pray tell?

EDIE: He was too handsy.

SHELLY: "Handsy"? He was posing you for a sex shoot!

EDIE: And then I posed him. Horizontally.

SHELLY: (laughing, lifts Edie's wrist) Edie Gann, born Ouida Gagné, "The Cajun Crusher!" (imitates crowd noise)

EDIE: (lingering upon every consonant) *Beck moi tchew.* (yanks loose)

SHELLY: One of these days I'm gonna look that up, slugger. Anyway, you are going to say "Yes" to me. (puffs a grayer ring encompassing the screen)

EDIE: Oh?

SHELLY: You know you are.

EDIE: Do I?

SHELLY: You should get it out of the way, Edie. Say "Yes" and it'll be over. Quick, and bordering on painless.

EDIE: Yikes.

SHELLY: Yikes, nothing. It's "Yoicks!" foxy girl! The hunt is on! (she exhales, and the letters "Y-O-I-C-K-S-!" bloom out of the smoke in the air about them) Why, the word actually contains "SICK, YO?" (she points at the letters, which rearrange themselves helpfully)

EDIE: It also contains "SO ICKY!" (she points, and the characters re-form again)

SHELLY: (waving away the smoke) Come on.

(Rising, Shelly puffs at the Camera the darkest smoke ring yet, which Dissolves into the edge of a camera lens creating a circular Frame, wherein a nude spread-eagled Edie is reflected. A series of clicks punctuate their dialogue.)

SHELLY'S VOICE: That's it. Open up and say "Ah." Smile and say "Cheese." *(click)*

EDIE: Hilariously entertaining.

SHELLY: Ooh, I love that you're not totally shaved. *(click)* Let ya freak flag fly, mama! (she sighs) I can't believe you give this pretty little kitten to boys.

EDIE: They have their uses.

SHELLY: Uses? Men? They barely have opposable thumbs.

EDIE: Spare me. You've rocked more cock than I ever did.

SHELLY: Bread 'n butter, sweetie. Nuthin' but. *(click)* "Zuni Fetish Doll Edie" understands.

EDIE: (baffled) What in the hell is a "Zuni Fetish Doll Edie"?

SHELLY: (the image tilts down) She's in my lens right now. Aren't you, puddin'? *(click)*

EDIE: Shelly! (the image tilts up) God, sometimes you're more like a guy than most guys are.

SHELLY: You wanna hear what put me off boys in the first place? I was doing one of Charlie's "swallow" videos.

EDIE: Ugh. Ugh.

SHELLY: *(click)* Mmm, it's so good for you, it's practically a meal in itself.

EDIE: "Waiter, send this back!"

SHELLY: (her hand enters the camera's field of view, international thumb-rubbing sign language) Gravy, gravy.

EDIE: Okay, you go follow your star, Shelly.

SHELLY: It's a red giant!

EDIE: Me, I'd just as soon not snarf down some jerk circle's load of phlogiston for a few hundred extra dollars.

SHELLY: The title was either "The World's Hottest Glottis," *(click)* or "Huey, Dewey, Louie, and Ptooey!" (the "lens" image fisheyes, and modulates from this moment onward like a crystal ball, painting illustrations of her remarks. Dissolve to tableau of a nude Shelly in Medium Shot, genuflecting before four rampant schlongs. Cut to Close Up.) There I am on my knees with four mopes, and a stiff neck and terminal carpet burns and penises hither and yon, and all I could think about was my puppies when I was a kid, Butcher and Holler.

(Dissolve to younger Shelly seen from the same Camera Angle, in Close Up, her animals licking her, she scratching their ears and pushing their snouts away in amusement. Cut to Medium Shot of her frolicking with them.)

SHELLY: I doted on those pups. I doted on 'em, but you could never pet one of them without his roomie nosing in and demanding to be petted, too. Annoying.

(Dissolve to Shelly in Medium Shot, phalluses everywhere, thrusting and angling for her approval.)

SHELLY: And similarly, the mopes, you couldn't give one a tug or a lick without getting poked in the cheek by another, and another. That's dudes: needy puppies pawing your skirt and begging for favors.

(Cut to Close Up, Shelly pushing the cocks away, not amused.)

SHELLY: And I'm not needy, not in the slightest, 'cause it's drippy and pathetic. That's when I resolved to swear off the stick, unless for professional purposes.

EDIE: Which is all the time, lately.

(Dissolve to Shelly at the lectern, holding up a biology textbook and tapping her yardstick on a diagram.)

SHELLY: Did you know everybody starts out female in the womb? Then about half of us *diverge*. What does this tell us? That males are mutations, at best.

EDIE: Uh-huh.

(Dissolve to Medium Shot, cowering Shelly and Edie clutching each other, menaced all around by naked big-pricked homunculi.)

SHELLY'S VOICE, feigning terror: Edie, the Earth has been invaded by mutants with dicks!

EDIE'S VOICE: Scary.

SHELLY: (lowering her camera as the Shot leaves the POV of her lens and assumes the Normal Perspective) And for your information, Eden Gann, the reason you and I are together is because I'm more like you than *you* are.

EDIE: Good, Shel'. That's good, since it brings us to a chat we had an hour ago.

SHELLY: Vogel.

EDIE: Who else?

SHELLY: You know the old saying. "Men: can't live with 'em; can't zip-tie their wrists and ankles, cement their jaws shut, beat them to death with a blacksmith hammer, torch the body, and bury the remains in an industrial landfill."

EDIE: That is horrifyingly specific.

SHELLY: Oh my god, girl, just give the man a "let's be friends" Bee-Jay. He'll forget about it. Forget his own name, I bet.

EDIE: I am not having sex with Charlie.

SHELLY: Oral is not sex. Oral is a presentation.

EDIE: I get it.

SHELLY: It's an opening session.

EDIE: Do go on.

SHELLY: It's a meat and greet.

EDIE: Don't stop now.

SHELLY: It's a cocktail reception!

EDIE: Yeah I know, I often like to serve coffee and knishes during a blowjob.

SHELLY: Oh Edie, my twisted rugelach, my milk chocolate babka...

EDIE: Shelly, are you going to help me or not?

SHELLY: What, by taking a week or two off, so you can summarily ram Charlie's face into the smoldering vermiculite? Of course I'll do that, Ed'. Didn't you think I would?

EDIE: (mild frustration) You could have told me when I asked you, instead of, "Oh, I'll weigh the outcome," "Ooh, it's such a tough decision," et cetera.

SHELLY: Babyface, you're a better lay when you want something.

EDIE: But what was all that about hating needy people who ask for favors?

SHELLY: That, my dear, was the justly celebrated Woman's Prerogative. (moving toward her) Now sit still, while I adjust your aperture...

(Edie NARRATES, affecting a flatter, more Shelly-esque diction, as we are shown a succession of photographs from a past web photoshoot:)

EDIE: The array of images far surpass my own, shot in a chiaroscuro style giving an effect both sensual and starkly immediate.

In the FIRST, we see a pillared room or set dressed in Gothic details: a black-white patterned floor, a vaulted ceiling reaching overhead, beneath it a bed of iron and a barred window, hung with red upholstery whose shimmering plaits catch and throw back the flare of a dozen torches, flickering in their brackets on the close creeping walls. A hazily religious significance envelopes the scene.

There on the left is a marble column; on the right, the bed; in the center, a chair in heavily stitched leather, where I sit, silent as a judge and in jet, my petticoat, my high heeled boots. My features are hidden under a white mask, the whitest stone-silent surface in the picture. The stiff unyielding visage is that of a waxwork, motionless, adamant as a cadaver, a bolt of light flashing in the night black. But through twin holes, the pupils are murkily vivid, inspirited. They measure their prey.

Gann, barefoot and virtually nude, in a flimsy colorless negligee, stockings and garters, hovers by the broad column. She clutches the hem of the skirt, tucking it into her thighs, as if daring the spectator to discover her sex. Her bust hangs forward in this position, and she may be panicked, she may be piqued: impossible to tell. The shoulder straps have fallen to her elbows, and her breasts, pale half moons, swell above the gauzy material.

Despite her awkward pose her limbs are elegant, fawnlike, her physique superb; her face, lips parted, expression pleading, at once invites and entreats.

The CAPTION reads: "Leanna gloated at pretty Edie, directing her to angle her head so her golden locks dappled a tan shoulder. The smallest movement of her enchanting face and figure was a seduction, the luminescent blue eyes, the peach-blown mouth, sweetly suggestive, the sheepish obedience, grist to the butcher's blade..."

In the SECOND PICTURE, the coal-black bed and its jumble of red blankets dominates. On it, pulled taut, her fingers and toes fretting at the dark detailed metalwork of the bedstead, Gann waits, a rabbit caught in a trellis. She lies prone in her negligee, face pressed in her pillow, her near leg and hip raised and her hands grappling at the cold uncaring iron. She is bared to the waist by the upswept slip. Over the garter belt her buttocks seem to ripen outward, even in a still shot, and between them a discreet darkness salutes the onlooker.

CAPTION: "Rising, Leanna arranged her conquest on the mattress with the mildest of touches, of candied phrases, noting with satisfaction the shiver which ran down her spine. She filled the air with symphonies of praise to Edie's expectant flesh, her delightful chamber sections, the arena through which her violent play soon would resound. Edie blushed..."

In the NEXT PICTURE, Gann is entirely and abjectly naked, on her haunches before me, her booted Governess, bowed, wrists chained, her hair thrown sideways to shield her sight and her neck disclosed, avid for the chopping block. Her ass juts out to balance smartly on her heels. A lambent nipple is exposed, forlorn, vulnerable. The same kind of slender chain as that at the wrists, binds the ankles.

A long, somber, curled whip of unworked leather rests by her, dismal on the white tile. The thicker handle also is of leather, and marked by regular usage.

CAPTION: "At Mistress's bidding, Edie retrieved the whip. Leanna was pleased. 'My slut chose a fine one. Kneel!'

Edie dropped to her knees, a well-observed ritual. Leanna smoothed the locks of flaxen hair obscuring her distress. 'I like you best this way,' she hissed. She coiled her fingers in the hair and, jerking, wrenched her head up, swatting the face to left and right.

Grasping her more tightly, she imparted a detailed prospectus on the evening's entertainments. Edie would be tied, she would be whipped, back, bosom and belly. She would be injured, defiled. Leanna recited in a deliberate manner, using the vilest terms with utmost precision, as Edie's shudders caused her to seem wonderfully ardent, and her eyes widened like a sacrificial lamb..."

NEXT, Gann, naked and chained, is secured to the bedpost. Seen from behind, her body shows the evidence of violent struggle. The neck is slack and the body canted slantwise, drooping from the shackles in exhaustion. The buttocks are trimmed with a network of whip marks, each defined in every particular, so defined that to the discerning eye, they are plainly cosmetic.

Nevertheless, little Gann in her pathetic display continues to lure the spectator to her dilemma.

CAPTION: "'I beg of you,' Edie groveled. 'No more.'

'Fool!' exclaimed the imperious Leanna, standing beside her, the whip slung around her arm. 'Is it for you to decide?'

Edie quavered, implored, in a misery without let or limit.

For her part, Leanna meant to feel as well as witness her terror. She reached around her to fondle her breasts, and felt the nipples spring up. As a hand amused itself there, the other asserted itself at chastity's bounding line. Edie's jaw fell and her breath came, strident.

'Get these legs out! I'm not done with you.'

'No, you mustn't. Please, please,' she whimpered.

Leanna tapped her shoulder blade with the whip handle. 'Why, don't you enjoy it?' she inquired.

'Yes,' Edie conceded. 'It's *nice*.'

'I live to serve!' and winding backward, Leanna made the lash fly so fierce a cavort that her victim leaped about, inciting the bed to groan in sympathy. 'This? You like it?' Edie could only dip her head..."

In the NEXT IMAGE, the girl is tethered to the stone column, her shape forming an "X." Stiff ropes bind her, wholly fixing her to the smooth pillar. New wounds appear, the bonds cutting at wrist and ankle, crimson rills on her waist expressing profounder injuries.

CAPTION: "Preening catlike in Edie's direction, Leanna soothed and petted her breasts, unpinning her reserves of delicacy. She tried the secret recess below and found it sticky and damp.

'Doesn't my wicked girl love when Mistress corrects her? It makes you hungry for more of the whip, I can tell,' and she insinuated deep within her.

Edie's eyes shut and her lips pressed together.

'They say you can't train a kitten, yet here you are, broken to my harness, ready to go any way I choose to goad you. Aren't I right, trollop?' She prodded her with the toe of her boot.

'Take me however, whenever you wish,' Edie breathed.

'Splendid,' Leanna said, and slapped her face to left and right.

Her contortions made Leanna salivate; never was she more captivating than at such moments. She untied one of Edie's wrists. 'Stroke yourself, slut!' and she flexed the lash, making her dance a furious allegro against her stony partner.

Edie's rhythm became that of orgasm, a countering of the tormentor's lash with an equal lashing of her torso, forcing the remaining wrist out of its restraint as a mournful lamentation escaped her and her fist belabored her sodden privates. She slid to the floor, a soulless thing, and abused herself..."

The FINAL PHOTO completes the sequence. Gann lies stretched on the tiles, on her side, blandly facing the camera. An awkward arm cramps under her, another extends toward the viewer in empty supplication. A thin trail of blood runs from the mouth's corner to the checkerboards. The vacancy in her eye is reassuring: the life force has gone, agony is at an end.

Close by, I sit caressing myself. My black underskirt covers all but my hand and my parted thighs. The middle finger disturbs the warm swollen flesh there, driven in to the last joint, and the nails on my outcast fingers loom a dark red on my white skin.

CAPTION: "Her anguish consummated, Edie wailed once and no more. Head flopping and jaw stuck open, she rolled to one side, straining her limbs as her breath clattered out. She lay unmoving on the black and white surface. Leanna's finger disappeared inside her sex, and she kicked at the shambles in sullen disregard. 'Check. Mate,' she muttered..."

CHAPTER 3

EDIE, back among the living, NARRATES: (coughing, clearing throat) *kof-kof* ...Anyhoo... See how easy, Charlie? It's Political Science 101: two people in, er, congress, and you've got a democracy. One person like you, getting so tightfisted with his business, it's a puppet dictatorship. I'm a freedom fighter, Charles, and as the Father of Our Country George Washington said, "You don't fuck with a freedom fighter!" Yet there you sat in your cubbyhole, you and Izzy, believing you ruled...

(Dissolve to Interior Charlie's Office, Wednesday Afternoon, Charlie and Izzy situated precisely as they were a day earlier, Charlie's chin propped on weary hands.)

IZZY: ...therefore in terms of Identity, sex toy x, and sex toy y, are the same predicate F but different predicate G's!

CHARLIE: You're killin' me with this subject. You are literally ending my life.

IZZY: I'm cutting off your wind?

CHARLIE: Prepare to call the time of death.

IZZY: (with an effort) "Next subject," fine. I wrote a script. 'Case you're interested.

CHARLIE: You wear many hats, Lombardo.

IZZY: It's a work of uncompromising brilliance. I wrote it on the pot, between two shits.

CHARLIE: Then I can name at least one guy who got considerable satisfaction from it. Unfortunately, we're going to all-sex videos hereafter. Cheaper.

IZZY: No more stories? My labors were wasted?

CHARLIE: (regret-free) Yeah, that's your lonely heartache, I guess.

IZZY: That's my row to hoe.

CHARLIE: "Row to hoe"?

IZZY: Yep. The row I hoe.

CHARLIE: The hell?

IZZY: I'm hoein' the row. I'm a row hoer.

CHARLIE: Hoer?

IZZY: Gimme a row, and watch me hoe.

CHARLIE: You devise that? Or did you read a book?

IZZY: I read a book yesterday. Small words. Big margins.

CHARLIE: Okay, as a friend, don't tax your cerebrum. You could herniate yourself.

IZZY: Nevermore.

(The telephone rings. Charlie picks up.)

CHARLIE: Pie-Rite Pictures, ecstasized to make your acquaintance! (purr of conversation) Who? (purr) I don't know you. (purr) *MEH?* I know all the guys there, ain't heard of you. Fuck off my phone. (hangs up) Sounded like a process server. Fool me once! (eases back in his chair) Now, who's lined up for our subsequential opus?

IZZY: So far I can't get Leanna L'Amour on the horn. I think she's brushing us off.

CHARLIE: Worry not. I'll characterize to you that girl: when it comes to the schwanz, she ain't quite iron willed. She craves cock like nobody I've seen. A few day's liberty, and she will fold like Granny's knickers. What more?

IZZY: We got Derrien Usagi of course, plus the two Hungarians, Ursa Major and Ursa Minor.

CHARLIE: Refresh my recollection.

IZZY: (searches his memory) The Hungarians, we haven't used them before. We discovered 'em in a German oral flick, "Der NudelStrudel."

CHARLIE: And?

IZZY: Derrien, you're familiar. We used her in our own oral series, "I Know When I'm Licked!" number twenty-two.

CHARLIE: Got it. We'll call 'em in a sec.

IZZY: Call?

CHARLIE: The Gabor sisters. But beforehand, (ticks the items off) since we're three short, and it's the middle of the week, and the Adult Entertainment Expo in Vegas starts in two days, and I'm a conservative man at heart, behold me covering my ass. (he dials the speaker phone. As it beeps:) Are you scrutinizing my ass?

IZZY: Like a hawk.

CHARLIE: Listen and learn. (buzzing sound)

IZZY: Call an agency? Why not check their web page?

CHARLIE: Because I'm old school, bub, and we're in an enterprise of relations in more ways than one. (buzzing) You understand what is a Luddite? Look it up. I'm a proud Luddite. Your generation and the internet, you finger your keyboard more often than I finger my dick. (buzzing) Not for me, pal.

Business only, and only after a crying jag and ten minutes at your mother's tit.

IZZY: I should use it less?

CHARLIE: This is the dulcet tone of hard won wisdom talking to you, dummy. (buzzing) Prick up your ear.

IZZY: Prick who?

CHARLIE: It's a British expression. It means, do what I say or I'll shove my prick up your ear.

SECRETARY'S VOICE huffs breathlessly from speaker: Fourth World Modeling!

CHARLIE: It's Charlie Vogel, gimme Ramsey please.

SECRETARY: One moment! (buzzing)

IZZY: I'll use it less. Cold turkey.

CHARLIE: Spoken like a Luddite.

PATRICK RAMSEY'S VOICE: Fourth World, Patrick Ramsey.

CHARLIE: (to speaker) Patsy, it's Charlie. I'm runnin' a couple of quarts low. Whattaya got?

PATRICK'S VOICE: Still shooting epics, are you, Charles? Not waiting for Papi to close the sale of the studio?

CHARLIE: That's in confidence, Pat, never you mind. Full speed ahead is the order. I say again: whattaya got?

PATRICK: What you crave, my darling. Big knobs under a pair of morning glory eyes. (pause) I'm talking about the skirt. Not me.

CHARLIE: Lovely. And I'm talking about both of you.

PATRICK: Name's Trudy Titmouse.

CHARLIE: Trudy Titmouse? Her parents oughta be shot!

PATRICK: (dripping sarcasm) Yeah, a porn chick who just happens to have been born with the name Trudy Titmouse. What are the odds?

CHARLIE: Astronomical, bud. Or is it infinitesimal?

PATRICK: A mere proton in the cosmic soup, my lad.

CHARLIE: Trudy Titmouse.

PATRICK: Well, on her 1040EZ it probably says "Gertrude Titmouse."

CHARLIE: What else, pray tell?

PATRICK: Dig: she can act, as well as fuck.

CHARLIE: So what?

PATRICK: So, so she's one up on Meryl Streep, right?

CHARLIE: Who can act, but will not fuck. I get it. Two things.

PATRICK: Yessir.

CHARLIE: First, email me some pictures. Her, and whomever else you got laying around. And second, call that deadbeat Meryl Streep and tell her she's out of a job.

PATRICK: Will do! (hangs up)

CHARLIE: There you are, Iz'. Bing-bang-boom!

(Cut To Interior, Wednesday Afternoon, Patrick Ramsey's neat small Office. Ramsey, a narrow-faced vulpine gentleman with slickered hair and a pinstriped suit, waxes an anemic mustache and pecks a rune or two on his computer. An attractive Woman of indeterminate age, tall, rail-thin, black-tressed and in a gleaming white business ensemble, carrying a smart white shoulder bag, enters.)

WOMAN: Your door was... Excuse me, I didn't see a secretary.

PATRICK: Just went to lunch.

WOMAN: My name is Moira At—

PATRICK: I recall.

MOIRA: I'm not interrupting? We had an appointment.

PATRICK: (all charm) How could you interrupt? A vision. You could maybe interrupt as sunlight interrupts a rainy day.

MOIRA: I won't use up too much of your time. (she extends her hand)

PATRICK: (takes it) You said you had a presentation of sorts, isn't it?

MOIRA: In brief.

PATRICK: I am at your disposal. (unlooses her) Regale me!

(She offers him a card.)

PATRICK: Cream linen paper. Very natty.

MOIRA: The web page is indicated at the bottom. See there? (she slings her bag onto a filing cabinet) Mind?

PATRICK: You're among friends.

(She opens the bag, disentombs a pocket reel of sixteen millimeter film.)

PATRICK: I've been to the web site. I'll tell you the truth. It's the tail wagging the dog, but you do your showpiece, I don't mind.

MOIRA: I'm seeing the essential players in the field, Mister Ramsey. Why? Because we, you and I and everyone at every level, in adult videos, we are here to bear witness to a Change. An Event, such as what scientists call a "Cataclysmic Event." The previous Event swept away the tyrannosaurs as if they were so many dead leaves, Mister Ramsey. Are you a tyrannosaur? No, you're not.

PATRICK: I have a thunder lizard between my legs. Do I qualify?

MOIRA: You may joke, however (she extracts a pair of shears from her bag and unleashes a section of film stock) for a hundred years, this was the medium of visual pornography. Photographic film. (she clips a row of frames, letting them flutter to the desktop) Fragile, flammable, brittle. (she sweeps the fragments into his wastepaper basket and returns the reel and scissors to her purse) Do you imagine film was the permanent medium for pornography, Mister Ramsey? Do you? Ask Johann Schwarzer.

PATRICK: (glances down) Is he under the desk?

MOIRA: Era by era, our industry has bent technology to its needs. But today technology is the greater need, and it is our industry which must bend.

PATRICK: I'm bent, believe me. Moira, now yours is an Irish name. Do you know "Moira" in Gaelic translates as "bitter"? What could they have been thinking when they named you Moira? Patrick, or Padraic if it wouldn't suffocate you, signifies a nobleman. A patrician fellow, this one.

MOIRA: You don't seem Irish.

PATRICK: And yet everybody who sees me, they say, "There goes the Auld Sod!"

MOIRA: Huh.

PATRICK: Sod this, sod that.

MOIRA: Yes.

PATRICK: Everywhere I go.

MOIRA: Can you see what I'm alluding to?

PATRICK: Me of all people, I certainly can. Did I begin my career in porn? Are you aware I once cast a theatrical movie which was *sans le jizz*, as the French say? A rousing adaptation of the nineteenth century classic book "Confessions of an English Opium-Eater."

MOIRA: Really?

PATRICK: He was always eating up the opium, that guy.

MOIRA: Okay, fine.

PATRICK: Never left room for dessert!

MOIRA: To the subject at hand. In a haphazard way, your industry has made use of streaming video as one more revenue stream.

PATRICK: The stream is overflowing!

MOIRA: Is the stream not transmuting into the wave of the future? No inventory. Sell the warehouse. Reject the ancient regime, join the revolution. Physical media are dying on the vine, Mister Ramsey! What I'm proposing is a web site assembling and curating video clips from studios big and small, and without charge to users. Based on the model of YouTube.

PATRICK: Studio content from you, for free? All you lack is the cutlass and a parrot on your shoulder.

MOIRA: When I visit them, I'll endeavor to clarify their position. They can't expect to enforce intellectual property rights. They have no champions in court or Congress. Sites like mine are at the vanguard, and there will be many more. Will they spend their resources on lawyers? It's better to let us offer a click-through driving a percentage of visitors to their sites. Of course, we'll then get a share of their subscriber revenue, too.

PATRICK: Sure, how could you not?

MOIRA: Your part would be to provide talent for the live webcam option. We want to touch all the bases.

PATRICK: (sympathetic smile) Miss, I'm telling you in person what I told you on the phone. You're an appealing lady. I'll be honest. This is the future, and you can bet the farm. There's a place, yes, for ten minute sex scenes on a tiny screen with dropouts and buffering lags and pixels the size of a yard bag. But most fans are very loyal and dedicated perverts. They won't abandon the studios or the studio model, and they'll hold onto that special moment of putting in the DVD and settling in for a nice dirty hour and a half revue with lots of dishy girls and the usual dozen or so studs. It's home to them. Now you run along to the next victim, and when the scales fall from your peepers someday and you can admit I'm right, swing on by. I'll find a spot for you here. Deal? (he resumes typing)

MOIRA: (gathers her effects) Good luck. You have my card.

PATRICK: (intent on his computer) Girls, girls, girls. (she leaves)

(Cut to Exterior, Wednesday Afternoon, Poolside by a spacious rented House. Edie reclines on a deck chair by two attractive exotic women each on their own chairs, with similar strongly sensual features but contrasting hair colors, Ursas Major and Minor, the three in swimsuits taking the sun.)

The Gabor sisters? Hungarians, yes, sisters, no: Ursa Major (the brunette) and Ursa Minor (blondie). Legal names: Czilla Galgoczi...um...Szilvia Gulacsy...or is it...Zsuzsa Gerloczy...er...you know what? Let's stick to porn names from now on.

The Ursas had never done a vid together, but when they left Euro-porn they came to the US side by side, raring to go, and convinced like a lot of foreign starlets that they could definitely teach us backward Americans a thing or two about sex.

Which they could. If your textbook is the Necronomicon...

URSA MAJOR: *Pincér! A számlát, kérem.*

URSA MINOR: *Nagyon finom volt.*

URSA MAJOR: *Gulyás a la Edie!* (they laugh)

EDIE: Give me a break, you two. It's an English speaking country.

URSA MAJOR: We are discussing goulash. This is a Hungarian food. You try this food?

EDIE: Kind of a stew?

URSA MINOR: Because you invite us to go for dinner, Edie, and all of us will be bosom friends. Not strangers anymore.

EDIE: Sure.

URSA MAJOR: And we are discussing a recipe for "Goulash a la Edie." Here it is: We take Edie the baby calf, and exercise her muscles for flavor. We coat her meat with oil and make her simmer for much times until she is moist and hot and tender. After we have warmed her juices, we spice her up and bring her to a boil. Then we eat her.

URSA MINOR: (beaming) Soup's on!

EDIE: Creative. You do that sort of thing in your videos, Major?

URSA MAJOR: No. I am with men in my films.

URSA MINOR: Crazy, no? She likes the butt sex. (elbows Edie) You too?

EDIE: I only occasionally partake, sorry.

URSA MAJOR: You heard of Otto Kálnocky? He has the best dick for the butt sex. His nickname is "*Lófasz.*" Means big giant horse dick. But also it means a big bullshit. He is both.

URSA MINOR: He was a janitor before he is a porn star. Everyone says, "Hey Otto, you brought the broomstick with you!"

EDIE: See, I'd think a smaller—

URSA MINOR: You would prefer Tibor Sipos. (thumb and forefinger) Teeny-tiny.

URSA MAJOR: I worked with Tibor! We didn't have a sexy-sexy. In the film, he did a "Billy Budd."

EDIE: A "Billy Budd"? What's that?

URSA MAJOR: Just what it sounds like. A guy fucks the nostrils of a goat while it licks his balls. Are you thick?

URSA MINOR: (protective) No, no, she's *inexperienced.*

URSA MAJOR: Ah.

EDIE: C'mon, I've seen a lot. You two can't have done that much more than I have.

URSA MAJOR: (appraising her) Have you ever attempted a "Hochzeitsnacht im Paradies"?

EDIE: Enlighten me.

URSA MAJOR: That's when one guy is in your face, one is in your ass, you jerk off two more guys, another puts his peeter in your left ear canal, another in your right, the seventh guy is in your pussy and the eighth pleasures himself onto your toes as you tongue an old man's puckered bunghole until he deposits a turd between your gums.

URSA MINOR: And you eat the turd.

URSA MAJOR: (impatient) Certainly you eat the turd. It's not a genuine Hochzeitsnacht if you don't eat the turd.

URSA MINOR: That's called a Pseudo-Hochzeitsnacht.

URSA MAJOR: (savage vehemence) Pseudo-Hochzeitsnachts are for losers!

EDIE: Okay, I stand corrected. Really.

URSA MINOR: Ursa, have you done a "Naughty Marietta"?

URSA MAJOR: Many times.

EDIE: Which is?

URSA MAJOR: You balance yourself on an altar with a candle inserted up your hoo-hah, which you must under no circumstances relinquish 'til you've said five Our Fathers and five Hail Marys.

URSA MINOR: Then you straddle a large crucifix and are fucked from behind while the head of Jesus noodles your clitoris. (beatific glow) It's very spiritual.

EDIE: (sitting up) This is becoming—

URSA MAJOR: Now a "Merry Widow," is one of my favorites. Six men strip you and put you in a coffin tied face to face to a corpse.

URSA MINOR: They lower you into a grave, throw dirt in your eyes, blow their noses, pass gas, spit, and sing, "When Margo lies in her pretty little boat, boys/Our claws will form a necklace 'round her throat, boys."

EDIE: That's, um, uh...

URSA MINOR: I know, not for everybody. Fortunately, I come from a musical family. (losing interest in Edie) Ursa, have you tried a "Snow Maiden"?

URSA MAJOR: Tried it? I practically invented it!

EDIE: I'm going—I'm going over *there*. (they tune out her presence from here onward)

URSA MAJOR: You have to lie on a dinner table so a guy with a razor-sharp fork can eat a fresh-cooked omelet off your rear end as you chew on a burning coal. Then he rinses your bowels with boiling oil. Yes?

URSA MINOR: That's not all!

URSA MAJOR: Not all? What more is there?

URSA MINOR: You forgot the gunpowder!

URSA MAJOR: Oh, yes yes. Last but not least, he pours gunpowder in your *punci*, lights the powder and when the flames shoot out, he pees on you like a human fire extinguisher.

EDIE: Going to walk away now... (collects her things)

URSA MAJOR: A "Schatzgräber," this is where a man hacks off an eighteen-year-old boy's prick and balls, and uses a hot poker to hollow a vagina between his thighs.

URSA MINOR: And right away he fucks the brand new clam.

URSA MAJOR: And strangles the boy.

URSA MINOR: Of course, strangling, this is strictly optional.

URSA MAJOR: Strangling is not optional. No way is strangling optional.

URSA MINOR: Look, how will she learn if you always argue?

URSA MAJOR: (tut-tutting) This is what comes of being a freethinker. A Schatzgräber without the strangling!

(Edie creeps toward the cabana. From the house, we can hear the faint sound of a telephone ringing. None of the three react.)

EDIE: Slowly walking away...

URSA MINOR: Okey-doke, fancy pants. How would you and Edie do a "Lulu"?

URSA MAJOR: A "Lulu"? "Lulu..."

URSA MINOR: Remember? The "High School Musical" wrap party?

URSA MAJOR: "Lulu," right! Okay, okay, first we get a sledgehammer and flatten her feet. Then we tie her to a stepladder, slit her lips and nostrils, slice off her clit with a razor, and shave off her ears. Then we bash in her teeth and hammer red-hot nails in their place. Then, we bind one of her wrists to a post, give her a wooden switch, and duel against her with a chainsaw. Then we douse melted wax on her eyeballs and when they dissolve, she's locked in a trunk with a key, but the key is in a cage full of scorpions. In conclusion, we shove a Roman candle in her, ignite the fuse, and up it goes, sending her limbs hurtling in all directions. Then we set the hounds to retrieve the chunks of flesh so we can roast them for dinner.

(The telephone stops ringing. Edie is by the white Cabana Wall, out of harm's way, speechless.)

URSA MINOR: You know, this pillow talk is making me feel extremely horny.

URSA MAJOR: I know! How is it that we never were together, before?

URSA MINOR: Let's try a couple something somethings, huh? (inviting smile) Edie? Chop-chop.

EDIE: Uh-uh.

URSA MAJOR: Your loss, baby girl. Ursa, I think we should start with a "Flying Dutchman."

URSA MINOR: Or a "Hairy János" would be better yet.

URSA MAJOR: Maybe a "Stiffelio"?

URSA MINOR: How about a "Knot Garden," and a "Turn of the Screw"?

URSA MAJOR: Are you trying to kill me? Let's do a "Fairy Queen," instead.

URSA MINOR: And top it off with a "Magic Flute!"

URSA MAJOR: (husky come-hither) *Csókolj meg.*

URSA MINOR: Goody! Time for *entyi-pentyi!*

(They pet each other. The Camera Pans to Edie at the Cabana Wall, staring aghast. The shadows of the Ursas, on the white wall close to her, assume various increasingly disturbing shapes as we overhear them speaking.)

URSA MAJOR'S VOICE: *Igen igen igen igen! Bal. Bal.* Okay. *Jobb.*

URSA MINOR'S VOICE: Mmmm, *hogy hívják azt?*

URSA MAJOR: Ooh, *a kedves húgom.* Ow! Ow! *Ribanc!*

URSA MINOR: Ouch! *Kurva!*

URSA MAJOR: *Nem! Megállj! Megállj!*

URSA MINOR: *Megsérültem!*

URSA MAJOR: *Kuss! Orvosi segítség kell!*

URSA MINOR: *Hagyj békén! Ne érj hozzám!*

MAJOR and MINOR: (menacing gravelly voices speaking in unison as their shadows morph into the face of Beelzebub) *SQUA TRONT!*

EDIE: Good Lord!

(Cut to Interior, Wednesday Night, a busy, dimly lit Strip Club decorated in Middle Period Elvis's Bedroom, music pumping, TV monitors burning, strobes flashing, patrons pullulating in the background, shadows of Shelly and Edie thrown on a wall thirty feet from the main stage. The Camera Pans, and we watch them converse in their booth, ignoring a gaggle of fans who hover nearby, gawping at Shelly's sexy spangly attire.)

EDIE: (wide staring eyes) "Squa tront." That's all it said. "Squa tront!"

SHELLY: C'mon, Popeye! Snap out of it! (jerks her arm)

EDIE: How much would it cost to have the inside of my skull sandblasted clean?

SHELLY: I asked you here to take a break from this crazy crusade of yours, Eden. Besides, you've got to keep a hand in the game.

EDIE: I might have to rethink my life choices...

SHELLY: When I do my next routine, you are to meet and greet the hoi polloi, screw Charlie and everything else, and clear your mind. Pose for pictures. Whatever they put in front of you, sign it. Cop some bills. Cozy up to the club rats.

EDIE: I gazed into the Abyss, Shelly. And the Abyss gazed back into me, deep into my soul. And the Abyss said, "Can I get fries with that?"

SHELLY: Quit moping, I have to get up there soon. (looks past her) Sydney!

(A house dancer appears, tanned, slender, well-toned, purpose-built, glitter-dusted, with ambitious breast implants and a long and improbable red dye job. She shoulders by the customers.)

SYDNEY: (antebellum accent) Shelly is here, y'all! (Shelly rises, they hug)

SHELLY: Hiya, cutie! How you been?

SYDNEY: Workin' a double, ya bitch, 'cuz you're such a big draw.

SHELLY: You're just now coming over? (to Edie) She's shy since we had a thing a year ago. (to Sydney) Where were you, that I didn't see you? Hiding in the locker room?

SYDNEY: Yeah, I'll kick yer heinie, I'm so shy.

SHELLY: I wasn't snubbing you, sweetness. I wasn't scouting the stage, either. You in the black for tonight?

SYDNEY: Back in black, hon.'

SHELLY: Edie here, (Sydney smiles at her) before she was hot shit Ariel Caliban, she didn't dance in a club, with a sound booth and a bouncer. She danced in hotels. To an iPod, with a bodyguard. (to Edie) Where's that no-goodnik gone to? He sleeps with the fishes, you told me.

EDIE: He's—Jake's not dead!

SHELLY: (to Sydney) No, but he does live behind a Red Lobster. (they laugh)

EDIE: Will you ever tire of that joke?

SHELLY: Never! I only go out with you as an excuse to tell that joke!

SYDNEY: Edie's one of the girls, though?

SHELLY: She's one of us. She's a crap dancer, but we'll let her in the treehouse. (to Edie) House dancers have to pay the clubs a house fee to dance there. Then if business is slow, or the dudes are broke, they've lost money. Capitalism strikes again.

SYDNEY: Or they spend it all on the feature act. But I got plenty of regulars here, they like me. I do fine most always. (she blows a kiss to the multitude)

SHELLY: She's too adorable, is why. (puts her arm around her)

SYDNEY: Hey, later I'll give you a lap dance. You too, Edie.

EDIE: Thanks. Not in the mood, Sydney, thanks anyhow.

SYDNEY: (lighthearted mockery) "I contend that at this impasse I am presently not of the mood to be nuzzled upon." (she and Shelly laugh) My ass is magical, kewpie doll. I do stuff with it.

SHELLY: No lie. Her butt practices the Black Arts.

SYDNEY: It has supernatural properties.

SHELLY: It does.

SYDNEY: It has raised the dead on more than one occasion.

SHELLY: It can pull the stick from your fanny, Edie, and whack the jizz out of you with it.

EDIE: I'll pass.

(Shelly plunks Sydney in their booth and sits beside her.)

SYDNEY: Remember, Shel,' that fella in Sacramento, you were giving a lap dance and you realized the guy had slipped his dick out before you sat backward onto him?

SHELLY: I warned him I'd wrench it sideways and down so hard, his erection'd look like a question mark and he'd have to stand on his head to fuck.

SYDNEY: Good times!

(Several of their beaux wince, dip into their pockets, reassure themselves that they are intact, and discover a fascination with other sections of the club. They leave.)

SYDNEY: And the grubby unwelcome fingers. Edie, I have had more fingers stuck in me than a regulation bowling ball. One jackass, I clambered off of, he upped and punched me!

SHELLY: Laid you flat.

SYDNEY: Shelly and the bouncer steered him outside and took turns discussing with him which body cavity he intended to excrete through for the rest of his life, 'cuz the customary outlet was no longer going to be an option.

SHELLY: You got an apology, and we both got the biggest tips of our whole misspent lives. (to Edie) Better to have fucked him up, I know, but I'm a moneymaker, babe. When I'm done, their wallets hurt.

SYDNEY: And the talkers.

SHELLY: Who said talk is cheap?

SYDNEY: Talk is not cheap.

SHELLY: Edie, you didn't see a lot of this on hotel gigs. Customers gotta feel like white knights, they talk to you like you're their part-time girlfriend. They are nice, at first, but sometimes the testosterone circulates to their brainstems and it becomes, "I want chest lifted, back arched, ass up, legs spread, and shut your trap you fat cow, drop on my cock and give me twenty, use your blowhole to make me sleepy in a good way, not from what comes out of it but what goes in!"

(Two of the adjacent bystanders recall more pressing concerns, and dissipate.)

SYDNEY: Tips. A client tipped you with a smoked kingfish mackerel, right? You called him "Lester Haddocks."

SHELLY: (to Edie) The fish, not the client. Who gives a shit what the men's names are?

(The once respectable coalition of devotees withers to a paltry few diehards.)

SHELLY: That mackerel, though, it was *yum*. (cupped hand) I miss you, Lester!

SYDNEY: What about the guy who couldn't get aroused unless he was covered in freshly baked macaroons?

SHELLY: I got the recipe. Delish!

SYDNEY: We ordered out, and you escorted him to the Champagne Lounge.

SHELLY: My job was to gradually expose him with my mouth as I de-cookiefied him. I gained a thousand dollars and two pounds on the same night.

SYDNEY: That reminds me. How 'bout the guy who trailed you to your house, 'member him?

SHELLY: (uncertain) Narrow it down.

SYDNEY: Pasadena. The ex-soldier. With the necklace.

SHELLY: Um.

SYDNEY: The *necklace*. He'd strung it—

SYDNEY and SHELLY: With the sun-dried ears of Iraqi children! (they laugh)

SHELLY: (to Edie) Yeah, we dated off and on for two months. I considered him to be a riddle wrapped in a mystery, wrapped in an enigma, wrapped in a suit made from his victims' skin.

EDIE: But—

SHELLY: He was a good lay, Edie. Try to keep up.

SYDNEY: The guy who put a cigar out in your hair?

SHELLY: In Yuba City. The guy who hocked green phlegm on your cleavage?

SYDNEY: Turlock. The guy who'd snorted so much blow, his nasal septum ignited into flames while you were reverse-motorboating him?

SHELLY: Chula Vista. The guy who got so wasted he ralphed up a complete twelve course dinner, including ceramic plates and assorted flatware?

SYDNEY: Brought it home. I afterward got many sincere compliments on my table arrangements. 'Member the guy, Shel,' the Texas boy, the salesman who would pass around two-pronged silicone dildos with the presidential seal on each end?

SHELLY: (scans the club, whispers) *Not a salesman. The actual President.*

SYDNEY: So thoughtful.

SHELLY: *So* thoughtful!

EDIE: I think—

SHELLY: Remember Christmas time, when Zwarte Piet kidnapped half the club's strippers, shoved them in his grumble bag, dragged them to his fire pit in the Underworld and fed them alive to Krampus the Goblin-Santa?

SYDNEY: They *were* very naughty girls.

SHELLY: They were!

(One fan remains.)

SHELLY: What about the guy who came in, never changed his clothes, and smelled like a sewer had backed up into a mass grave? And yet his breath was always minty-fresh. Huh?

SYDNEY: 'Cuz of the schnapps.

SHELLY: Was that it?

SYDNEY: (to Edie) He didn't drink it. Before an evening out, he would fill a large enema bag with peppermint schnapps and—

(The last of their paramours evaporates.)

SHELLY: (standing) See there, Edie? This is how you get back to your old self. Forget the Hungarians. Focus on normal relations between men and women, the way we do!

EDIE: Shelly, I think you're wanted onstage.

(Shelly hugs Sydney from behind and tongues her ear.)

SHELLY: Take care of my honey, Syd'. Get the suckers lined up for her.

SYDNEY: Make it rain, girl!

(Camera Follows Shelly as she struts onto the main stage, tears off her booty shorts to flaunt the G-string underneath, and launches her routine by smacking the gobs of gobsmacked patrons with the shorts to the rhythm of "I'm a Slave 4 U." They dutifully counter by placing bills on the waist-high rail circling the stage. Winking at her two compatriots, she flings her body around the center pole.)

SYDNEY: (looking on) Shelly, she's a classic, in't she? Everything I know, she taught me. How long you guys been fraternizing?

EDIE: About nine months. Can I get something to drink?

SYDNEY: Oh dang, where's my p's and q's? Poppy seed, you can have your heart's desire, long as it's non-alcoholic, 'cuz... (she nods at Shelly, somehow already jaybird naked)

EDIE: Coffee.

SYDNEY: Coffee in the VIP booth. You go there. There? Right. And I'll square it with the manager, and I'll send some big tippers to you, too. Come on. (she pulls on Edie's arm) Come on come on come on come on. (herding her to a Booth in the recesses of the club. She scurries off.)

(Cut to VIP Booth. Edie occupies the next ten minutes watching Shelly snag banknotes from admirers using any part of her anatomy but her fingers. Sydney reappears with steaming hot mugs, sets Edie's in front of her, and slides in next to her. She gives the OK to a man lingering at the margins.)

MAN 1: (pussyfooting, nonexistent hat in hand) Miss Caliban, major fan, major major.

EDIE: Thanks.

MAN 1: I didn't realize you're here, I apologize. I don't got a camera. I do got a cocktail napkin for you to sign, if you could honor me like such. It's a drawring which I myself drew of you, that is, an artist's representation.

EDIE: (examines it) It's a sketch of the Incredible Hulk, with boobs added.

MAN 1: Because I done the sketch earlier, and I was in a hurry to get the autograph. I said it was an artist's representation, how *I* see you.

EDIE: You see me as a green monster hulk with boobs.

MAN 1: In a manner of speech.

EDIE: Twenty dollars. (signs it)

SYDNEY: I like it! Do one of me later? I'm a She-Hulk too! Aaarrrgghh!

(Man 1 exits smiling. Man 2 wanders by, sizing up the stage.)

EDIE: If you're waiting to talk to Leanna, she'll be here soon.

MAN 2: Dandy by me. I like you better anyway.

EDIE: Bully for you.

SYDNEY: How come?

MAN 2: (looks at the stage) She's older.

EDIE: (to Sydney) Older. (to Man 2) She's attractive, what's the diff'?

MAN 2: Probably none, but I've charlie-horsed my junk muscle to her so often through the years, I prefer fresh skank to get my balls a'rollin'. She's kinda played out. She's past her sell-by date. My cock analyst valuates her as a poor investment.

EDIE: And how old are you?

MAN 2: I'm on this end of the camera, and you're on that end. That's how old I am.

EDIE: Would you like to get any older?

MAN 2: What's that mean?

EDIE: Keep moving.

(MAN 2 starts to reply, sees the club's beefy Manager hovering yards out with a bouncer, catches Sydney staring daggers at him, and retreats, outnumbered. The Manager waddles up to their booth.)

MANAGER: (leans over Edie, raspy-throated mutter) Okay. I let you have that one, he's an asshole. Okay? But we are doing business. Conduct yourself. Comport yourself. But that bird? Okay. (he trundles himself away)

SYDNEY: (to Edie) Okay? Okay! (nudges her)

EDIE: Sydney, this just isn't my night.

SYDNEY: Hon', I have grinded my behind here, this club alone, for 'bout two months, and what I have learned is I don't have a night. What I got is a bank statement. Now that there, he looks like not a complete waste of Wildroot Cream. You!

(MAN 3 steps from the gathering throng, grinning, glad-handing his brethren.)

SYDNEY: C'mere, baby, you sit right in amongst us girls.

(They redistribute themselves.)

EDIE: Or, Leanna will be here soon, if you'd rather wait for the featured dancer.

MAN 3: You kiddin'? I love you! I got tennis elbow, I whiffed my stiffy so much to your escapades!

EDIE: Charmed, I'm sure.

MAN 3: You're a doll, a china doll, without the extra makeup. I hardly recognized you.

EDIE: Seems like that was the idea.

MAN 3: I can get a photo with you?

EDIE: Of course, but twenty dollars.

(He ponies up, chucks his phone to a helpful fellow onanist.)

MAN 3: Cheap at the price! (reaching, he soul-crushes them together into a triple scoop totem pole. To the photog:) Got it? (snap) Awright! (sets them free)

SYDNEY: Sugar, Ariel doesn't intend to get too neighborly this evening. Pictures are acceptable and she can sign DVDs from the store upstairs if any of you all want. Lap dances, though, are extracurricular. Anybody who requests one, I can escort 'em to a private room.

MAN 3: (strong arms her close) I bet you can. Look at those apple cheeks! (he blurphs his lips against the side of her face)

EDIE: Maybe that's from the blood rushing to her head.

MAN 3: (to Sydney) I'll call you "Ariel" while you do me. You'll be my imitation Ariel Caliban. (he Captain Queegs her breast)

BOUNCER: Hey! (springs forward)

EDIE: (umbrage taken) Hey, man, hands to yourself. Why don't you come back after someone explains to you how a strip club works?

SYDNEY: It's fine, hon.' Don't mind him.

EDIE: It's not fine. It is *not* fine.

MAN 3: (to the cameraman) Immortalize us once more! (to Edie) Why carry the agita? We three can go to a private room, and we can get extra private for the man with extra big dough. (he forces apart Sydney's knees, his thumb spelunking in her daisy dukes) That private enough for you, Almost-Ariel? (uncomfortable snickering from the onlookers, as Sydney squirms in dismay. The bouncer charges the booth.) Me, you, and Real-Ariel can—

EDIE: Or *you* could do a lap dance for *us*. Check it out.

(She swipes her cupful of scalding coffee onto his crotch.)

MAN 3: (detonating out of the booth) What the fuck! What the—what the fuck!

(The bouncer jumps him, wrestles his arms behind him.)

EDIE: That private enough for you?

MAN 3: What in the fuck! I'll strangle you, fucking bitch!

EDIE: Bring it on. I've got a cup left, and you've got a testicle left.

MAN 3: (twerking inside his chinos) Bitch!

EDIE: (rotates the mug) With your name on it. Says right there: "Contents property of fire engine red useless hairless inept impotent scrotum with larger man-shaped scrotum attached."

MAN 3: Where's the manager?

(The Manager returns, intervenes.)

MANAGER: (to Man 3) Did I warn you before? You do not touch. They touch.

MAN 3: I'll call a lawyer!

MANAGER: Who will explicate to you that laying your paws on a female without permission is also pronounced "assault." Here's your phone. Toss the dice, see what your future holds.

MAN 3: I'll call the cops!

MANAGER: Several of LA's finest are present. Should I invite their company?

(Shelly descends into the fray, in street clothes.)

MAN 3: (to Edie) You and me will cross paths again one dark day.

EDIE: Pray that never happens, Buster, 'cause next time I'm gonna find a blasting cap and some C4, and give you the mother of all circumcisions!

MANAGER: Out. Out you go.

(The bouncer escorts Man 3 off the premises.)

MANAGER: (to Edie) You too. Use the service entrance, avoid your new boyfriend.

EDIE: Like hell.

SYDNEY: She was defending me!

MANAGER: I'm a reasonable man. I talk to reasonable people. The unreasonable must go.

SHELLY: She's going. Me too, that was my final dance.

MANAGER: Okay, you too. Drama, I don't need.

SHELLY: Dude, we, you, everybody made money tonight, and, c'mon, occasionally an example should be set. Fuckers have to know their place. It's all good.

MANAGER: I pay a bouncer to show fuckers places. (to Edie) You want to be a bouncer? I am presuming the answer is "No."

EDIE: I'll bounce. I'll bounce right now. (she rises) Want to bounce, Shelly? Let's go.

(She forsakes the booth.)

EDIE: It was nice meeting you, Sydney.

(Sydney waves goodbye.)

SHELLY: 'Bye, Sydney!

EDIE: Call me.

MANAGER: Yes, call her at her extension inside the Thunderdome.

(Edie and Shelly pass among the rabble, eliciting a spontaneous roar of applause, Shelly reciprocating with the Queen Elizabeth wave. As they glide outside and into the history books:)

EDIE: *Please* still be out there, loverboy. I'm beggin' ya.

SHELLY: (laughing) Didn't I tell you this would bring you back, Popeye? Dopey guys are your spinach!

CHAPTER 4

(Dissolve to Exterior, Izzy's small House, sunny Early Thursday Morning. Izzy enters the Shot in workout togs, swinging a gym bag. Before he can access the door, Ed sidles in.)

ED: Lombardo! Friend. Knight errant! Master of men! Reaver of women!

IZZY: Make it quick, Eddie. I gotta take a leak last *September.*

ED: Your urgency is noted. But realize, won't you Iz,' that we are naught but painted horses hobbled on the Great Carousel? Neither our roundabout globe, nor life's whirligig, care a jot—

IZZY: Jesus Christ! (he fumbles at the knob)

ED: Medieval scribes we are, toiling to illuminate the parched skin of our book of hours while the Earth turns out its dark age.

IZZY: Fuck! (he gives it up, drops his bag, scrabbles at his shorts)

ED: (browsing the environs) No Toms a-Peeping, you'll observe? Just a quiet spot and the pressing need. Have at it, buddy. I'm your squire, look. (he unzips his slacks) By the way, when you go to Pie-Rite this morning, think I could accompany you? I have a question or two for your boss, courtesy of, um, *MEH*, but I can't get past the security guard. It'll be a soft focus puff piece, the typical lightweight verbiage.

(They free their hogs. Izzy's stream sizzles into the wall. Ed uses his baton to conduct a larghissimo. As their bladders depressurize, Izzy's eyeballs creep downward in astonishment.)

IZZY: Holy shit, Ed. How do you get it through the door?

ED: I wrap it round my leg forty or fifty times. You?

IZZY: You're being kind.

ED: Poppycock. I might even envy you. Five years ago, Iz,' when we met, when we were young and succulent with possibility, you and I, the country bumpkin and the trouser lumpkin, I thought, Porn Star Izzy? Okay, what if he did draw the short straw? That nugatory nubbin—

IZZY: I don't know what that means, but I'm offended.

ED: That picayune pickle will do the job. Nobody's holding a T-square to the screen when you haul it out, my lad.

IZZY: Terrific. Appreciate that.

ED: (gently) No complaints from the ladies, I hope?

IZZY: No! I'm good on the magnitude when I'm, you know, when the ball game is "batter up" I'm sizable.

ED: In real life? Enchanting to hear. On a porn set, of course, it's a non-issue.

(They lean on the wall. Izzy joggles out a reluctant ounce, and coaxes his minutiae into his briefs. Ed wiggles his, too, bespattering much of the Eastern Seaboard.)

IZZY: About access. Bro, Charlie'd kill me. He treats the place like it's a friggin' fortress.

ED: And here my siege engine is at the shop getting a tune-up. (casually inspecting his still-aerated member) Let me ask *you*. What's going on with Charlie and one of your demoiselles, Eden Gann?

IZZY: Eddie, I can't talk about office shenanigans and what-all, without permission. (wipes his hands on his jeans) Porn sex, "real" sex, I'm turned around, man. What'd you say, it's a non-issue?

ED: It is, because they're opposites.

IZZY: Opposites?

ED: (gesturing with his pecker) What is a tool, but its function? What is an act, but its object? Define things by what they seek to achieve. Tell me the object, the goal of sex.

IZZY: Gittin' off!

ED: Woman's pleasure. (he taps his horn section) Men are defective slot machines: every time you yank the handle, it's jackpot. Orgasm is a cinch. Pleasing women, contrarily, is a round of liar's poker, all bluff and guesswork with a chancy outcome. If sex is about mutual pleasure, and man's pleasure is assured, the goal of good sex is woman's pleasure. If an act is its object, the sex act exists to gratify the woman. Now, what is the goal of porn sex?

IZZY: Woman's pleasure?

(He pauses for effect. They share a hearty laugh.)

IZZY: Sorry, I couldn't resist.

ED: Porn sex is about the visual. It must conclude with the conspicuous, the manifest, proof of orgasm. That's seldom provided by the lady. The endgame of porn sex is the male orgasm. Opposites!

IZZY: You get that from a video, or a girl sometimes? (he jams his key in the lock and reclaims his bag)

ED: (sighing, he embarks upon the time-consuming process of cramming Big Ed back in his pants) Sadly I, yes I, once loved and lost.

IZZY: Didn't pan out?

ED: No, our backgrounds were too dissimilar. Her people were Visigoths, and I come from a long line of Ostrogoths. Such was the gulf, the chasm, separating us. Our families disapproved. Ultimately my mater, Crotechilde daughter of Theodoric wife of Brunulphe, relented and blessed our union—actually, she slaughtered a vulture and sprinkled us with its blood, but six of one, half a dozen of the other... (zips up) However—

IZZY: Is any of that true?

ED: Everything I tell you is a lie, including what I'm telling you at this moment.

IZZY: (confused stare)

ED: (sensing an opportunity) Furthermore, did you know that like Pinocchio, lying, and lying alone, compels a part of my anatomy to grow longer? I wonder, if I say "My phallus will grow," will it?

IZZY: It, uh, if you're lying, it will. But if it does, how could you be lying?

ED: Precisely. This recalls to me an anecdote from erotica's jazzier quarter, the realm of gay porn. A popular headliner was renowned for his ability to satisfy himself orally. One day our limber Lothario resolved to blow all those, and only those, performers who didn't blow themselves. I ask you: did he blow himself?

IZZY: Um, if he didn't, then he must have, but then if he does, then he can't.

ED: And I'm reminded of Edie Gann, whom I believe might have sidled into our colloquy a twinkling ago. Perhaps you could ask her something, when you see her. You may have heard that she essayed a few Bondage and Discipline shoots before Vogel brought her on board. In a photo-story, she was dominatrix to a submissive. As the two flitted from argy to bargy, he quite advanced himself in her regard until, moved as she was by his dogsbody ways, she decided to requite him with the command, "Do not obey my orders anymore!" Could he have obeyed her order?

IZZY: ...Obeyed?

ED: He does, so he doesn't, and if he doesn't, he does. Simple.

IZZY: Simple...

ED: You should ask her about it, Izzy, when you see her. Ask her. Right?

IZZY: I...can't ask...

ED: Can't?

IZZY: She's...I shouldn't say...

ED: No? Yes or no? Answer the question: will the next word you say be "No"?

IZZY: (goggle-eyed) If I say "No," the answer is "Yes..."

ED: Edie Gann. What's the deal?

IZZY: She's out. Charlie fired her...

ED: Fired! And the others? Fired, too?

IZZY: No, some flakes, lately, that's the business.

ED: Of course. It inclines to the undertaking, I'd venture.

(A defeated Izzy turns to the door.)

ED: Just between you and me, my friend, right?

IZZY: (wandering inside) All's I know is, I don't know!

(Ed whips out his notebook and pen.)

ED: "Eden Gann, the former Ariel Caliban, released unceremoniously from her contract with Pie-Rite Pics. Lubricating the egress of her confreres, as well? *Sub rosa* skullduggery indeed." (he closes the book. Thinking aloud:) Follow up calls to place, yes. And on to the cybercafé!

I'm sorry, my sympathy goes to Izzy here. He wasn't trying to out me, and Tragos leading somebody like him into a state of confusion is like a freezer leading a tray of water into the state of ice. He was doing what came naturally. Being an idiot. Ed gets no credit, that one is on God.

He was filling up his damned notebook, though.

Meanwhile Shelly had agreed, a while ago, to help educate the unwashed masses that day by talking to a battalion of coke-bottle-lens nudniks at a (shanty)town hall/community discussion site called Threadum, *and with my anonymous assist, her speaking and me taking dictation, we opened the floor...*

(Dissolve to Interior, at a table in the Dining Room of Edie's Condo, Thursday Noon. Edie is seen from behind, typing expertly on a laptop. An animated Shelly paces around her, chattering energetically, too low to be heard. Camera Pushes In to a Close Up of the screen, far along in their Q&A.)

ENTER LEANNA'S...CONFIDENCES

Submitted by L'AmourRoars

Is that—No, it can't be—Yes, it's her. *That* chick. Leanna L'Amour, narsty-ass videowhoor, ridding the queendom of possible pornguy progeny two hundred million tadpoles at a time. A random mouse in the maze, lovin' the left-hand rule. (Meeep-meeep.) Curious? Inquisitive? Brilliant insights? Gimme!

COMMENTS

...will do for a few months up 'til you puncture it and the air rushes out, and I've patched up romantic relationships with people but never with inanimate objects. My advice: respect the flesh. Anyway, those staring eyes and round mouths give me night sweats.

Q: (Tunnelvision) 12:01pm

Thanks.

Q: (CanReachItFromHere) 12:01pm

Leanna, can you describe how you got in this biz.

A: (L'AmourRoars)

I had passed my LSAT and applying to law schools (really? yup!) when I accompanied my boyfriend to a gentlemen's club, where I didn't see a whole lot of gentlemen, but I did see the featured dancer, who did vids for Pie-Rite studio, and after he got a pic and an autograph she discreetly slipped me her number. I suppose my slut vibe was strong even mid 20's. To start, artcore with girl/girl. Soon I branched out into everything.

Q: (RumSodomyRash) 12:02pm

You intend to practice law when your career in adult is finished?

A: (L'AmourRoars)

Yeah uh huh.

I think that ship has sailed.

Q: (LezIsMore) 12:02pm

Regrets?

A: (L'AmourRoars)

The pornos don't pay that well and when you're contracted to a studio, you don't do a ton of them. That leaves me lots of opp's to hooch my choochie in joints all around. The profit margin is better, there.

Pie-Rite raised my profile, now I search for various ways to market it. "Leannalube." "Vibrator a L'Amour." And the love doll (I'm looking at you, Tunnelvision), though that didn't fly off the shelves. Too pricey? You tell me.

Q: (LezIsMore) 12:03pm

Didn't buy it, bought it, didn't buy it. More for guys than gals.

A: (L'AmourRoars)

Plus, I've saved and invested prudently, which I suspect is uncommon in my occupation. May the Lord bless and keep you, pointy-headed Silicon Valley nerdlingers! I estimate in a couple more years, I'll be of "retirement age." (In porn, that's not wrong.) How many individuals can you name who in their late thirties can stop working, kick back, travel, and have a future wide as the horizon?

Q: (LezIsMore) 12:03pm

Good for you!

Q: (PulledPork) 12:03pm

Massive fan, Leanna. Glad you're participating in this. I bet you've been asked b4. Here goes. If you weren't in videos, what might you be doing?

A: (L'AmourRoars)

I dunno, maybe I'd be here grilling you, porn stud.

Kidding aside, I believe in capital-F Fate and that we discern alternative paths but don't get to choose them, freedom of choice is an illusion, we are trapped in a cause and effect chain extending from before we were born which can be broken only by random events that don't restore free will to the equation because randomness is not willed, and we die alone in a cold and meaningless universe, and... S'mores, anyone?

Q: (PulledPork) 12:04pm

Excuse me while I go kill myself.

Q: (ChewOnThis) 12:04pm

She said the law.

Q: (PulledPork) 12:04pm

Right, apologies. Justice Leanna, I instead throw myself on the mercy of the court.

Q: ((L'AmourRoars))

I'd hang ya, but I see you're already hung. Case dismissed!

Q: (CraftBeerCanDick) 12:05pm

I'm a presentable guy, who can get it up in the most exceedingly trying circumstances. What's the trick to being cast in a porno?

A: (L'AmourRoars)

Truly I don't know, man. The unhelpful formula is, pretty girls = no problem breaking into straight porn, cute boys = easily get in gay porn, cute boys = *might* get in straight porn, pretty girls in gay porn? = don't call us we'll call you.

Q: (BigglesInThePants) 12:05pm

Spit or swallow?

A: (L'AmourRoars)

Swish, swallow, repeat. Not thrilled by the taste... Something about the act. I don't analyze it. My sig oth don't cotton, though.

Q: (BigglesInThePants) 12:05pm

I hope it's a lady! You're with a woman? (Also in porn?)

A: (L'AmourRoars)

Yeah, sorry opposite sex, it's hot girl-on-girl action these days. Nuttin' but pillow fights, sharing each other's perfume, and synchronized periods. I knew you wanted to hear that last part.

Q: (DoesDistressMakeMeLookFat) 12:06pm

I understand you're into BDSM in IRL. Expound, please. (details)

A: (L'AmourRoars)

WIITWD? TNG, "in IRL" I'm a 24/7 abrasive, figging, cupping, OTK spanking electro-play-maintenance RACK-preferring top (never a switch) with an auctioned, collared, mummified bottom, sometimes nyotaimori, sometimes shibari hogtied, no need for a DM or munch or black sheeters, with Gorean impact play until subspace then subdrop then aftercare occur.

Or just cuddling is nice, too.

As long as it includes breast torture and nose hooks.

Q: (DesitivelyBone-aroo) 12:06pm

You've got to be a domme. You made my brain hurt.

A: (L'AmourRoars)

Rejoice, painslut!

Q: (BuiltSpiltKilt) 12:07pm

Leanna! Dinner?

A: (L'AmourRoars)

Hells yeah, bring some for everyone. Hawaiian pizza. (I told you I like to make people suffer.)

Q: (CreamSoup) 12:07pm

Do you have a favorite penis

size?

A: (L'AmourRoars)

1-Yes. I keep it in a jewelry box near my bed.

2-Six and three eighth inches, as that is the largest box I own.

Q: (NardnPat) 12:07pm

First time/long time. Indulge me:

1-Best star to do scenes with?

2-Will you ever sell your own artificial vagina?

3-Where do you see the industry going, the next several years?

4-Marry me!

A: (L'AmourRoars)

1-Ariel Caliban.

2-What I do with my artificial vagina is none of your concern, Sir. (How did you know?)

3-It's forever evolving. 70's bush baby films don't look like 80's hairspray vids, the 80's don't look like the stripper-fit 90's, the 90's don't look like today.

4-Take me, I'm yours! June wedding?

Q: (TheUdderWoman) 12:08pm

He asked, though, where the industry was going.

A: (L'AmourRoars)

Yeah. Dodging the question. The internet is a game changer, I don't doubt it. I predict it will be the sole delivery system soon. And after that, we'll be fucking Matrix-style.

Q: (BugSplat) 12:08pm

And having tentacle sex with the machines' ships.

A: (L'AmourRoars)

Squidgy. Don't push the analogy, dude.

Q: (ThoseLipsThoseEyes) 12:08pm

Seriously ambivalent, Leanna. How do you, an obviously no-BS person, reconcile to a profession which objectifies women? I'm a fan (and a woman) but it's never been easy for me to justify.

A: (L'AmourRoars)

That's okay. But we're performers, and the objectification is a performance, too. It's someone else's fantasy, and they get to have it because they're paying me to enact it for them. If they have to come to me and give me money and ask me to do this, and I can say yes or go to hell or pay me more, who's in charge? And I don't mind repeatedly bringing up the money to you guys, in any job they must pay you to do what you wouldn't do for them gratis.

Q: (PulledPork) 12:09pm

Excuse me again while I go kill myself again.

A: (L'AmourRoars)

Sure the business is run by men as a rule, no different than most businesses. Customers? They empty their wallets for the women. We have the power, if we'll use it.

And if the porn is created by and purchased by women—there are a few estrogen-centric studios—the process of "objectification" is consensual end to end. Who's victimized?

Q: (StiffyBits) 12:09pm

You're officially harshing my buzz, Leanna. (sound of hand quitting lap)

A: (L'AmourRoars)

Soapbox, please!

Since the conversation is about women's bodies and in what ways they ought to be used or viewed, and it assumes the question is to be answered by women themselves and not men, it follows that the owner of the actual body, the woman, should get final say (even when said body is embedded in a patriarchy, since we now enter into the topic of personal responsibility IMO. Unblinking, ask yourself whether you're submitting to the "male gaze," or are doing your thing, and behave accordingly).

Q: (MoreThanEnoughMuff) 12:10pm

That could be called a kind of old-school feminism, I guess.

Q: (CheezWiz) 12:10pm

Wondering if we could possibly return to the subject of tentacle sex...

A: (L'AmourRoars)

I don't believe sex is something men "get" from women, or women "give" to men. It's a transaction whether cash or emotion or fluid is exchanged, and it's a good transaction if both parties are left equally satisfied. That's it.

Q: (Caprichorale) 12:10pm

Brava! We are collections of parts. It's the reductive aspect which may offend.

A: (L'AmourRoars)

Most often, I'm asked to do what I call "Tiger Woods Porn": three holes in one. If that's all some fans require of a woman, it's their weakness. And it is a weakness. I don't embrace it, I do use it.

Q: (IronIsHot) 12:10pm

Use me, Mistress Leanna!

Q: (TeaterTotter) 12:11pm

This convo got more interesting than I expected. Would you say, as some have, that you're depicting the act of reclaiming female pleasure?

A: (L'AmourRoars)

Nope, practically never do chicks in adult videos really have orgasms, and they don't do the videos for that, and I think our audience gets it and isn't bothered by it. If it's a depiction, it's a depiction of negative space.

I'll be honest. I'm definitely there to reinforce adolescent ideas about sexuality in the arrested development cases among you, through my videos. I admit it.

You'll still buy 'em.

If anything, I have to view it as an act of victimization in the opposite direction. Of you, not me.

Q: (MilkyWhiteDischarge) 12:11pm

...What?

Q: (SuperDrool) 12:12pm

Yup, I'm outta here. Been a slice.

A: (L'AmourRoars)

I notice some ladies present. Welcome. This line of thought tends to pit us against each other—against ourselves! If you check the mirror, and are happy with what you see, is it because you've internalized masculine notions about feminine attractiveness? How do you even know for certain? How do you look, or dress, or act, if you don't know? Do you join the club, whichever club, and let it decide? Where's the agency in that?

And if any man, or woman, lets my vids determine their ideas about sexuality, where's the agency in that?

Q: (Azz4Dayz) 12:12pm

Preach, girl!

A: (L'AmourRoars)

I'm fully responsible for my choices. To myself. All I ask of you ladies is the same.

Q: (Caprichorale) 12:13pm

Would you ask the same of, say, Ariel Caliban? I presume she's the "sig oth" you alluded to, am I correct?

A: (L'AmourRoars)

Of everybody, but that girl least of all needs my advice.

Q: (Caprichorale) 12:13pm

Perhaps, perhaps not. Exercising poor judgment lately, don't you agree?

Q: (StiffyBits) 12:13pm

Officially re-interested. What did Ariel C do now?

Q: (Caprichorale) 12:13pm

Rumor has it she's out on the street, so to speak. Received the sack from Pie-Rite. Comments?

A: (L'AmourRoars)

If my extremely good friend Ariel is reviewing her options, that's her privilege.

Who are you? Besides a big mouth troublemaker, that is.

Q: (Caprichorale) 12:13pm

I'm the Road to Damascus, the Appian Way. I'm the crack of dawn, light of a new day. A journalist, in plain language. Example: since her departure, rumor has it no fewer than four contractors with Pie-Rite have disembarked too, each time shortly after a visit from Caliban. Stirring the pot, is she?

Q: (OiWhatsAllThisThen) 12:13pm

Oi, what's all this then?

A: (L'AmourRoars)

A "journalist" with nothing but rumors to pass around to impressionable idiots. –AC.

Q: (FlangeRod) 12:14pm

Hey hold on a minute, did she call me an idiot? I know when I'm being called an idiot.

Due to the fact that she just did that.

Q: (Caprichorale) 12:14pm

Here is my impression. Rumor has it you, Ms. L'Amour, have, unheralded and without alerting Pie-Rite, initiated a sabbatical from the studio. Again, shortly after Caliban's disengagement. And as to the matter of credentials, my name is Ed Tragos, of *Mature Entertainment Headlines*, and other publications, I have butts waiting to scuttle, and I anticipate with bated breath your response.

A: (L'AmourRoars)

Ariel Caliban here. Want my response?

If you're a journalist, I'm the Queen Mother of Atlantis and Prime Minister of Mars. And even to the extent that you're an asswipe reviewer for asswipe *MEH*, you were always the droopiest dicked wallflower at the hottest ever orgy. And rumor and innuendo are for lazy writers and court eunuchs. Both of which you are. And if anybody does someday locate your balls, I will personally cut them off, throw them on a pan, fry them in garlic butter, garnish them with sprigs of parsley, shove them in your cheeks and punch you in the jaw so hard that semen will shoot out of your ears, which will open them up sufficiently that you'll experience no hardship understanding me when I scream, Consume Shit And Die!

End of discussion.

Ariel & Leanna OUT!

Q: (ShreddedNed) 12:15pm

Pow!

Q: (Caprichorale) 12:15pm

A pleasant day to you. See you, as they say, in the funny papers.

Q: (FurryTurtle) 12:15pm

What. Just. Happened?

Q: (FeatherDuster) 12:15pm

WTF?

12:15pm

12:15pm

12:15pm

12:15pm

Q: (FlangeRod) 12:16pm

She seemed nice...

(Camera Pulls Back from the computer screen. Edie swivels in her chair, meets Shelly's eyes, and shakes her head.)

Thanks, Shel'. Now I knew, and the next thing to do was to put away my Charlie Vogel revenge fantasy and protect my interests by signing as soon as I could with a studio before my quote was affected by talk about Tragos's scummy bottom-feeder article. I executed a U-turn and sprinted to the offices of Jewelpaste Productions, where the bossman, a half-a-giraffe boy wonder with a bonus pituitary gland and a Harvard MBA, was kind enough to see me and give me the cook's tour before we got down to brass tacks...

(Dissolve to a substantial, well-organized Office, Early Afternoon Thursday. A gangling Man of about twenty-five years, goateed, wearing a man bun and a blazer over a Radiohead T-shirt, slouches under the doorway and enters accompanied by Edie, flipping his fedora onto his desk as they sit.)

MAN: (in the midst of conversation) ...media, as I've shown you. Shelf on shelf of DVDs. Or no tangible media: frictionless, or thereabouts. No friction is better.

EDIE: You're in the wrong line!

MAN: Friction between my pockets. Inside my pocket, no. Companies producing Blu-rays. It's a mistake, it lacks direction. They're treading water. What is the result if you tread water too long.

EDIE: You get tired? You sink?

MAN: You sink. You drown. You're a fan of hi-def?

EDIE: High definition is no friend to a naked lady, Mister Scas—

MAN: You'll get it. Pronounced Sha-CAH-loh. I prefer the one name. Sciacallo. One name and you're unique. Think fashion designers. Think Banksy. Prince.

EDIE: Attila? Boudica?

SCIACALLO: Yes! Because they're warriors. This industry. Eleven thousand hardcore movies annually, thirty percent of video rentals, sales and rentals together, billions of dollars per year earned. Behind the scenes? General Motors, through Direct TV. Time Warner, through cable. Marriott, Hilton, Westin. I'm a pornographer. The two of us. Our interests coincide at present. Later? More prosaic interests will supersede. I plan to be liquid. To have liquidity. To move sideways among these companies. Then upward. Am I a pornographer? I'm a capitalist. Jewelpaste, my releases average seven hundred units sold per annum. Total releases industry-wide? Fourteen thousand last year. And the internet. (he draws her attention to a pie chart on the wall) Note the demographics. Income less than fifteen thousand, six-point-two-three percent of users. Note the percentage goes up with each income level. At an increasing velocity. Income above seventy-five thousand? Thirty-five-point-three-zero percent of users. What to do with that market.

EDIE: What businesses do, figure out what they'll pay for and give it to them? (she scans another chart) "Most Searched Terms by Country." "Lesbian." "Lesbian." "Teen." "Mom." "Teen." "Beurette?" "Novinha?" I'm afraid to ask.

SCIACALLO: No. No. It's online. It's the algorithm. What is your search history. Keywords? Start there. Who are you. Where is your job, your home. What do you like. Support your appetites, yes. But mold them, too. Ads. The menu of content we display. Very limited. Shape your desires. Create an addict. Addicted to the content. "Content wants to be free"? Not when the content is yours alone.

EDIE: With you as the man behind the curtain.

SCIACALLO: Some man will be behind the curtain. Be glad you know the man.

EDIE: I'd be happier if I worked for the man.

SCIACALLO: Not a possibility.

EDIE: W-what? Why is it not a possibility?

SCIACALLO: Rumors of troublemaking. Damaging your employer's brand. A story making the rounds, the studios. An exposé to be published.

EDIE: I heard the story. It can't hurt you, or me if you hire me.

SCIACALLO: No major studio will sign you. Or Pie-Rite, either, no re-sign. After the sale at AEE in Vegas concludes.

EDIE: What sale? Charlie is selling the studio?

SCIACALLO: Gonzalez, the owner. Studio treading water, as I said.

EDIE: He'll have to parade his ladies for the buyer.

SCIACALLO: Remaining ladies, yes. Not you. Too much grief. No major will sign you after the sale. Neither will the midlevel studios. Not a loose cannon performer.

EDIE: I'm a loose cannon.

SCIACALLO: I can recommend several lower echelon studios. As a favor. Let's see. There's Anaphylactic Video. Zero Pretenses Entertainment. Excruciating Associates.

EDIE: One article, that doesn't exist yet.

SCIACALLO: It's proactivity. I'm a disinterested party. Where you go or what you do. I can advise, since you're here.

EDIE: Feel free.

SCIACALLO: Bigger breasts. Fewer reservations. Anal is back on the table. Bukkake is on the table. It's a crowded table. The table is groaning. What you've got to sell from here on. You'll do it all. The porn star, brought low. Fans love it.

EDIE: Is that what I am? Low?

SCIACALLO: You can't take it personally. When my day is done, I leave this at the office. Not a pornographer. I'm a husband and a father. (he taps a family portrait)

EDIE: That's your son?

SCIACALLO: It is. Four years.

EDIE: Ladykiller.

SCIACALLO: Thank you.

EDIE: Who broke the jar?

SCIACALLO: I don't—

EDIE: You, or your wife?

SCIACALLO: The jar?

EDIE: The jar of formaldehyde he was floating in when you visited the freak museum.

SCIACALLO: (thousand yard stare) No jar.

EDIE: No jar? All right. How long *has* your family lived downstream from a nuclear waste dump?

SCIACALLO: You'll insist on dragging in the personal. My innocent intentions notwithstanding.

EDIE: Do you think they'll make him their king?

SCIACALLO: Who will?

EDIE: When he's finally reclaimed by his wandering tribe of Yeti relatives—

SCIACALLO: The doorway swings in two directions. You can walk straight through it.

EDIE: You can watch me. (she stands and pauses by the door) You're betting you can regiment lust, but you can't. It's not like gambling or other vices. People will surprise you. They'll surprise themselves sometimes. Sex is bottomless. (she steps out, sticks her head in) Here's a rule to live by: in all of recorded history, not one guy with a man bun was an expert on fucking. You can look it up! (she exits)

Okay, badass ballsy girl accepts no shit, takes no prisoners. Yay. Except that was the moment when impulse turned into necessity. Suddenly I no longer wanted *to demobilize Pie-Rite's contract stars, I* had *to do it, before you caught on to me and by Expo time, be the only woman to show up there, and wait for you and that Gonzalez guy to see the error of your ways and beg me to come home.*

Not that there weren't problems enough to go around...

CHAPTER 5

(Cut to Early Evening Thursday, Exterior, a cybercafé. Ed quits the establishment, lips smacking, warmed to the pith by a leisurely supper and an aperitif or three, and windy as an Irish orator. He expels a molar-rattling belch in the general direction of the setting orange sun. Descending to the sidewalk, he is accosted at once by a freckle-punctuated boxy blonde gamine, post-winsome, with klieg light eyeballs and the grin of a gap-toothed carnivore. He stops short.)

GIRL: Mister Tragos?

ED: The same, to my great good fortune. Your servant, madam.

GIRL: (talons outstretched) Hello. (they shake) Hi. My name is Possum Oakley? I don't believe we've met. Are you, do you have a ride? I've got a car. Um, I'm from *MEH*, a different cubicle than you. Can I drive you?

ED: You certainly may. I am in the way of being a convinced boulevardier, you know, my little marmosa. (an epic burp) However, today I shall hew to the directive of, I'm going to say, Buddha or Bazooka Joe, not sure which, who warned, "There are two mistakes one can make on the road to truth; not going all the way, and not starting." Let's hit the road.

(Possum opens her car door, unlocking the passenger side. Ed wriggles in. Cut to Interior, Possum's Car.)

ED: How did His Nibs deduce where—

POSSUM: Mister Corbetti? It's a bit embarrassing to repeat. (she joins the traffic) You can direct me to your place.

ED: North. North as is the North Star. You're fine.

POSSUM: Mister Corbetti understands that you're onto a scoop, due to some postings at a web forum? He understands you're not sick at all. He said to me, "Possum, you're new, an intern, you're a gofer basically, but you aspire to be a journalist," (I'm studying journalism at school) "you get Ed," (he knew you'd be here because [his words] "it's one of the known branches that tree dwelling ape likes to hang from," sorry) "you find Tragos and you will learn specifically what not to do. Because we are here to prop up an industry, not to bulldoze it," (he's thinking of firing you) "and you tell that malingering, malodorous son of a bitch excuse for an ink-stained wretch to come in Monday with a puff piece and I'll ruminate on the possibility of not butchering his entire family and dancing the moonwalk on their coffins. Or maybe don't ever come in again." Am I still going north?

ED: ...Clarifying. You're an intern through your school, and they sent you to *Mature Entertainment Headlines* magazine?

POSSUM: University of California.

ED: At Los Angeles? A laudable institution.

POSSUM: At Irvine.

ED: Oh! That explains it.

POSSUM: Go Anteaters!

ED: Go, indeed.

POSSUM: And I feel guilty.

ED: Because you're an inkjet away from pandering pornography? Hogwash. Is there even such a critter?

POSSUM: No, because I'm the messenger, the bearer of bad tidings.

ED: You are both a possum and a catspaw, yes. I forgive you, messenger. I'll shoot you some other time. (stentorian belch)

POSSUM: (visibly relieved) Thank you so much for letting me off the hook. And I can concede the appeal of an interesting story. (pause) Did you just say there's no such thing as pornography?

ED: (tipping his car seat) I reject the designation. Do we in the field mean to arouse? Undeniable. Not a convincing argument, though. Shall I use the example of fetish material? Yes: it sets up the thorniest objections.

POSSUM: Fetishes. Hmmm.

ED: (waxing pedagogical) Say you and I each contrive a video showcasing a woman's bare foot. My monument to cinema goes to the San Francisco Museum of Art, part of a series illuminating the commonplaces of everyday life. Additional images include my teapot, a birdhouse outside my window, a taxicab to our office, et cetera. My aim was not sexual stimulation. But your filmic masterpiece goes to a web site for fetishists, you bad girl! (she laughs) Our work is identical in content and craftsmanship. Uninformed creatures, examining them together, sans context, cannot locate a disparity in purpose, and if purpose should brand one of them as pornography, and purpose is absent, neither effort is pornographic. (he wrestles his seat farther back)

POSSUM: I never thought of it that way.

ED: (stretching his legs) Or, both are. "It's the reaction evoked," you say. "I am a devout advocate of the site you allude to, 'Ho's-and-toes dot com,' and both collections of images get me bothered, to me they're erotica. To someone else, perhaps not, but to me."

POSSUM: Isn't the reaction important?

ED: Should it be? Gay porn doesn't arouse straights, or vice versa, and any given fetish representation, to the unconcerned majority, is about as hot as Doc's stethoscope.

POSSUM: Yeah, fetish. (grips the steering wheel) Why can't eroticism be intrinsic? Still north?

ED: You're good. Here we have a photo of a man's genitalia. From a medical tome. There, a description of copulation. In a textbook on sexuality. Neither are pornographic. We've returned to the theme of context and motive. (a final gaseous eructation)

POSSUM: But why not? (she passes him a breath mint) An idea, or a state of mind, can be "transferred" to a physical thing. That's the essence of communication, isn't it?

ED: Yes. But the thing must present the idea successfully. *That's* communication. It's a two-headed beast. If I assert an idea and you're unreceptive, we've communicated nothing. Left at the next light. (unwraps his mint)

POSSUM: You—

ED: I admit to being a hopeless draftsman. My sketches of lovers *in media res* invariably end up resembling a walrus doing pushups in a Barcalounger. To say a doodle of a sea mammal in a recliner is erotica because I wish it to be, is to taffy-pull the definition beyond recognition. (pops the mint. Continues speaking as it skids across his bicuspids.) You see, since the concept of "erotic" involves an esthetic judgment, an actual judge is required, not just the creator and the thing-to-be-judged.

POSSUM: Okay. (turns the wheel)

ED: Therefore if the quality marking a thing as erotic can't necessarily be found in the thing itself, nor in the conception of the thing, nor in the reception, then it isn't anywhere!

POSSUM: What about if I create erotica and view it myself? That satisfies all the criteria. I'm the creator and the judge.

ED: Ridiculous.

POSSUM: Why?

ED: Each time you had an amorous dream, or a sexy thought, you'd be a pornographer. Erotica must be disseminated, to *be* erotica.

POSSUM: You're ridiculous.

ED: How so?

POSSUM: Because "porno-graphy." It's in the definition. "Sex made graphic."

ED: Literally, "harlotry in writing."

POSSUM: I commit my thought to a physical medium, not just think it, and I view it.

ED: Look up that definition of pornography. "Writings, pictures, films, etc., designed to stimulate erotic feelings." If you create it, you have these feelings. It must be produced for others, to stimulate the same reaction. And if you look at it afterward when you're not already stimulated, you're not identical to the person who created it. You might not be aroused by it anymore. By yourself, you don't "satisfy all the criteria." Now, suppose you wake from your spicy dream and relate it to me, in speech alone. Talking is committing to a physical medium, sound.

POSSUM: Not permanent.

ED: No physical entity is permanent. Celluloid, canvas, paper, simply are longer in fading to oblivion.

POSSUM: Okay, I tell you my dream, I'm a pornographer. If I created it, purpose is apparent to me.

ED: Not necessarily.

POSSUM: How not?

ED: What if, instead, you talk in your sleep and I overhear you? What's the difference?

POSSUM: Intention. I can't be an unintentional pornographer!

ED: (lecturing around his mint) Exactly. You created it, yet you're not a pornographer, therefore, how can you have created pornography? You didn't, so it isn't, even if I am aroused by it.

POSSUM: "I know—"

ED: The author of the essay on "Erotic Art" in the *Stanford Encyclopedia of Philosophy* gropes in his drawers—escritoire-ally speaking—for an adequate definition: "...erotic art is art that is made with the intention to stimulate its target audience sexually, and that succeeds to some extent in doing so."

POSSUM: He's quoting an encyclopedia to me.

ED: This is tenuous at best. If it stimulates me successfully on Monday and Wednesday but fails on Tuesday, where did its identity as erotica go?

POSSUM: Ugh! C'mon. Porn exists because "I know porn when I see it!"

ED: Yes? Who died and made *you* boss?

POSSUM: I'm saying we all know porn when we see it.

ED: Do we? Empty noise, unless you imply that an absolute reference exists against which we each can judge whether a work is pornographic, or not, and come to a like conclusion. And doesn't that sentiment always pack the extra baggage of a moral component? Porn is good, or porn is bad. Never neutral. Where is that absolute reference?

POSSUM: Can I make a detour? (spins the wheel)

ED: Not in our nature, as I demonstrated. Then it must be an esthetic and moral absolute outside of ourselves. And what name do we give to the absolute arbiter external to ourselves, and acting as a moral coordinate? Why, God, of course.

POSSUM: (searching the streets) I'll grant, you're very confident about sexuality.

ED: There, you've persuaded me. Every work of hardcore pornography is proof of the existence of God. (he crunches the mint to a pulverulence) *Reductio ad absurdum!*

POSSUM: You speak with such authority. Such an air of... (she enters a parking lot) ...command, Mister Tragos.

ED: Ed, please.

POSSUM: It's quite sexy. (stops the engine)

ED: Pish tosh.

(She scrambles out and waits for him. Cut to Exterior, a Parking Lot. They converge on an unremarkable single story shuttered concrete box.)

ED: I use the terms interchangeably for variety, but I do recognize a distinction between erotica and pornography.

POSSUM: Oh?

ED: Erotica, a subspecies of Art, is suggestive. It demands that the aficionado meet it halfway, imaginatively, emotionally. It doesn't do everything for you.

POSSUM: I guess not.

(Exterior, Building. They arrive at a Door with a slot at eye level)

ED: Pornography is definite. It reduces one to a spectator. It does all you need it to do, asking little of you. This is the source of Schopenhauer's dishonorable discharge, from Art, of things that *necessarily* stimulate without the *entre nous* of aesthetic contemplation.

(Possum raps on the door.)

ED: Note that before the internet, self-abusers had to start with the erotic—say, bodies in swimsuits—and graduate to the pornographic—bodies, period—later, because access to explicit matter was controlled until they came of age.

(The slot clacks open, revealing two glittering basilisk irises.)

POSSUM: *"Terwilliger."*

(A rusty-sounding lock bolt scrapes out of its strike plate.)

ED: I mentioned Art. Art, say I, is a letter of intent to the world.

(The door creaks inward.)

ED: And The World, I define as anything that is not Me. And is thus unworthy of any further consideration—

(Possum grabs his shirt and hustles him in. The door slams shut.)

(Cut to Interior, Thursday Evening. A Sex Dungeon.)

Edie NARRATES in Possum's newly breathless delivery:

EDIE: *Craptarts.* What's this effect the man has on me? Damn my impertinence! I release his jacket apologetically, my cheeks flushing. A smile flutters on Mr. Tragos's lips. He's possibly the sexiest male I've ever seen. *Quit being so good looking, you.*

I swallow. "I bet this kind of place is a desperate bore to someone like you!" I blurt out over the racket of techno music.

"Not at all," he says, peering at the dimly lit interior, more curious than annoyed. "Beyond my normal areas of interest, dear girl."

Crushed, I search for a hole to crawl into. *Get it together, Oakley.*

I'm saved by the doorman, a muscular, bald-pated specimen in leather shorts, his nipple clamps strung on a skinny chain whose center dangles from a screw poking through his pierced tongue. He jabs a clipboard at Tragos without a peep and gives him a pen. Ed scans the page. I peek past his shoulder, though I've memorized every word in my many visits here.

Is that his aftershave? Gosh. My hair is about to catch on fire. *I want to be your hairy fireball woman.* We read:

THIS WAIVER EXEMPTS OUR ESTABLISHMENT FROM LEGAL RESPONSIBILITY FOR ACTS COMMITTED ON ITS PREMISES. PATRONS ARE EXPECTED TO ADHERE TO THE RULES AND GUIDELINES PRESENTED HEREIN. INITIAL EACH LINE, AND SIGN AND DATE AT THE END OF THE FORM.

SUBMISSIVES:

1) Submissive attests that they suffer from no life threatening illnesses. Submissives omitting to disclose said illnesses to management, and subsequently dying in the course of a session, are at risk of permanently losing their membership.

2) Submissive must demonstrate obedience to Dominant at all times (see: Appendix). Failure to show obedience may entail the sacrifice of an appendix (see: Appendix).

3) Submissive's eyes must remain downcast in the presence of their Dominant. Blindfolded Submissives must cut eyeholes in blindfolds so that Dominants may ascertain whether rule is obeyed (see: Zorro, Mark of).

4) Conduct of Submissives reflects on their Dominants. Common courtesy, while being flayed alive, is a hallmark of civilized behavior. "Please" (throttle me) and "Thank

you" (for chiseling the Serenity Prayer into my epidermis) are simple words that go a long way.

5) Checkmark. Submissive agrees to be restrained with:

    a)   wrists fixed in front

    b)   wrists fixed behind back

    c)   knees bound

    d)   right wrist affixed behind back to left knee

    e)   left ankle affixed to right shoulder

    f)   right kidney affixed to hot air balloon

DOMINANTS:

1) Dominants are responsible for wiping down equipment after a session. Leaving gore for the next Dominant to clean up is considered the height of rudeness.

2) Dominant may loan his Submissive to another Dominant, so long as Dominant follows prevailing international exchange rates (examples):

    a)   two English ponygirls = four Canadian adult babies

    b)   six German commodes, human = one Tibetan monk, immolated

3) Use of safe words is solely at the discretion of Dominants, but should be settled upon in advance. Clientele are welcome to employ the safe words below, ordered by severity of pain inflicted:

    a)   "humina-humina"

    b)   "d'oh!"

    c)   "thanks a lot, Gilligan!"

4) Erotic humiliation: comments can be equally as hurtful as instruments of torture. (Little known fact: during World War Two, Lieutenant General Bernard Montgomery won the Battle of El Alamein against Field Marshall Erwin Rommel not by superior weaponry or strategy, but by declaring to Rommel in a communiqué dated 1 July, 1942, "My dear Winnie: owing to our two nations' recent and most regrettable donnybrook, I feel myself obliged to inform you that my beret says it should very much like to eat your swagger stick. Wishing you all the best, Monty.") Truly devastating. However, the ability to use statements effectively is an aptitude given to few Dominants. This dungeon is happy to provide suggestions to Dominants in need of effective insults. Example insults:

a)   "Your sister sells *blini* to the Cossacks."

b)   "Your sainted grandmother has a mug like an armpit bubo." Et cetera.

ALL PATRONS:

1) Bodily organs left on the premises will be held for thirty (30) days. Organs not claimed within thirty (30) days become property of the sex dungeon.

2) Hard Limit: No acts may involve a baby or an animal unless express written consent is obtained beforehand from said baby or animal.

3) Patrons who enjoy being subjected to Face Sitting are discouraged from interacting with patrons undergoing Bladder Desperation.

4) For the last and final time: We implore patrons to choose comfortable footwear prior to leaving home. Our specula are intended for vaginal use only. A vaginal speculum is not, and has never been, "The Poor Man's Shoe Stretcher."

Signed: _____

Tragos scratches on the signature line, and aims his impassive glance at me. "I am at your disposal, Miss Oakley," he says. "After you." I go a fierce red at the sound of my name on his perfect lips. *Thank God for bad lighting.*

My feet wait patiently for a signal from the pyramidal cell axons in my frontal primary motor cortex. I pilot him through the club on licorice twist legs. We pass a flat screen TV monitor showing eight women on a dog track, on all fours, straining at their leashes as a carrot whizzes by along a rail. Eight Masters in breeches crop them forward.

"You like it?" I murmur, husky-voiced.

"Ah! What are new pursuits," he muses, "but sweetmeats from life's buffet, to be savored at leisure?"

I'm pretty sure that's a Yes.

We proceed past a brunette in Nazi regalia, lording it over a pair of Young Republican bottoms draped on a pommel horse, their britches at their ankles. She pokes the naked rumps with the coil end of an electrical wand, and they yelp their appreciation.

"I have to apologize," I say. We progress inward. "I'm afraid we're here hours early. But I might be able to occupy you 'til things pick up."

"Perchance I shall occupy you," he says with a mysterious grin, "as Antigonus occupied Lacedaemon, yes?"

Golly, I think. We're going to do it, and it's going to be Mister Arrogant But Handsome Ed Tragos, and it's going to happen on this spot.

He scans the décor as we walk to the beverage bar—no alcohol allowed—pursing his lips, admiring an iron maiden here, a strappado rigging there. We stop at the bar. "Bear with me!" I say. He smiles that smile. *Gimme him, on a sesame seed bun, with a side of more him.* I beat a hasty retreat, escaping into the dressing room area.

Soon I'm back, threading through a mini obstacle course of chained submissives and their dommes, and find him sipping a chicory coffee and puffing a clove cigarette. Glancing my way, his flawless forehead knits in surprise. Beyond flawless. Flawless could take lessons from his forehead. His forehead could offer a Postgraduate Oxford University Fellowship in flawless. *Cool your jets, Possum.*

"What in Heaven's name are you wearing?" he asks.

Tilting my eyepatch, I throw off my cape and cowl.

"It's my body hugging latex rubber Marga the Panther Woman costume," I say, because it clearly is, "and you are to speak when spoken to!" and I wrap the loop of my snare pole around his collar and yank it taut, ending the discussion. "And sexy stuff *is* proof of the existence of my inner goddess, whom you will now worship! *Reductio ad servitium!*"

"Gakk," he replies.

I rest the pole in the crook of my neck and drag him to a wooden A-frame in a corner of the dungeon. He staggers onto the low platform, tripping on his feet, dizzy from the sudden lack of blood flow to his head. "At this station, you will abase yourself before me. Understood?" He lets me trap his wrists in padded steel cuffs, left and right.

His dismay and confusion gape at me. Yes, the man is lost in confusion, in endless night, and none but I can penetrate his shadows and carry him screaming, newborn, into day.

Hanging on the wall nearby are many instruments of the Art. Shoving the handcuff key in my belt, I slide a riding crop from its bracket. "Hand."

He squints, and zigzags his shackled hand as if waving. I smack it hard with the crop. He flinches and bucks at his restraints.

"Feels good, yes?"

"No!" he bleats.

I smack his other hand, double hard. "No?"

"I...Yes?" Cowed, he awaits his next tutelage.

Can he see how I'm flushed, can he hear how my heart is pounding? I'm wet already.

Determinedly, I squat, sweep his pants down and off, and rise. His attitude is that of a penitent knelling before his confessor. Good. "Refresh my memory. Who is it you belong to?" I say, all innocence.

"I..."

I prod his ribs with the crop. "Who?"

"You!"

"You, what?"

"You, Mistress!"

"Good boy. Or, are you a bad boy?" I jerk the snare swinging from his neck. "Answer me!"

"Ur," he says in a strangled gnarl, surreptitiously attempting to wriggle loose, "A mingy suitor I may have been in some youthful gambols," I stroll behind him while he speaks, pulling on the snare, "if my demission pleases, uh," his eyes dart sideways as I disengage an item from the rack by the wall, "uh, I, uh, might yet equal your most perfervid exploits—" I tap the wooden paddle on his chin.

"Mister Tragos, I am going to display to you the depths of your devotion to me. I'm going—did you just roll your eyes at me?"

"No!"

"And you call me a liar? For that alone you deserve be severely punished!" and I hide his ass until it's bright red.

He wails. But he knows that all I've done is radiate outward the flame smoldering deep inside him. He wants this. He wants to be reduced to an instrument, an apparatus built to amuse Mistress.

I thrash him, thirteen blows in total, twelve strikes and a spare. "We'll do an even twenty, shall we? You will assist me by counting. Count!" I raise the paddle.

"One?" he ventures. I smack him.

"Two!" and again, harder.

"Three!" The tears flow.

"Four!" He flails against his restraints.

He can't say it.

"No? I'll help you. Five!" Groaning, he snatches at the chains by his wrists.

"Six!" He gnashes his teeth, bites his lip.

"Seven!" He slumps backward, swaying from his cuffs. The snare loop urges him upright. "Good."

I forage in my costume, and lift my cupped palm: a string of corded silver metal balls, each the size of a serpent's egg.

He whines in disbelief. "Oh yes. I'm popping these balls in your butthole, one by one, and then snapping them out. How do you like that?" His buttocks tighten. "If you try to resist me, I'm going to jam the handle of my riding crop up there so far you'll taste hay. Which is it to be?"

My eyes never leaving his, I reach around and punch the balls in, one, two, three, four, methodically, listening to his breath whistle through his nostrils.

He freezes, and instinctively tightens up. "That just makes it worse. But be my guest," I say, and I wrench everything out. He shrieks and almost topples the A-frame, wresting the right side cuff off its chain completely.

"Oh my gosh!" I say. He really is too big and strong.

I jerk the snare again. Before I can snag the loose chain on his free hand, he grapples at my waist, holding me close, steals the key from my belt, unlocks the other cuff and forces my wrist toward it. Pushing me away, he steps from the platform.

He throws off the snare and gathers his trousers. "I...articulation fails," he says. "Psychological hugger-mugger on such a stratospheric level has got to be...who's your role model, Vlad the Impaler?" He zips up.

I stare at him, so beautiful. In our interlude here, we've created something terribly special. But it's time to let him go.

"Is it truly meant to last, you and I? I'm not convinced it can, my darling. You should go."

"Right, I'm going," he says, buckling his belt.

He's about to crumble.

"It's not what either of us expected, it's how it has to be."

"Yeah, I'm good," he says, wincing as he touches his backside.

"I've transformed you, though, haven't I?"

"Nope," he says, his throat catching. The agony is printed all over him.

"Don't. Don't stay."

"I'm definitely not," he turns so I won't see his anguish.

"Goodbye, Ed."

"Whatever," he says, hobbling out the door.

It slams shut. He's left me. My perfect man has abandoned me. The thought sends tears pouring down. Yes, we've collaborated on the tragedy that is my lot, and now the book has closed and I am alone. Alone! I yield to misery, weeping openly and unashamed. Weeping, weeping, and sensing the cuff bite my wrist most uncomfortably. I blink at my feet, where a metallic glint shines at me.

"KEY!" I holler at the doorman...

(Dissolve to Interior, Thursday Evening, Charlie in his Office by a blank dry erase board, on a phone call.)

CHARLIE: *Traction*? How could they *both* be in the hospital, in traction, at once? (sound of buzzing from earpiece) What sort of accident? (long death march of buzzes. Charlie scowls, his eyebrows climbing upward) Okay, okay, I get the gist.

Hungarians. Sheesh! (he stops to think) Listen, you're a nurse. Lemme ask you a serious query. (genial badinage) Could you contemplate a career in the adult film industry? You've already got the wardrobe— (a loud click, dial tone from the earpiece) Fer the love o'... (as a still-fuddled Izzy wobbles in, Charlie tries another number. Cut Back and Forth from Charlie to Patrick Ramsey in their respective Offices.)

PATRICK: Yeah, Ramsey, Fourth World.

CHARLIE: Patsy, what's the story? It's Thursday evening, why haven't I heard back? You been ducking my calls?

PATRICK: My angel, now's not a favorable time for you. The word is out.

CHARLIE: Word? What word would that be?

PATRICK: That you're poison, of the worst kind. Combination pirate-ship roach-bait poison. Everybody looks at you, they see a skull and crossbones on a black flag with cyanide dripping down the pole.

CHARLIE: What'd I do?

PATRICK: Somebody at one of the agencies has spread the word. Who, I don't know.

CHARLIE: The Word, again.

PATRICK: Word is, you don't pay your agency fees. You're everywhere in arrears. Nobody in town will sell you talent.

CHARLIE: Pat, you of all people comprehend I always pay. I'm stately, but the check always comes.

PATRICK: Like a funeral, you're stately. But arguing with me is fruitless, my treasure. I'm a cog. Who argues with a cog?

CHARLIE: I *NEED GIRLS!*

PATRICK: Welcome to the male gender. Dear heart, currently you are untouchable. In a year, who can say?

CHARLIE: Year? *Year?* You lowlife rat fuck.

PATRICK: That's the spirit, boy-o. Now I've got a call coming in, so keep cozy, and don't you ever change. (hangs up)

CHARLIE: (yelling at the receiver) Fink!

(Cut to Patrick Ramsey's Office, Thursday Evening, Ramsey reclining in luxurious indolence in his chair, exhibiting a satisfied grin. He props his legs on his desk, on the far edge of which roosts Shelly in a handsome sable wrap.)

SHELLY: Cut. Print! Bravo!

PATRICK: Didn't I tell you? Brando, DeNiro, Pacino, all the O's? Patzers, next to me.

SHELLY: And you made certain Charlie's name is wet dirt at the agencies?

PATRICK: He walks in, they wouldn't validate his parking.

SHELLY: And if he tries to recruit at a strip club?

PATRICK: Strip joints, and escort services too. I have breathed my plague throughout the land. (rueful frown) I feel to an extent bad about it. Charlie Vogel is one of my oldest and dearest boon companions. I'd take a bullet for the man. What am I doing? Why?

SHELLY: Please.

PATRICK: I'd take a bullet and give a lung! My right lung and my left nut, I'd give!

SHELLY: What you're doing at the moment is pretending to give a shit, to remind me I promised you a reward for each day this situation goes on.

PATRICK: There you go. Slipped my mind. But, chicken, why are we doing this?

SHELLY: Favor for a friend.

PATRICK: Uh-huh. Would that friend be the late lamented Eden Gann?

SHELLY: How...?

PATRICK: Rumors abound, ducky. What say we call her up and suggest a threesome? I'm positively pyrotechnic today.

SHELLY: Edie's social calendar is pretty full this week. (she gets up and circumnavigates his desk) Besides, you might not survive me alone.

PATRICK: (indicating himself) We playing it the way Patsy likey?

SHELLY: I didn't dress like this for my health.

PATRICK: (as she commences removing his suit jacket) You know, lovebird, not only can I act. I can also fuck.

SHELLY: You be quiet.

PATRICK: (finger and thumb along mouth) Zip!

(Edie NARRATES, employing a fast-talking nasal affect:)

EDIE: Shelly stood before me in her sable coat. An Amazon queen, her palm swept the glistening fur. She tossed her long locks and challenged me, "Can you stand before Aphrodite herself—No! Kali! who will surely destroy you—and sanction her every dictate?"
   "Yes."
   With a feral smile, she struck a stinging blow to my cheek, backhanded, and grinned in a mix of contempt and approval as the water started from my eyes. She threw the fur off of an arm and struck again, and again.

"Kali in sable," I breathed. "I beg of you, crush this slave beneath your boot-heel!" I knelt and peered upward.

"You will dedicate your life, your whole self, now and future, to my slightest wish?"

"You need but to ask!"

She smirked at me in her witching way, sliding the fur to her throat. "You tremble? Capital. I prefer you so," and her face became a white mask under the flame red hair. She put her heel to my ear and pressed my head into the floor.

I heard chuckling, harsh, exciting, then in even inflections, "I accept. You claim to be my servant in all things? I'll show you what that means! You fool, you broken toy, dangling on a string from my fingertip! Your education begins in earnest!" and taking a metal ruler from my drawer she whipped my shoulder blades repeatedly.

I bit my lip.

"No? Aren't you loving it?"

I cringed, silent.

"I'll make you bark soon enough."

She covered my back with applications of the ruler, stinting nothing. I howled in despair, and her reply was high laughter. "Don't you adore me? And haven't I given you all you desired? It amuses me to unveil you to yourself—whine, I want to hear it—" the ruler whistled through the air— "the man who dreamed of being treated like an insect, only to wake and realize he is merely an insect who dreamed he was a man!"

I gaped at her, blinking tears. Her foot was extended.

"Well?"

Grateful, I touched my lips to it: never was she more enticing, nestled in her furs.

I felt the blood beat in my temples as she lowered her foot and sauntered to the divan by the wall, draping her figure along it.

"No stool? How rude you are. What are you going to do about it?"

Scrambling to her, I dropped to my knees and presented my clasped hands. She rested a heel there, sighing. I dared a kiss.

"You presume on my benevolence. I understand, this is your office. I am a guest here. You can tell me to go anytime. Can't you? Tell me to go, I command it!"

I burst out recklessly, "That is the sole command I cannot obey. Flog me if you must!"

"But I am behaving monstrously toward you. Is that all you care for? Cruelty? What a bore!"

She withdrew her foot and leaned forward, making me cower.

"There, you've caused my fur to slip. Replace it."

I swaddled her in the warm fur, gazing at the black gown underneath, the ivory skin, unwilling to meet her eye. I was visited by the oddest sensation, as if I'd entered the den of a feral beast, a predator which reveled in its strength and savagery, and yet my survival depended upon petting the animal that could snap and rend in an instant.

"Look at me."

When I obeyed, she examined me with vivid curiosity.

"Pull off my shoes."

I liberated one ideally turned ankle after the other.

At that she cast away her wrap, baring the long pale neck, the graceful, curved arms: the living sculpture of an Attic goddess.

Her perfume filled my nares so heavily I sniffed at the stolid air. I crawled at her feet, as much dog as man.

"Poor doggie," she said.

I saw she had the ruler close by, batting it on the cushion beside her. "Have you no mercy?"

"None!" she exclaimed, treating me to another quick whipping. "There! A variation on the old headline: Woman Bites Dog! You are my dog, and you must adore me utterly, as dogs do, yes?"

"Yes! Perfectly and unto death!"

She scourged me in brutal disregard, a Nero plucking at her instrument while I seared and raved and shriveled to an ash.

"Think carefully before you say that. I may or I may not ever free you."

"Cane me to death, but never release me!" I cried, clinging to her leg.

"Be my slave, then, now and evermore!"

She waved to the left and my reverent gaze followed, to the full length mirror on the adjoining wall, where we two appeared as in a panel from a medieval triptych: she on the couch with her sable like a dark frozen lake spread all around, and I, the happy consort, dancing kisses on the steel ruler and thinking, "If she could be this eternally, a vampiress ravaging men with her green eyes, her flawless body, her devil's tresses—Oh, to be a cinder burnt on her altar!" And I heard

Shelly's wild pitiless laughter raining down on me from above, silver coins from an Empress's hoard...

Ah, friendship. The funny thing is, Charlie, you were right. Despite her protests to the contrary, Shelly was a dog lover after all. So it worked out fine.

And while I relaxed at a colleague's home, you were at last beginning to feel an ex-contract starlet's 6-inch Dolce & Gabbana stiletto spike heel, nailing your ass to a doorpost...

CHAPTER 6

(Dissolve to Interior, Thursday Evening, Charlie seated in his Office, staring at his phone in anger. He looks up to where Izzy loiters in his chair with a girlie magazine, absently fondling himself.)

CHARLIE: Can I offer you a moist towelette?

IZZY: Uh, sorry.

CHARLIE: Buddy, when I said you were my right hand man, this is not what I had in mind.

IZZY: Yeah, sorry.

CHARLIE: You're over there ridin' your clutch, and meanwhile my bank account is coughing blood.

IZZY: Sorry.

CHARLIE: Is that what you're putting your attention to, since you swore off the internet?

IZZY: It's a magical age for me.

CHARLIE: I'm overjoyed for you, but please sprinkle your pixie dust somewheres else. There's a suitable moment lacking.

IZZY: It's a natural function?

CHARLIE: So's leprosy. No judgment, I'm no choirboy. But stealing the odd moment? No. I'm one who likes to take his time during sex. Five or six hours, even.

IZZY: Who would put up with that?

CHARLIE: When I'm alone, anyhow.

IZZY: You must've gotta rich fantasy life! (thumbs up) Cheers!

CHARLIE: You're welcome. But tell me, where's my stars I'm bringing to Vegas later tonight, if I'm almost altogether starless? Ramsey ain't chippin' in, that toefucker. And I was partial to the guy. You confront some obnoxious types in the business, but he was, whaddaya call, the reverse antithesis.

IZZY: Noxious.

CHARLIE: Exactly! He was a very noxious person. The issue is, we have to stabilize the situation before it catches up to our moneyman, "Papi Toro" Gonzalez.

IZZY: "The Mattress King"? From TV?

CHARLIE: The same, except he's got a sideline. He finances our concern, and is Not To Be Fucked With. His mattresses may be soft. He's a hard character, I shit you not. He's lined up a couple of likely rubes for the studio sale at the Expo, with the usual deep pockets and low morals, but before he can wine, dine, and give their ass a shine, he's got to stampede the cattle past them.

IZZY: We could go downtown and draft a few working girls. Instant artistes.

CHARLIE: Always you miss the distinction between a slut and a whore. I'm telling you, it's a question of gentility. Girl has to be easy, without bein' sleazy. Got to be polluted, without bein' prostituted!

IZZY: Still.

CHARLIE: If I tried to weasel some loose lip Hollywood Boulevard skank on Gonzalez as the embodiment of this studio? It wouldn't fly. But I would. Right out the nearest window!

IZZY: Or I'm thinking we could use the Italian, with the boyfriend phoned us, remember? Pecora alla-Pecorina. She's got a terrific attitude, no drama whichsoever.

CHARLIE: Oooh, yeah, a small speed bump there. Last week she was getting her tits redone from 34-D to 34-triple-Z, when in a tragic surgical mishap, she exploded.

IZZY: She died?

CHARLIE: No, oddly enough she exploded and instead of blood and guts, root beer sundaes came out. Of course she's dead, moron.

IZZY: It's a shock.

CHARLIE: Yes.

IZZY: When someone in the trade dies, and it's not from suicide.

CHARLIE: Or liver failure.

IZZY: Or Aids.

CHARLIE: Or embarrassment.

IZZY: And we've had calls from Banshie Phoenix's representation. She's a free agent, and she's got lots of fans.

CHARLIE: Thanks for nuthin'. Every fortnight, a studio disemploys her. Know why? 'Cause she's a raging hellbitch!

IZZY: I can—

CHARLIE: She's a demon fuck goddess from Darkest Hades!

IZZY: (snorts) Compose yourself. I can control her. I can be forceful when the necessity arises.

CHARLIE: Iz,' you are no match for Banshie. (sour laugh) Forceful! You gonna kick her ass?

IZZY: It's under review.

CHARLIE: Trust me, you're outta your league. The only thing more fearsome than retard strength is coke fiend strength.

IZZY: (as the insult soars above his head) Ah, she's been off that crap for a long time.

CHARLIE: See? (miming the movement) I'm hereby placing her on the back burner. Let her agitate a while. What else you got?

IZZY: We've got Derrien, she's a real sweetheart. We can promote a line of gangbang videos. One chick is plenty.

CHARLIE: Yeah?

IZZY: I've got the series' title. We can call it: "The Blizzard of Ooze."

CHARLIE: That'll pack 'em in.

IZZY: It trips lightly off the tongue.

CHARLIE: And after?

IZZY: Tomorrow it's Friday. After that is the weekend. Three days before the Expo ends. You deliver her to Vegas, to the

AEE, and she'll be the figurehead, right? Meanwhile I'll collect the AWOLs and meet you there.

CHARLIE: (nodding) Right, right. She signs the photos and box covers, and I give her the big push. Yeah. Our new featured star. Build a whole line around her. "Derrien for Dessert."

IZZY: "Derrien Does Des Moines."

CHARLIE: "Derrien Delights Duluth."

IZZY: "Derrien is Dicked by Delta Force."

CHARLIE: "Derrien Drains the Dresden Philharmonic."

IZZY: "Derrien at a Distance!"

CHARLIE: ...Why would she be at a distance?

IZZY: Well–

CHARLIE: Don't quit yer day job.

IZZY: And this gets us through Friday at least. We can regroup on the last days.

CHARLIE: Hmmm. Phone my leading lady, Isidoro, won't you please?

(Izzy punches a number on his cell phone, listens. Charlie waits.)

IZZY: No answer. (hangs up)

CHARLIE: (dialing his desk phone. Sound of buzzing from the speaker.) Have I taught you nothing? Let it ring unto Ragnarok, as The Mighty Thor would say. Show 'em who's boss! (buzzing continues) Porn stars! When I'm elected the next Pope, we'll round 'em all up and put 'em in a *petting zoo.* (buzzing) Let 'em out to do a scene, then their ass goes right back in the slammer. (someone on the other end picks up, and we Cut between Charlie and Derrien Usagi, a gentle, twentyish young Asian American, a small town Southwestern émigré with an guileless expression on her face and a disarming lack of cynicism in her manner, at her Apartment on her sitting room couch.)

DERRIEN: (wearily polite) Hello?

CHARLIE: (butter-wouldn't-melt) Derrien, my dumpling.

DERRIEN: I'm kinda low today, Mister Vogel. I'll be at the Expo later, I guess, on my own. Don't send a car.

CHARLIE: Did I ask? Mayhaps I called because you're my favorite of all my girls. Mayhaps I'm paying my respects to my salty dumpling Derrien, simply because you deserve the solicitation.

DERRIEN: Charlie, come on. You know, I like you and all, but... (searching for the words) ...the truth is, people don't respect you much, and you don't respect me. It's...

CHARLIE: Buttercup, what I do for a living, you think I give a nightly fuck whether I'm respected? I got your respect, right here!

DERRIEN: I want someone to care about me and love me, no matter what. And I can't get it. Not many men can handle what I do.

CHARLIE: (not helping) 'Course not, angel cake, you're a porn star. That's like a septic tank with hooters!

DERRIEN: What!

CHARLIE: It's as if I'm talking to an anthrax colony, here.

DERRIEN: Shut up!

CHARLIE: You'll get over it, sugar. It's just most guys are of the opinion, "Ooof! She's probably got everything but roadkill up in there."

DERRIEN: Don't you dare say that, Charlie. I'm careful. I'm tested every month. And I'm clean.

CHARLIE: (striving to soothe her feelings) Sure you are, peanut. I bet I could eat dinner off your cooch.

(Camera Pulls Back from Derrien to include Edie, next to her on the couch, shoulder to shoulder, her ear near the receiver.)

EDIE: In your dreams!

CHARLIE: Who the...Ariel? Is that you?

EDIE: Hey, Charlie-bird.

CHARLIE: You gotta be shittin' me.

EDIE: It's Edie, by the way. E-D-I-E. Say my name, bitch.

CHARLIE: All along, it's been you, right? (marveling) The fog lifts. Life makes sense.

EDIE: Glad I could clear it up for you.

CHARLIE: And here I was beginnin' to wonder if, I dunno, God hated me.

EDIE: Oh, She does, boy. She does.

CHARLIE: (getting his dander up) So what is this? What do you call this?

EDIE: I call it cheating the cheaters. What do you call it?

CHARLIE: I call it a desperate act. I call it a hollow gesture.

EDIE: Squaring accounts, Charlie.

CHARLIE: Nah, you're trying to square the circle, is what you're trying. Nobody told you that's impossible? Where's your schooling?

EDIE: Maybe—

CHARLIE: Go peruse a book, ya pack mule! Advance to the rear of the class!

EDIE: (a pause; in a tougher, before-I-was-so-rudely-interrupted tone) Maybe I'll take you to school.

CHARLIE: You ain't up to it.

EDIE: Vegas is looking awfully lonely these days.

CHARLIE: You heard about the sale, big whoop. You can't scare me with that. More tail? Ogle out your window. I have it on good authority, fifty percent of the population is female.

EDIE: Keep on dreaming, man, and look closely, and you'll realize I'm your one and only dream girl.

CHARLIE: I will never rehire you.

EDIE: "Never" is a day and a half away.

CHARLIE: The buyers don't show 'til Sunday. Good luck.

EDIE: Luck is for leprechauns. (she reaches for the telephone cradle)

CHARLIE: Wait a minute. Is this a "hanging up" voice I'm hearing? Are you contemplating to hang up on me?

EDIE: (adopting a milder tone) Did I ever mention, Charlie, that you exude a funk?

CHARLIE: A *funk*?

EDIE: An effluvium. You exude an effluvium.

CHARLIE: "Funk," as in "funk"?

EDIE: As in, you don't have a pleasant stink about you. As in, your body odor fouls the air, offends the nostrils, and motivates the eyes to water.

CHARLIE: Funk.

EDIE: It's like they hung a shirt and tie on a canister of tear gas. (she cradles the receiver) Only a true pal would break it to you!

(Close Up on Charlie as a click is heard and the dial tone hums.)

IZZY: (after an uncomfortable moment of mutual silence) What do we do? (Charlie, lost in thought, doesn't respond.) Boss?

(Glaring downward, Charlie hits a button, cutting the noise.)

CHARLIE: "The Enemy of My Enemy is My Friend."

IZZY: Beg pardon?

CHARLIE: It's an old saying. I repeat: "The Enemy of My Enemy is My Friend."

IZZY: So what?

CHARLIE: So are you my friend, or not? Decide now.

IZZY: Huh?

CHARLIE: (dangerously) Now! You my friend, or my enemy?

IZZY: Your friend, okay? Jeez.

CHARLIE: It seems I got a wild hair up my crack. And it's a blonde hair.

IZZY: What—

CHARLIE: With black roots!

IZZY: I—

CHARLIE: I entrust you to pay a call on Little Miss Muffet. Time to carry the fight to the enemy.

IZZY: Edie?

CHARLIE: She's at Derrien's. A couple blocks from here. She likes you, doesn't she?

IZZY: Yeah, we get along.

CHARLIE: If she can use her evil charms to jam up my operation, could be we can use yours to unjam it.

IZZY: Oh...I get it. You want *me* to seduce *her* so *she'll* lose interest in seducing *them*. (estimates) It's doable.

CHARLIE: Sure it is. You're an inbred pinheaded Hoboken hillbilly with a flyspeck for a cerebrum, but this you can do, right? You were born to it, if you think about it.

IZZY: Genius, Boss.

CHARLIE: Ain't it, though?

IZZY: Indubitably.

CHARLIE: I laugh at Einstein.

IZZY: You should.

CHARLIE: I guffaw at Mozart.

IZZY: Fuck him.

CHARLIE: All right, get going.

IZZY: Right! (stands up, snuggling the skin rag maternally)

CHARLIE: But leave the magazine.

IZZY: ...Right. (lays it down, gives it a tender pat, and exits)

(Cut to Interior, a Hospital Corridor, Late Evening Thursday. A recovered Ed Tragos careens around a corner, whistling, flowers and a notepad at the ready. An Orderly rolls past steering an unused gurney.)

ED: (buttonholing him) Pardon me, Ensign? I understand I'm in the correct section, that is, I believe so.

(The Orderly halts.)

ED: I've forgotten the room number.

ORDERLY: Name?

ED: I ought to have written—um, Ursa? As I told the receptionist, I don't know their real names.

ORDERLY: Nature of injury? Description?

ED: Description, yes. Two temptresses, Slavic cheekbones, attractive, well proportioned, one fair, one inclement, Hungarian accents.

ORDERLY: Don't ring a bell.

ED: Come, sirrah, they're in this hallway somewhere, and you couldn't miss either of them from a mile away.

ORDERLY: Nature of injury?

ED: Um, that is an affair of some delicacy. In the course of... as the two exchanged what I inferred to be outsized and perhaps too woolly affections... "universal torsion" might be the appropriate term... skeleton and musculature effecting positions previously unknown to humankind...

ORDERLY: Room thirty-eight C. (he rolls out of sight)

ED: Best regards!

(He continues apace, whistling, parsing the digits as they dart by until he attains the unit.)

ED: (polishing the 38-C placard with his shirt cuff) Tell me to "Blow"? Blow yourself, Eden Gann! (he swans in)

(Interior, Hospital Room. Ed enters on the panorama of two women lying in twin beds, ossified from head to foot in body casts, their arms and legs swaying from wires. They spot him through their eyeholes and burble at him through mouth slots.)

URSAS: (together) Mrrrrrphh!!

(He ventures in, puts the flowers on the trays of uneaten food between them.)

URSAS: Flloophh!!

(He bows, kowtowing out of the room.)

ED: Yes, ladies, to you too.

(Exterior, Hallway outside the door. Ed rips out his notebook, scanning the contents.)

ED: Last possible lead. And if this doesn't pay off, I'm unemployed.

(Cut to Interior, Late Evening Thursday, Derrien's Abode. Edie and Derrien sit on her couch, part of the apartment visible behind them, the walls decorated with posters from romantic flicks, the shelves bearing a selection of porcelain figurines in bridal raiment. Two glasses of pink Zinfandel rest on the coffee table in front of them.)

DERRIEN: ...I'm depressed, but not low enough I'd consider quitting the industry, Edie.

EDIE: We don't have to discuss it.

DERRIEN: 'Kay. (she lifts her glass) Some mood Charlie was in! (drinks)

EDIE: I know, right? Maybe his back is having a bad hair day.

DERRIEN: Wait. You and Charlie, what was that argument about?

EDIE: (offhand, dismissive) Tough love, sweetie.

DERRIEN: Love!

EDIE: Yeah, well, in most cases love's a toughie. (sips her wine)

DERRIEN: Tell me about it. What's so awful about me?

EDIE: Not a thing.

DERRIEN: No?

EDIE: Derrien, have I not been hitting on you for, oh, an hour or more? Much good it's done me.

DERRIEN: (shifts in place) I'm sorry, Edie. I don't go that way.

EDIE: South, you mean?

DERRIEN: Not with girls. I'm so straight, I won't even have sex with girls in front of an *audience*. That's super straight. It's almost straight-laced! Whereas, your laces are kind of, you know, kind of crooked. And I'm not judging. But when I dream about what turns me on, it's got to be, you know, big and hard, and red, and full of seed.

EDIE: You're turned on by watermelons?

DERRIEN: I want a specific guy to be attached to my ideal penis. And it's, you know, it's someone you've met, too. And, um, we've done videos together a few times...

EDIE: Not my business, but you ought to steer clear of boys who fuck for bucks. As a rule, they tend to be a bunch of low rent, low IQ, suitcase-pimping pond scum knuckle-draggers.

DERRIEN: Please. My guy is a director!

EDIE: Same as a performer, except the third leg of their tripod is an inch or two shorter.

DERRIEN: You're right, I guess...I s'pose this is what happens to you, when you're young and your parents aren't there like they should be, out partying and junk.

EDIE: Preachin' to the choir. My personal babysitter was "Nick at Nite."

DERRIEN: Who was he, your uncle?

EDIE: Uncle? No...

DERRIEN: I had one of those. Uncle Rufus.

EDIE: Oh?

DERRIEN: He used to pop in at two o'clock in the morning with a camera, a pastry gun, a shaved ferret, and a copy of "Barry White's Greatest Hits."

EDIE: Um...

DERRIEN: Edie, I'm realizing you and I are a lot alike. In another world, we could've practically been each other. Like the Prince and the Pauper!

EDIE: (nodding enthusiastically) Or like in that other world, where you chug a potion and transform into me, and I put on a top hat and go murder people!

DERRIEN: (she drains her wine) Never mind. Never mind. Talking about it exhausts me. I'm going to have a nap before I leave for the Expo. (she stands) Edie, you should stay. There's a second bedroom down the hall on the left, past mine, okay?

EDIE: Okay. We'll talk later.

DERRIEN: Mmm. Goodnight.

EDIE: 'Night. (Derrien exits)

(Edie sips from her glass as Narration is heard.)

EDIE: *Charles, I will not lie to you. Corrupting the semi-innocent is a difficult and thankless task. And listening to Derrien's repeated use of the L-Word—the only remaining four letter word in Pornland—had me wondering if she wasn't right. Maybe the supreme turn-on isn't the repetitious clash of private parts, the anonymous bump and grind, the windup fuckdolls. Maybe it's the gentle drumbeat of love, blossoming in the depths of the soul.*

CHARLIE: *Really?*

EDIE: Nah, just fuckin' with ya. What I was actually thinking was, who's this guy, this director she's so gooey for? How many movies has she done? And who is Charlie's major go-to director boy?

(A cannonade rattles the apartment door. Edie walks to the door, grimaces through the peephole, we see Izzy from her perspective.)

EDIE: Speak of the devil. (she lets him in)

IZZY: (surging forth) Eden, honey, don't talk. There's a thing I've got to tell you from the heart. A thing I've been feeling ever since—

EDIE: You want to bone me.

IZZY: Well, make love.

EDIE: Same difference. Here's the plan, Krazy Kat. Hang here for a minute. Walk down the hall to the first bedroom on the left. Engage in sexual intercourse. Got it?

IZZY: F-first on the left. (he points)

EDIE: Your other left.

IZZY: Affirmative.

EDIE: Where I'll be waiting for you. Don't switch on the light, 'cause I'm kinda shy as I suspect you've realized. Say "It's Izzy" so I'll know it's you and not Derrien coming in. And then don't you say another thing: she told me she might be napping, let's not wake her up.

IZZY: Roger that.

EDIE: You'll remember the whole shebang?

IZZY: If it involves getting laid, suddenly I become an idiot savant.

EDIE: Baby, you get credit for being half right. Now go hang out on the couch and I'll change into something sexy for you, darling.

IZZY: Sure!

(Edie exits. Crosscut from Izzy on the Living Room couch to Edie in the Hallway outside the two bedrooms.)

No reason to make your lab rat navigate a maze, is there, if the goal is for him to cop the cheese?

(Interior, Hallway. Edie locates a circuit box and cuts off a breaker. The bulb in the ceiling dies, rendering the hall far dimmer.)

Besides, here's two somebodies who, near as I could tell, had already been stumbling blindly through life up 'til then.

(Living Room. Izzy spies Edie's unfinished glass of wine on the coffee table. He picks it up, sniffs, and drinks it.)

I figured, one shove from me, and they might stumble on each other.

(Hallway. Edie tests the knob on Derrien's bedroom door, finds it unlocked, and cracks it.)

You say I'm manipulative? So what? Who was more manipulative than Cupid himself?

(Living Room. Izzy puts his feet up, sipping and whistling tunelessly.)

All I was doing was ending a thought Derrien started: "I hanker," "I pine," "I love." I was sticking Izzy and a honking big exclamation point at the end of her sentence.

(Hallway. Edie cups her hand.)

EDIE: (softly) *Izzy?* (she dematerializes into the second bedroom)

(Living Room. Izzy vaults off of the couch, tripping, and replaces the empty glass on the table. He wanders out of the room.)

(Hallway. Izzy enters the darkened hall, tries the wall switch to no avail. He opens Derrien's door six inches and pushes his face in.)

IZZY: (hissing) *It's me. Izzy.*

DERRIEN'S VOICE from within, sounding drowsy, hissing: *Iz—Izzy?*

IZZY: *Shhh.* (he creeps in)

(Interior. Derrien's Bedroom. The remainder of the scene is spookily greenlit, as if shot by night with a low light camera. Izzy approaches her bed, a veritable menagerie of stuffed animals, rummaging his way while she clicks the lamp on her nightstand to no effect. She shrinks back when he plops on the bedside and slouches over her.)

DERRIEN: *What are you doing?*

IZZY: *I have to show you how I feel. Don't I, honey?* (kisses her)

DERRIEN: *Feel?*

IZZY: *Don't you want it?*

DERRIEN: *I...yes, I want it.*

IZZY: *Then shhh, and let me.*

(Sex scene, warmer and more heartfelt than the previous such.)

CHARLIE: *Cupid and his bow my ass. More like Lizzie Borden with an even bigger ax to grind.*

*EDIE: Shut your custard hole, Mister, I gotta see this. I missed it
the first time.*

(Edie SPEAKS in a voice of feathery whispers.)

EDIE: The walls leaned far away. We were alone. We lay on a
raft. The waters churned. Izzy's hand rested on the incurve of
my hip. It lingered there. It was a leaf drifting, in the satiny bay
between my hips and belly. My mouth wanted No. His caress
bid Yes from my body.

Birds glided overhead, they glinted white. They melted into
nothings.

His lips sought. In kisses we communed without speaking,
in ancient dialects. He urged us into the mattress. His urge
pressed on mine. On my naughty. His hand found my tailbone.
I shivered. We were infants lost in a dark wood, shivering.

Bending low, his breath misted the breach of my cave. He
would be safe there. I traced his shirt collar. But he must go in
naked, it would be too sultry for clothes. I pulled his shirt off. I
was awkward—slow, and bad. I should be corrected. He would
teach me.

I bent, undid his jeans. I yearned. The bed raged and
pitched as he seesawed out of his trousers. The bedsprings
were cries of nightbirds, concealed in the firmament. We
kissed. Our bodies touched, twined, and knew. We were Adam
and Eve, we were explorers braving a cliff's verge.

His attentions sank to my breasts, my downturned chalices.
I quivered in my quivering. My eyes were stars looking down
at us. I saw my hair on the pillow framing my head, a black

radiance. I saw my knees rise. My pelvis tilted, my priestess bowl with its gentle creature for sacrifice.

He ceased. My nipples were damp in the cool. It was cool back home in Flagstaff. The desert sky is cloudless, the north wind keen. Clouds lolled above us here, but we were the only warm.

His nose brushed the curls hiding my crevasse. He kissed there. *Baiser-baiser*, his lips formed. Kiss-fuck. His tongue went in, was a liquid pleasure. I forgot. I spoke nonsense. I felt him grinning. My thighs shuddered and ached. He soothed them with more kisses.

His tongue then trailed to my navel, my nook, darting in and out, and between my legs, where it slid languorous round my little button, telling lurid tales.

Phantoms scurried on my skin, raising goosebumps. Oh! I made my hips rock, I made him sure I was ready. He licked at my dreamy wet. I was bereft, beguiled, forsaken. He released me. One more patter of kisses fluttered up to my lips, and I sampled the smoky musk.

His staff grazed my hip, insistent: his pikestaff, his pizzle. It needed guidance. A ghostly hand composed of hints and wishes swelled within my own, caused it to meet his prick. It was another's hand gripping. I was elsewhere, dancing through ranks of blossoms in a cloistered garden. A child, larking about. Lofty, tinkling laughter descended in flurries. It hastened skyward, hung like a banner. It was dewy morning.

My breasts were dewy. My other, dewy. My murmurs bore flowery scents of hibiscus, and lilac, and the stirrings of unseen beings.

The top sheet hied up, a kite flapping in the still atmosphere. My stuffed animals retreated to the shadows, turning their backs. Izzy parted my legs.

I lay limp as a bolt of cloth. Someone's dull grasp led his cock to my entrance. It glowed and burned. I was afraid of it. It jounced on my tummy. My knees rose higher, feet shuffling, the fitted undersheet protesting mildly. I closed around him. Our secrets tangled together, soughing.

My gaze softened past vast distances to faraway throngs. We bumped. I bit his shoulder. He moaned. He worked and played within me. Silky movements of our loins meeting, root to furrow. I tossed my hair, swung my bottom. His mouth tickled my ear, speaking syllables without words, intimate as an inner voice. My nails ran across his chest.

His lightness became a heaviness, his movements sharper.

I saw his pleasure, I floated it in my fancy, a mote tumbling on currents of desire. I sighed it aloft. I could please him. If I could please him, I would be happy.

Delicious heat burgeoned in my vitals. His cheek smudged my cheek. I grappled him behind, aided his striving. Sensual pulses of his presence in me, safe, secure. He was there inside me, he would be there forever. Time fell away. Our steaming filled the air, rose in our heads like fog. We were adrift, unmoored, in an expanse strange and yet homespun.

In the darkness a scream called. A woman's scream. Did I know the woman who screamed so?

Huffing, I bit my lip. A gasp raked my throat, my lungs. I wanted to be a seed flitting through vagrant winds, I wanted to lie in a field and taste the marrow in a maple twig. Then all of me spilled out and I was spent, shaken, as our play quickened into joyful harmony.

'Ah!' he cried, 'I'm cumming!'

My arms enclosed his neck so that when he stiffened, he lifted us up. Nebulae swam by, a rush of light entered and splintered into a thousand dazzling particles. 'Oh, Izzy!'

A last thrust to the hilt, and his sticky pipings left trills of tingling music in me. Tendrils crept down my thighs, slick, damp. He was done. He was undone, done in. The walls resumed their proportions. The world was solid.

He lazed beside me, his penis-pendant furled at my hip, no longer rigid. Too weak to try my cavern. I heard myself mumble, full of cobwebs: 'Sleep tight.' I shut my eyes. Colors, old and new, pinwheeled. I lay watching them, dozily...

CHAPTER 7

You must be a belt and suspender type, Charlie, right? Sending Izzy to do your dirty deeds wasn't enough. While I derailed him, I understand you broke your Internet Commandment and went chasing after a very special pretty girl you did a quick search for online, and as always, those pictures and stats simply cannot be trusted...

(Dissolve to Interior, Thursday Night, University of California [Irvine] Campus, a drab Lecture Hall. Fluorescent panels, frowsty students. Close Up of a hastily assembled inscription on a signboard: "'I read four books and massacred two pints so I could give this goddamn speech. Listen up!' Feminism, the Internet and the Digital Post-Post-Restant. Speaker, Adult Actress Leanna L'Amour." Camera Pans to Shelly on an elevated dais, speechifying, wearing subliminal makeup, a baggy floral dress and granny glasses, hair pinned up, sexiness dialed to "Mute," droning on and on from a spiral notebook.)

SHELLY: ...we've examined proto-sex images, clay statues and cave art exalting fertility. Embryonic erotic fiction, written as much to provoke as to arouse, priapism as political act. More sophisticated representational paintings and sculptures, often idealizing the body. Photography, by contrast, started as a mirror to reality, illustrating sex both familiar and off brand.

(Charlie enters at the rear of the Hall and joins the somnolent devotees, mostly masculine, primarily undergrads, with a sprinkling of more mature novelty seekers, and sits.)

SHELLY: (reading) The original pornos, stags, depicted sex as recreation and prostitution: love and commerce, legal and illegal tender, the two sides of the social equation. Golden age movies from about '75 to '85, influenced structurally by Hollywood musicals and in turn influencing splatter horror flicks. Here, sex had context in the form of plot, therefore a point of view, intentionally or not. Early videotapes, shot on the cheap, sold cheap, felt cheap, and cheapened the fans' experience, (looks up) and for good measure the shitload of shitty compilation tapes that conditioned the audience to buy the later shitstorm of shitty all-sex videos, which have just about finished annihilating plot forever.

(She surveys the congregation, hoping the profanity will goose her spectators' interest. No luck. Charlie, eying his chance, flaps an arm. Shelly, startled to see him, willfully ignores him.)

SHELLY: Because—

CHARLIE: Plot, shmot! It's the bumpity-bumpity!

SHELLY: *Because*, (reading) every sex scene is a documentary. It's happening. Absent narrative, what is left but a low budget industrial training film for fucking? Cain Todd wrote, the awareness of fictionality produces imagined desire-like states, rather than simple voyeurism. Do imaginative desires, or "i-desires," sanction or tease out the abrogation of constraints that real-life desires are subject to?

CHARLIE: Cain, the guy from the "Kung Fu" TV show?

(Several students titter.)

SHELLY: I will beat you until you die.

CHARLIE: Okay, okay, I'm a pacifist! Go on with your thing. (he nudges the lady next to him)

SHELLY: (having lost her place, scours through her notes, gives up, continues at random) Marshall McLuhan wrote, "Print technology created the public. Electric technology created the mass." Digital technology? Has created the mob. To be in a mob, you barely have to comprehend what defines and delineates the mob. More important is to be carried on a slick, soupy wave of compliance to the mob mentality. How do I, an agent of the sex industry, positivize this negativity?

CHARLIE: (to the lady on his right) Is that a word, "positivize"? (to the boy on his left) Brainiac. She made that up, yeah?

SHELLY: (reading) When you click on an adult web site, does the internet reach out to you, or do you reach out to it? One of you is requesting the connection, and this matters. Any sex worker can tell you who is in charge of the act. And the act of visiting my web site is a capitulation to my idea of sex. Enough discrete visits, and a mob reflex may arise that ramps up the volume of clicks without betraying my inherent behavioral precepts. How can I assist this reflex?

CHARLIE: (arm flapping) You mentioned soup. Will a hot meal be provided soon?

SHELLY: Charlie.

CHARLIE: I missed dinner to be here.

(She holds her notebook high, lets it go, it flutters to the platform.)

SHELLY: Right. Get up here.

(The audience perks up, smelling blood.)

CHARLIE: Me, up there?

SHELLY: Get up here.

(Charlie crosses his wrists and perp walks across the auditorium and onstage, to much snickering.)

SHELLY: (to onlookers) This hard-on with a haircut is Charlie Vogel, the boss of my studio. Not the boss of me, mind you, Charlie, if you can recognize the distinction.

CHARLIE: I would never boss you around. (playing to the crowd) I asked my dentist. He said thirty-two teeth is my lucky number, and not to change it. (laughter)

SHELLY: What brought you here tonight?

CHARLIE: I followed the gaper's block! (laughter) And, you know, I'm knowledgeable. I been toiling in this enterprise for three decades. (he scans the audience) You. The longhair guy who, if Cousin Itt dies, you got the job. Ask me a question pertaining to the industry.

LONGHAIR: Um, okay, she brought up plot. Why was plot important, even during the so-called Golden Age?

CHARLIE: Good question. 'Me ask you a question. Say it's nineteen seventy-eight, you're sittin' in that carbuncle you call a dorm, and it's Friday night but you can't get a date because most women look at you and decide that they prefer to mate within their own species. But you're a fan of my starlet, here.

SHELLY: Who was age six, creepozoid.

CHARLIE: It's a fer instance. (to Longhair) Do you pay for transportation to downtown where is an adult theater, buy a ticket while the world sees you and says, "Ho, Skeevatz!", slither into a joint that smells like a jockstrap died, relax between the guy in the open raincoat and the guy with palms so furry they have a salon appointment, the feature starts and you commence to knock one out in, my best guess here, three or four minutes tops, and then comes the walk of shame back home on account of it'll be a month before the testosterone builds up again in your raisin-like gonads? Or do you stay? You stay if there's a plot, and characters, and production values, you got your twenty pieces' worth, and you can sit in a tiny puddle of your own *schmaltz* being entertained and writing your dissertation entitled "I Can't Get Laid But This Will Do for Now."

LONGHAIR: I'm writing that dissertation, because Leanna! (he smiles at her)

CHARLIE: Exactly. Plot gave you an eighty minute reason to be inconvenienced. I'm surprised it hung around for so long once video came in.

LONGHAIR: Credible.

SHELLY: Very instructive. But I see we're about out of time—

CHARLIE: I could divulge one more. (to a pale Ruthvenesque blonde) You, Draculina.

DRAC: What's the main difference you find in modern porn stars, versus the classic era?

CHARLIE: Easy. They always have thought of themselves as outlaws. Today they're bullshit cultural outlaws, they can't walk in a room, right. The old guard? They were actual outlaws. They could be arrested. We all could.

DRAC: It was legal!

CHARLIE: Legal to exhibit, not to film, which was called pandering, which is sex for remuneration. You could be shooting your masterwork, and after the guy disgorges his port nutsack but before he disgorges his starboard, the cops would smash the door in and you have to call the lawyer you pay to bail you out after every third spooge, he's part of the cost of doing business. And it irks me, these schmucks, these Johnny Cum Lately guys who think they are Kid Curry with crabs, and these broads who think they're Calamity Jane with chlamydia. They're not outlaws. They're outcasts!

SHELLY: That's my cue. Thanks for your consideration, kiddies. Don't forget to floss.

(She clinches an armful of Charlie, wrangling him offstage as the crowd disperses.)

(Cut to Exterior, the Lecture Hall Parking Lot, Thursday Night. A car bounces off the road and into the Lot, Moira visible through the windshield.)

(Cut to Interior, the Lecture Hall, a third floor Window reflecting on the dais and looking out on the Lot below. Shelly pressgangs Charlie into the Shot. They stand by a table laden with Shelly's lecture aids: a laptop computer patched to a

projector aimed at a screen on the wall, and various media—
books, art prints, tapes, laser discs, DVDs. The two
communicate double-fast:)

SHELLY: (she pockets her glasses) Get it out of your system.

CHARLIE: No, I'm impressed. You have a bright future.

SHELLY: Go on.

CHARLIE: Either as a public speaker, or as an over the counter
alternative to knockout drops.

SHELLY: They saw an opinion I posted online and I got an
invite. Hey, I took a chance, and also fuck you.

CHARLIE: I *applaud* you for that. You misread the
circumstance, is all. And since you're here blazing new trails,
allow me to add another macadamia to the trail mix.

SHELLY: What's that?

CHARLIE: Schlepp that trail to Las Vegas tomorrow. Come
with me back into the loving clutches of Pie-Rite.

SHELLY: (loosens her hair) Back? Was I mislaid?

CHARLIE: Extend me some credit. I'm cognizant you're with
my other broads, following the pied piper Ariel Caliban off the
reservation.

SHELLY: *Rats* followed the Pied Piper. (she pilfers a brush from the table, brushes her coiffure)

CHARLIE: L'Amour, I know you better than you know yourself. Unlike most of my girls, you're a reasonable person. You're negotiable. You're a well-honed sharpie about the money angle on things.

SHELLY: You buying me something? Or just buying me? (brushing) Why would I sell out a friend?

CHARLIE: Friendship is negotiable.

SHELLY: More than a friend. (done brushing, she flips her compact, applies war paint)

CHARLIE: "More" is eminently negotiable. We're in such an endeavor, is "more" not the main subject we negotiate?

SHELLY: (talking around her lipstick) Seduce me. What's your offer?

CHARLIE: (conspiratorial undertone) Listen, I'm undergoing second thoughts about whom I deputized as my rear admiral. He's a place keeper at best. I deemed him a blank slate, which is good, but it turns out his medulla oblongata is so calcified it's more of a concrete slab. No thanks. Now you and me, we're peas in a pod. We could move mountains.

SHELLY: (inscribing eyeliner) Peas that move mountains? They call that an avalanche. (folds her compact, pirouettes)

Make yourself useful. (Charlie unzips her dress) Gonna fire Izzy and give me the job?

CHARLIE: At a substantial bump. I'll quote you the only sort of figures (admiring her derriere) that arouse me anymore, in our occupation.

SHELLY: Don't bother. (lets the dress hit the floor, revealing a denim skirt and a crop top)

CHARLIE: You're in?

SHELLY: (spins to face him, kicking the dress beneath the table) Due diligence, Charlie. I heard the studio is up for grabs. You might not have a job either, in a day or two.

CHARLIE: Toro the owner guarantees I'm grandfathered in. Stick with me, and I'll make you a grandmother. You wanna hear the quote, or not?

SHELLY: Not. I'll draw the line at throwing Edie under the bus.

CHARLIE: Or don't come back at all. See what you made me do? Don't come back, but I'll hold you to your contract and prevent you from working anyplace else. This too is negotiable.

(Shelly's stare peels him from aught to naught.)

SHELLY: I bet Pie-Rite is a steal, nowadays.

CHARLIE: Huh?

SHELLY: Maybe I will go to Vegas, arrange financing, place some calls, form a consortium, and put in my own bid. I can afford it, or didn't you realize? As you said, I've been smart about money.

CHARLIE: Er...

SHELLY: Have my accountant audit your statements.

CHARLIE: What I intended...

SHELLY: Determine the investment capital required. Evaluate your cash flow and operating expenses. Initiate a credit check. Find any hidden liabilities.

CHARLIE: Could we...

SHELLY: (angry) Calculate the fifteen year goodwill amortization! Compare your financials with the average in the RMA's Annual Statistical Report!

CHARLIE: I'm discerning hostility...

SHELLY: (angrier) Then you'll be working for me, Grandpa!

CHARLIE: I gather we got off on the wrong foot, here...

SHELLY: (angriest) Or I could hold you to your contract, and prevent *you* from working.

CHARLIE: Have I said, Leanna, how beautiful you are when you're angry?

SHELLY: (furiouser) Or let's wait and see who's on the unemployment line Monday, if I happen to call Edie and make sure she doesn't show up to help the close the sale, either!

CHARLIE: Sweetheart.

SHELLY: (furiousest) Git!

(Charlie, unable to summon a reply, trudges out of the Hall among a group of stragglers. Cut to Exit Door. Threading through the group on her way in, Moira, in her white-on-white business suit, passes Charlie like a rogue comet, not recognizing him. She gesticulates at Shelly and advances.)

(Cut to Window behind the stage, Shelly packing her materials.)

MOIRA: Miss L'Amour?

SHELLY: Sorry, you snoozed, you loosed. Lecture's ended.

MOIRA: (pouting) I apologize, I tried half the auditoriums before I found you here. It wasn't well publicized.

SHELLY: Eleventh hour shit. (packing) Late breaking news.

MOIRA: I'm glad I—

SHELLY: History was made, young minds inspired. You missed it all. (concludes her packing) The school paper sent you?

MOIRA: What? No.

SHELLY: You're how I picture a reporter, I suppose. The Voice of Fate. The Harbinger of Doom. No, Doctor Doom just left.

MOIRA: My name is Moira Atrop—

SHELLY: Moira, did you ever have a day?

MOIRA: Day?

SHELLY: Moira, you look to me like, oh, you look like you oughta gotta unbuckle a couple of ribs on your corset. Want to hit the nearest bar with me? Blow out your ribs with a pitcher of beer? We'll talk.

MOIRA: I...okay.

SHELLY: I'll spot you a pitcher myself. After that, you're on your own. You get drunk, land on the planks, no matter how scabby and vomitous, or on some dude, no matter how scabby and vomitous, don't you blame me.

MOIRA: I wouldn't think I'd—

SHELLY: All you have to do is grab my box.

MOIRA: Okay.

SHELLY: That's a line from my last video. (dumps the box in her arms) Get it?

MOIRA: (carrying the weight of the world) Mmmppphhh. Thanks.

(Shelly glances out the window.)

SHELLY: It's awfully heavy, I bet.

MOIRA: It's kind of heavy, yes.

SHELLY: Put it down a sec.

(Moira disencumbers.)

SHELLY: You see—with me, through the window—you see the guy hauling ass in the parking lot? Middle-aged, balding?

MOIRA: Uh-huh.

SHELLY: We're going to spend some quality time, Moira, because I like you. I think you're cute. But you have to do something for me. Will you do something for me?

MOIRA: Okay.

(Shelly slips six laser discs out of the box.)

SHELLY: Lighter now, right?

MOIRA: Probably not much.

SHELLY: I'll give you six chances to bean that asshole down there with one of these hi-tech Frisbees.

MOIRA: It doesn't appear quite safe.

SHELLY: He'll be fine. Head like an anvil. (she slides the discs into Moira's bag.) One at a time, mind.

MOIRA: Really, I came here to ask whether you'd want to do videos for a tube site I'm—

SHELLY: Got my own site. Bu-ut, I know someone who'd be perfect for you. I have her address. This first, though. Earn my trust.

MOIRA: Okay, I...okay. It goes no further, what I did?

SHELLY: We're the only two ladies on Earth, darling. Hurry, he's getting out of range.

(Moira lets fly. A metallic splash reverberates.)

MOIRA: Pooh!

SHELLY: Put some English on the next pitch. I'm clocking the wind at ten knots.

(Moira throws a curveball.)

MOIRA: (caught up in the spirit) I almost got him!

SHELLY: Almost took an ear off. Check it—we've got a runner!

MOIRA: Are those six discs all you brought?

SHELLY: Unless you plan to throw my computer at him.

(Moira whips the remaining discs in rapid succession. Four crashes are attended by a distant shout.)

MOIRA: I did it!

SHELLY: Game, set, and match! (hugs her, busses her cheek)

MOIRA: Bang on the face!

SHELLY: Must've thought he was out of range. Ya stone killa, girl!

(She picks up the box herself, they stride to the exit in tandem.)

SHELLY: Write it now, because later you'll be too drunk to remember—I promise. (Moira ransacks her purse, a notepad crystalizes) I lied, I don't have her address, but don't be cross, her name is Derrien Usagi, we recently did a scene together and, no shit, she's listed under that name!

(Dissolve to Interior, Derrien's tiny Kitchen. Friday Morning. Edie sits in the dinette, quaffing an orange juice and buttering a slice of toast, as Derrien and Izzy enter arm in arm, she in a robe and he, like Edie, in yesterday's clothes.)

EDIE: Look what the pussycat dragged in.

IZZY: You're indisputably sly. I suspect I should be pissed at you. Why am I not?

EDIE: You know why. (chomps a big bite of her toast, chews)

IZZY: That's your current mission in life, huh? Making everybody do what they were eventually going to do anyhow?

EDIE: (talking swampily through her food) Jus' caw me the Vickle Vinger of Vate.

IZZY: And then, oh crafty one?

EDIE: (swallows) I imagine you both circle back to Charlie, and have sex with lots and lots of people. Perfect way to begin a relationship.

DERRIEN: (to Izzy) No!

IZZY: Babe, it's just sex.

DERRIEN: I'm done with "just sex." And from the stuff you did last night, I assumed you were, too!

IZZY: But that was when I thought you were—

EDIE: (clears her throat)

IZZY: —Uh...

DERRIEN: Thought what?

EDIE: Go on, Izzy. (she holds Derrien's hand) We're listening.

IZZY: (scanning from Edie to Derrien to Edie) "Too smart for porn."

EDIE: That's what they tell me. Did I do wrong? Look at Derrien, and describe what you see.

IZZY: (examining her fondly) She's beautiful.

DERRIEN: I'm not!

EDIE: She is. She is beautiful.

IZZY: She's so pretty. (struggles to express) If she were any prettier, I'd...I'd chop off her head and use it as a table centerpiece!

DERRIEN: Aw...

EDIE: Okay, you've got two projects.

IZZY: Yeah?

EDIE: First, call Charlie and break the news to him. It's only fair.

IZZY: Yeah.

EDIE: And second, you might want to work on your sweet talk a little bit.

IZZY: Really?

EDIE: Li'l bit.

(Izzy retires to place his call in private. Derrien sits in the chair by Edie, who reaches for the loaf.)

DERRIEN: You do believe it could be a success, don't you, Edie?

EDIE: Stranger things have happened. (extricates a slice from the bag) Pigs have flown. Yogi and Boo-Boo have, undeniably, shit in the woods.

DERRIEN: Huh?

EDIE: But you've got to be willing to take the leap, Derrien. "Nothing ventured," et cetera.

DERRIEN: I s'pose.

EDIE: Guess who else took that leap. (twirling her butter knife with surgical dexterity) How about the world's great lovers? Romeo and Juliet. Antony and Cleopatra. Pyramus and Thisbe.

DERRIEN: Didn't...didn't all those people end up killing themselves?

EDIE: Is that what you're going to do? Waste your youth reading the fine print? (pokes the knife in her direction) Great lovers don't read the fine print!

DERRIEN: S'pose not. You understand so much more than me. I'm a high school dropout. You?

EDIE: (eyebrows knit, mouth screwed, she butters her bread as attentively as an artist at her easel) College dropout. UL of Lafayette, Lit Studies, two semesters in. Bored.

DERRIEN: (abject admiration) A *college* drop out! GOSH. But, you sound like a local girl.

EDIE: (amused) Here, I'll make your ears bleed: (adopting a thick-as-soup southwestern Louisiana patois) "Dat *couillon* Charlie, Ah'm gonna make him da *misere!*"

DERRIEN: (giggling) How'd you get rid of that?

EDIE: (pats her) It's California, kiddo. Be who you wanna be. (she slides the plate of buttered bread in front of her)

(Izzy returns, shell-shocked.)

IZZY: I completed the dreaded call.

EDIE: Charlie cool with it?

IZZY: You tell me. He said I was a miserable fuck and a motherless son of a bitch.

EDIE: Oops.

IZZY: The miserable fuck, it didn't bother me too much. I admit I was perplexed by the second. How can I be both motherless, and additionally be a son of a bitch?

EDIE: This is a conundrum which has stupefied the noblest intellects since the birth of mankind.

IZZY: (seeking encouragement) Does that make me an Intellect?

EDIE: In the sense that you're often stupefied, yes. (She leaves her seat) Derrien—

DERRIEN: (speaking to Edie, gazing up at Izzy) Actually my first name is Usagi. I switched them when I got signed.

IZZY: Okay, Usagi Derrien. Right. (he sits in Edie's vacated chair)

USAGI: But my real last name is Deguchi, not Derrien.

IZZY: Usagi Deguchi. Perfect.

USAGI: (to Edie) But my friends call me Usa, not Usagi.

EDIE: (hands on hips) Have we met?

USA: (to Izzy) But you can call me Usa-chan, or Usako.

IZZY: I, uh... (neurons emit *banzai* charge)

USA: Or Ko-Usagi.

IZZY: Um... (synapses commit *seppuku*)

USA: Or Usa-pyon, or Usa-Usa.

IZZY: Ehh... (mental plane goes *kamikaze*)

EDIE: (no-nonsense) Anyway, you two have to stop cuddling and start huddling. The future is wide open, why not give it a chance? What if there's something unique, and permanent, here?

IZZY: (contemplative, nodding agreement) Your tongue in God's ear.

EDIE: Uh, that's not how that...never mind.

(She continues advising them, her speech indistinct under the Narration as Usagi, without looking, bisects her slice of buttered bread and passes half to Izzy.)

What can I say, Charlie? I know the standard porn industry romance has the life span of a microbe. It's Der— um, Usa, who didn't know it yet. I liked Usa, and I was doing the best I could: I was giving her happiness in the short term, and wisdom in the long run. That's all anybody gets from love, isn't it?

Even Izzy, I was steering out of Hoochie Harbor and into a sea of possibilities. Maybe one day it'll be his time to hold the strings. "Senator Lombardo." "Governor Lombardo." "President Lombardo." As I said, stranger things have happened: I was reading the other day, they've begun building an ice rink down in Hell...

CHARLIE: *You gloss over it, but betrayal is no joke. It pierced me to the core, I tell you.*

EDIE: *Poor Charlie. I've got something that'll make you feel better, munchkin. How about a proper goodbye scene for you and Izzy?*

CHARLIE: *Yeah? Let's have it.*

(Edie NARRATES, imitating Charlie's gruff East Coast accent:)

EDIE: Izzy beheld me at the last. His eyes were of the deepest brown, near black, and broadcast a seductive power wherever he directed them; my heart blazed bright and fiery as a bar in a furnace.

He appeared a singular handsome fellow. His discourse when he spoke was melodic, its rhythms insistent as the cadenza in a concerto, wherein the composer heightens his effects to conduct the listener into a state of exaltation, releasing him from the heavens to drift, note by emphatic note, to a finale of happy exhaustion. A sensation *fortissimo!* shocked me to the ground of myself, and my vocal organ quietly *strohbassed* as it registered the caress of his *flageolet*. I understood that I must sup at that Passion whose frenzies are the Illuminati's veridical lodestone, and his comeliness called to me like an incantation:

Socket and helve, the blade in his bed,
Cockerel, kettle-wise, stir the fowl head.
Hecat' or colt-pixie, progress did swell,
Now stroke follow stroke, that the lech gate may tell.

CHARLIE'S VOICE: Nice.

EDIE: Sweat sprang out. My gorge thickened, my knees shook, my ears roared, I was addled with lust, enraptured, and like the saints of old, I saw a vision. Izzy stood undraped before me, a Pan twiddling his pipe. The blood flew from my bellows to my brain, and I was his utterly.

'Like me,' quoth he, 'You pledge to nothing less than the Love which annihilates. No woman can grant this love.'

CHARLIE: Say what now?

EDIE: Without another word he seized me and we grappled. He was aroused: our erections pressed together. I felt myself a wretch, a phantasm, beaten by a desert sun and in a crawl to the outskirts of an oasis, eager to dabble my tongue on the life-giving fluid there.

His sigh rasped in my ear. Our bodies intertwined, and I stopped his breath with kisses for long minutes. We parted and I whispered, 'Yes, I fought my desire all this time but the contest is turned, and I gladly surrender my flag!' 'Come,' he said, taking my wrist, ushering me to a convenient unadorned wall.

CHARLIE: *Having fun, are you?*

EDIE: He unbuttoned my trousers, glided within, my manhood stood to meet him, and his sure and agile ministrations brought the seminal charge to such a boil that it well-nigh spouted out extempore. He slowed, withdrew, and in a trice we both were stripped. My gaze devoured every inch of him. His dark Italianate complexion, his silky hair, the liquid elegance of his demarche, were the very absolute of carnal perfection.

Groaning, I sank to the floor, marshalling him onto me. He explored my flesh in fervent kisses as I discerned a questing hand behind me and a finger pressing at the entrance there. I writhed like a specimen on a pin.

CHARLIE: *(...)*

EDIE: The room spun about me. Still I had wit enough to recall his wondrous phallus, and yearned to sample its flavour. By look and touch I guided him to a position straddling my chest. His prick swayed before me, and I exclaimed at its suavity, its majesty. The shaft was ample and spiring, the skin glossy on the prominent glans, the battle-hardened helmet. I rubbed my cheek against it, murmuring endearments. It sought shelter between my lips and I tasted a faint drop of his liquor, of that aniseed fairy which intoxicates before sending one mad. I pulled at it frantically, and each thrust tempted it further in, until I was quite transfixed.

CHARLIE: *I'm gonna take a dump. (sound of slamming door)*

EDIE: (raising her voice) Faster and faster I sucked, as if to drag his sperm out by main force, when of a sudden Izzy tensed, cried aloud, and the pent up stream burst on my palate, I drowned in the salty spray, and again and again, Izzy twisting and wanting no more, I wanting nothing more, he calling 'Give way! You are drinking the life out of me!' as I feasted on his plasm, his musky soul-stuff. He collapsed beside me, exhausted.

CHARLIE: (echoey rejoinder from the washroom) I CAN'T HEAR YOU! CONE OF SILENCE!

EDIE: But I knew my man. Like Antaeus, contact with the earthiest part of me would restore his vigour.

'Darling,' said I, 'Will you catechize me in Celestial Love as Pausanias did his *erastes*?'

His eyes lit up at once, and in a whirlwind of newborn lubricity he rolled me so I faced away, and tapped at the Portal which resists all intruders. I perceived his fingertip at my cranny, the rosy slot stretched to accommodate two, a third, and a fourth finger tried my steadfastness. I twitched powerfully at his enquiries, the little mouth found itself wrapped round his massive turgid penis, and clung to it with so fierce an ardor that it was arrested in its progress.

'Ought I cease? Do I presume upon your person?'

'Carry on,' I cried, 'I wish to absorb you to the root!'

CHARLIE: (flushing sound)

EDIE: He dove in hard. I was giddy from the mounting pain, ready almost to rebuff him, when he traversed the narrowest rut of the pass and slid with a neat and resolute push into my bum, and marvelous pleasure outstripped any sense of discomfort. Back and forth he moved, my hind parts answering in nimble shudders. My blood bubbled in my veins, my brow was aflame, and I merged into the Godhead as I sank my fists in the carpet piles, a man in a pillory. I died; I was more alive than ever before; I shouted out joy. I felt his teeth gritting in my shoulder and volley after volley of his elemental fire scorching my bowels.

CHARLIE: *(sound of opening door)*

EDIE: (lowering her voice) He uttered my name a final time, wavered from me and, when I spun to face him, fell into my arms. 'Goodbye, my beloved. I adore you,' I sobbed.

How could any man, debating such motions as we had done, choose other and lesser? And if an angry and impetuous Deity had thought, then and there, to shake us both into dust, so long as it be one dust, we could have expired—happy!

CHARLIE: (resuming his chair) It's astonishing how much you suck.

EDIE: (snickers)

CHAPTER 8

(Dissolve to Interior, Hallway outside of Usagi's tenth floor Apartment door, Friday Morning. Edie, exiting, shuts the door and sets off from the far end of the hall to the elevator, passing a bleary-eyed Moira in the most optic-nerve-roasting luminescent white suit yet, halfway along, neither minding the other. At Usagi's door Moira halts, puzzled, and squints across the passageway but doesn't attempt to break Edie's trajectory. Edie punches the elevator button, and while she waits for the car to arrive she pokes at her phone.)

(Cut to Patrick Ramsey's Office. A mellowed-out Shelly unwinds on the divan in heavy furs, feet up, suspicious-looking cigarette in mouth. She inhales a long tranquil drag and propels it at the ceiling, glances at her phone, puts it to her ear. Cut between the two.)

SHELLY: (muzzy-voiced) Moe's Pancake House.

EDIE: Shelly?

SHELLY: Shelly the Shellgame Dame, they calls me. Where's the pea, never where you think it'll be. Whom might I say is speaking?

EDIE: Where are you?

SHELLY: I'm visiting, Edie. I'm comforting a sick friend. (she sneers downward) You are sickly and weak, aren't you? You're a low, crawling animal, you can't stand up and walk like a man.

EDIE: It's finished. You can cut him off.

SHELLY: (sighs) Right-E-O, Kitty. (hangs up)

(Camera Pulls Back to reveal human ottoman Patrick, nude on all fours, bound and gagged and propping up Shelly's legs. Shelly finds a hidden slipknot and retreats as the ropes disintegrate.)

SHELLY: Upsy-daisy, Patrick.

PATRICK: (loosening his ball gag) Eden Gann's coming, Mistress? The more the merrier!

SHELLY: Mistress hell. Our love affair for the ages—

PATRICK: I say, what good is a cat o' nine tails when I've only got the one tail?

SHELLY: —has run its course. We're parting ways. (she stands)

PATRICK: (jumping upright) You're abandoning me?

SHELLY: We've made some memories, haven't we? (she strolls to the door) Remember that time you were on your knees on the carpet? Or the time you were on your knees, behind the desk? Or when you were sitting over there on the sofa, having recently gotten up from being on your knees right next to the sofa? (at the door) You're gonna get a neck crick in your entire body, you keep that up. Memories! Let's leave them in the past, shall we? (exits)

PATRICK: (incensed) Go on, go, see if I care! (he rears up to his full naked height, ball gag swinging) At least I have my dignity!

(Cut to Usagi's Hallway by the elevator. Edie notices the button isn't lighting; she pokes it twice more and makes for the stairwell at the end of the corridor. At her end, Moira raises her hand to knock.)

IZZY'S VOICE: (muffled conversation from within) ...old saying? Go big, or go home!

USAGI'S VOICE: Oh, you can *definitely* stay.

IZZY: I spy with my little eye...

USAGI: (giggling) Get away!

(Moira raps. The flutter of rustling fabric intermingles with footsteps: the door is pried by an unkempt Usagi.)

USAGI: Hi?

MOIRA: I'm sorry to interrupt you. I am. Can I have a moment? I've been in touch with Charles Vogel, my name is Moira Atropos—

(Izzy, disheveled, emerges.)

IZZY: You were on the phone with Charlie a couple days ago. About a meeting.

MOIRA: Yes. Except I found that the address he gave me was a miniature golf course. I doubt he has his meetings there.

IZZY: Yeah, he'll do that. The phony trail. Considered yourself avoided.

MOIRA: I intend to have our meeting. It's my job. And Pie-Rite's address is not listed anywhere I've checked, online, public records, anywhere, which I've never heard of in a reputable firm. I was lucky to get his cell number before, but that was unlisted too, and now it's been changed.

IZZY: (to Usagi) The guy goes way back in the industry, to the late seventies in New York when he was a stockroom kid. Can't shake that rabbity, better-travel-light paranoia in his subconscious, where the cops are busting in any second.

MOIRA: And he's instructed his colleagues not to help me, either.

IZZY: (nodding) Every time a politician burns some airtime, it's "Grab yer boysenberries and hold tight! The jig is up!" And then he works in a joint that shady mattress guy Gonzalez owns. Go figure.

MOIRA: So I took what I realize is a liberty, a major liberty, and I looked up anybody who might be employed by Pie-Rite Studios, and the solitary entry I saw was right here.

IZZY: (to Usagi) You listed your home under your porn name? Are you nuts?

USAGI: It wasn't always my porn name. I've done more than pornos. People might contact me with offers, I'm a real actress. I did a serious movie.

IZZY: You did?

USAGI: Certainly! It was called "Vampire Strippers from the Planet Boobula."

IZZY: (tumorous with pride) How 'bout that? (rests his arm around her shoulders)

USAGI: See the poster?

IZZY: (squinching at the wall) "Bodacious Blood-Guzzlers Shimmy 'Round the Poles of Pluto!"

USAGI: I played Lactia, Defender of the High Holy Hemoglobes.

MOIRA: I don't have to come in, but would it be possible to get that address?

USAGI: Of course you can come in, Morta. (opens the door, smoothing her hair)

MOIRA: Thanks. (she enters) Uh, Moira, though.

(Cut to Interior, Usagi's Apartment. She and Izzy settle in the couch facing Moira.)

IZZY: Here's the deal. Give us your pitch, I'm curious. Then the address.

MOIRA: Why not? (she slides the bag off her shoulder and grubs inside, withdraws the shears and an empty canister.) Darn it, I forgot. I ran out of film two calls ago.

USAGI: I've got a videotape, will that do?

MOIRA: That'll do fine, thanks.

(Usagi rises and stoops by the cabinet near the television set.)

IZZY: Videotape. She's an old fashioned girl.

(She passes Moira a cassette, sits.)

USAGI: It's my demo reel, for casting agents. But all it is, is my one scene from the only movie I've done. I should probably just mail them the DVD, right?

IZZY: Always thinking, isn't she?

(Moira clears her throat, holding the cassette up. She worries the scissors under the tape guard and snips the tape.)

USAGI: Oh.

MOIRA: There. Have I not now sundered the umbilical connecting generations of fans of adult entertainment? (she pinches a section of tape) Could I not now do as much with the crystal and vinegar of your ancient film stock? Here. (she scrapes the tip of her scissor blade on the surface) Vanished is a century of toil, the history of sexuality writ in light and shadow. Nothing to remain but the silvered plastic you call the digital d—

USAGI: And, you know, live sex shows.

MOIRA: Huh?

USAGI: Live sex shows. We do that, too.

IZZY: (alarmed) You don't plan on chopping off anything there, do you?

MOIRA: This is a chronicle of technology, which up 'til this moment has transformed you, Miss Usagi, into an ephemeral avatar of yourself, a courtier to the passing fancies of your studio. What if they tap the Delete key? Content at our tube site has a permanent home. I'm offering you two the immanence of a god in cyberspace, the infallible, inevitable bits and bots of online theogenesis. Performers remade in another world as immortal Animi.

USAGI: (confused) I can hold onto my apartment, can't I? It's a decent neighborhood for the price.

MOIRA: No, that isn't...I'm saying—look, all of us, you'll admit, your time here will end and you'll be gone soon enough.

USAGI: (to Izzy) She's kicking me out!

IZZY: (suspicious) Who are you really?

MOIRA: No, you misunderstand. It's as if I'm carrying a message from a future where nobody need ever see themselves fade and die away in...

(Usagi dissolves into tears.)

IZZY: You threatening my girl? Fuck you, she's not going anywhere!

(Moira returns her scissors to her purse. She picks it up.)

IZZY: But you can go, though, to whoever it was sent you, and tell 'em we're staying put, right? (his arms enclose Usagi) Yeah, grab your shit and go.

(Moira recedes to the door.)

IZZY: You still crave an address for your filthy business? I wouldn't give my darkest enemy's to you, but here's one on account: The Mattress Emporium on Hollywood and Jeffries, ask for Mister Gonzalez, see where that gets you. Right? Now you owe me. The payback is we don't hear from you again.

(Moira vacates apartment.)

IZZY: (to Usagi) Fuckin' hater motherfuckers. Envy us because we do what they can't. We're special.

USAGI: (through tears) We are? We really are like gods?

IZZY: We're fuckin' golden gods, yeah. We're the chosen ones. (he wipes her nose)

USAGI: (snuffs) That's right. We are gods.

IZZY: Right, we're gods. (scans the carpet) Now, where's my argyle socks?

(Cut to Interior, Patrick Ramsey's Office, Mid-Morning Friday. Patrick, his anatomy under wraps, is regaling a matched set of bottle blondes on his sofa, one middle-aged and one barely-of-age. A fusillade is heard.)

PATRICK: Enter!

(Ed Tragos cracks the door and slithers in.)

PATRICK: (polished, professional) Ladies. Allow me to introduce to you Ed Tragos, my secretary said? Intrepid reporter for *MEH*, our primary news organ in an industry that has more than its share, heh, of organs I'm saying, get it?

ED: Well met, ladies. (he tips an imaginary cap, waits by the entrance, deferential to a fault)

PATRICK: Edward my darling baby boy, this will interest you. Here we have the captivating Martha (the older woman nods), and there at her hip is a fiery pistol by the name of Desiree, her daughter (the younger woman is engrossed by her shoelaces). Is that some tag, Desiree? I'm tempted to tell you to use your real name, my hatchling. And she is eighteen today, and of newly legal vintage therefore, and ready to be resoundingly corked.

MARTHA: (to Ed) See every since she's in rompers, she wants to be a star and ya know, she takes after her mama, not that disgrace in his prison cell where he should rot to bits and die in that order who shot me full of his hot glue and my legs have been stuck together every since, where men are concerned, but I says if she is got a gift, oughtn't she? Ought she not? And I'm online and I see she's a goodtime gal which I was back when, the fabulous tales the boys would tell about her, the length and breadth of her blowjobbing skills fer example, where she's like, "I gotta hole in the back of my skull, do your worst, buddy!"

DESIREE: Ma-a-a-a!!

MARTHA: I figure, lemme be the manager, keep an eye on the till, and we hire an agency to get her started and promoted proper. Which is him.

PATRICK: You will tweet like the tweety birds, dear ladies, at how I guide you to the gilded door. (he passes the debutante a pen. She flattens a document on the sofa cushion and signs multiple pages without bothering to read them.) There you are. (he gathers the papers, stands, files them in a cabinet, and turns toward the pair) This is a contract with myself as your representative, and not with any studio. The setup is, you are a private contractor for whom I secure jobs with many studios, and much exposure ensues. Think of it as the kind of arrangement used by, for example, a Helen Mirren.

MARTHA: (to Desiree) Another Helen Mirren right here!

PATRICK: I admit we've been through it once, but bear with me, for the education of Mister Tragos. When you walked in, I asked you a series of questions, Desiree. You had the answers. You proved to me your head is bolted on straight between your collarbones. I asked, "What do you hope to gain from this job? Surrender yourself to new experiences? Revenge on a boyfriend? Seek out pleasures given to few? Fall in love?"

DESIREE: (bored) Bank some cash.

PATRICK: "What studio is your heart set on working for? Which stars do you fantasize about doing sex with? What sorts of fans do you look forward to meeting, when your moniker is on the public's lips?"

DESIREE: Anybody putsa most cash inna bank.

PATRICK: "And what awards do you covet? *Mature Entertainment Headlines?* Triple-X Critics Association? Do you dream of being a lion in the trade, famous and respected in all quarters? In short, where do you see yourself in five to ten years?"

DESIREE: Lotsa cash inna bank.

PATRICK: (to Martha) Congrats, Ma'am, on the fine upbringing you have given your child. (he pushes a button on his phone) Say, call Jewelpaste Productions and tell 'em I'll be sending a virgin, be respectful, for Monday's big orgy. Name of, um, (smiles at Desiree) name's "Helen Meerkat," got it? Boffo. (hangs up, escorts the women to the exit) You've calligraphized the dotted line, you brought your test results too, I'm grateful, as the studio will demand them. My girl will give you the location and the schedule. (sees them out) You embark on a wondrous journey, twin butterflies!

(He sits at his desk and directs Ed to the sofa.)

PATRICK: Admittedly, a door could have on the opposite side Heaven, or it could have Hell. But that's the beauty of doors, *n'est-ce pas?*

ED: (sitting) And of people, sir, who can be heaven from one angle and hell from the other.

PATRICK: Anyone we know, you're referring to?

ED: You are a perceptive man. You must be, in your line. I hesitate to pronounce the name. I recall to you our brief, and mutually advantageous, dialogue by phone this morning. Suffice to say that an owlish, hoydenish starlet of your acquaintance has engaged her energies upon the expectation of reducing her studio to so much whit and flinder.

PATRICK: Eden Gann and Charlie Vogel, all right. You can't be subtle with me, I don't respond kindly, I'm not a patient man.

ED: I can tell you I've spoken to an editor at *MEH.*

PATRICK: I've got big ears. You are writing an article for *Wangler.*

ED: *Wangler Magazine,* then. And they'll publish, with a putative long term job in the offing, on the proviso of additional detail, and sources, attribution.

PATRICK: Which is me, to quote the Mother of Darkness. (he squares the papers in front of him) Good! I will explain to you the reasons I shouldn't help you. Knock 'em flat if you can. First, Vogel's ledger sheet will be hurt by your story, and he's a friend, a loyal friend, the paragon of friends.

ED: Your agency could benefit from free advertising.

PATRICK: Fuck him. Reason two, Gann schedules her occasional appearances and ancillary income through my firm and not Pie-Rite, and if her reputation and livelihood and income take a hit, don't I suffer?

ED: (uncomfortably) That, I didn't know.

PATRICK: Never fear, Edmund my adorable milk-faced urchin. Here's a secret, hide it in your hope chest. Out of all the oily Oliviers and the downmarket Denches you'll brush shoulders with in our rat's nest enterprise, I am the cleverest actor you'll encounter. Do you think you're talking to a captain of industry, a titan of the boardroom?

ED: Yes?

PATRICK: You're talking to a wreck, an earthquake, a temblor in a retail tweed. This smile? Seven-point-nine on the rictus scale!

ED: Your secret is a secret heartache.

PATRICK: A simpatico companion, I'm telling you, was in my grasp and kidnapped to parts unknown (snaps his fingers) not fifteen minutes before you came in, and who by? Eden Gann!

ED: Typical! You formed an attachment. And on Eden Gann's say so, your lady cut you dead.

PATRICK: Cut me off and threw me away, like the tags on my tweed suit I just mentioned!

ED: It is a handsome suit.

PATRICK: Forget the suit. When you stumble on the right person in romantic matters, you don't wish to lose them. I'm not a young man. I'm not old, don't worry, but young, no.

ED: In my—

PATRICK: A guy in my position has very specific urges!

ED: Understood. People say: as one ages, one develops more and more into the fellow one really is. I won't opine. I do suspect that, as you age, the things which most aroused are the only things which continue to arouse, because arousal is harder to achieve. Sexually, you are drilled down to the man you were always fated to be.

PATRICK: "Arousal is harder to achieve?" When did it become a catheter convention? I'm fifty, not a hundred and fifty.

ED: I was attempting to buttress your dictum.

PATRICK: Buttress your own dictum. I told you, don't try subtlety on me. Stop being intelligent. Gann has finished sidetracking Charlie's contract-ettes and due to this, as of this day, I'm high and dry. I'm stranded on a beach with no signs of a love life. I'll tell you about Miss Eden Gann, the complete sordid saga for your notebook. If she's a pain to Charlie, she's been an agony to me, this girl, and more poisonous still to her fans at her toxic personal appearances where an unwise word from some innocent admirer can lead to the wreaking of widespread death and devastation, and don't ask me about the photographer at a shoot who she smashed in the mush and now he wears his schnoz on the other side of his scalp and has to part his hair before he sneezes, and there's the prospective sale of Pie-Rite on the weekend which she may well end up sabotaging.

ED: Pie-Rite is going on the block?

PATRICK: That's the idea. It will be her latest atrocity, if I'm a judge.

ED: Shameful! I want all of it. All of it. Every scrap of bad behavior up to the present.

PATRICK: Edwin my delightful button-nosed panda bear, you shall have it! I tell you, before you arrived I was tempted to send yon Desiree chippie to Pie-Rite, not Jewelpaste. And "toodle-oo" (snaps his fingers again) to Eden Gann. But I'm in a bind. I played my part in Gann's machinations, and as I'm sure she's aware, this I can't have publicly divulged. It doesn't make me a prince to the studios. And then it occurs to me that if I whisper a sweet something to you, and you call on the proprietor of a certain gentlemen's establishment, and call a certain photographer, and you might discreetly pay a visit to Papi Gonzalez the owner of Pie-Rite I'll give you his address, I will be the Cheshire Cat, out of sight with my smile left dangling, and what's more I don't have to scramble on a Friday to assemble the troops for a Vegas showdown. You'll misplace my name?

ED: They'll need a detective to find a search party to find a scavenger hunt to find a bloodhound to find you! I shall embosom you beneath the mighty Grawlix! You will join the vaunted company of "Unidentified Sources" who have toppled presidents, prime ministers, and Pee Wees!

PATRICK: Deal!

ED: Also. I hesitate once more, but after we speak and I interrogate these notables, professionalism dictates I obtain Gann's comments before I submit my *billet-tout* to *Wangler*. Could you advise where she might be found?

PATRICK: Easy. Don't bother with her condo, that's a maybe at best. On most days, come the evening, she hits a bar—

ED: —I believe I might know the place.

"Know the place"? They built it around him. He was literally hiding under the foosball table the whole time. But if he was coming to confront me, good, that meant I'd be up to date on his underhanded monkey business and I'd be able to act to protect myself. Meanwhile, though, I had just walked down what was obviously the world's longest apartment stairwell for the purposes of this story...

(Cut to Exterior, Usagi's Apartment Building, Mid-Morning Friday. Edie exits the building, ducks her head and catches a whiff of her clothes, and shrugs. As she descends the steps she spots a slender, lank limbed, cobalt black Man waiting for her curbside by a black limo, the striking effect of his jet black uniform and shiny-brimmed cap magnified by his regal bearing. He argues with a Cabbie in an awkwardly parked vehicle.)

CAB DRIVER: Bottom line, you got no special privileges. You are one more hack, with a bigger dry cleaning bill.

LIMO DRIVER: (thunderous basso profundo delivery, musical East African accent) And what, what you are, my dear sir? Are you king of the catwalk? Are you the hereditary Caesar?

CAB DRIVER: Bet your ass I'll call the cops!

LIMO DRIVER: As any fool can tell you, the crown belongs to him who can seize it!

CAB DRIVER: (seeing Edie) A half hour, the asshole has been sitting here. Because of you? You two have no civility!

LIMO DRIVER: (scorning him, tipping his hat brim) You are Miss Gann?

EDIE: That's me.

LIMO DRIVER: I am to say that your presence is requested by my Mistress, the famous Golden Age sex goddess Punaise de Lit. Her name is in English "The Bedbug." She was in the classic erotic picture "*Infesté de Punaise.*" You have seen it? But she should be called Araignée, you see? *Toile d'araignée mondiale*, yes? Or perhaps *araignée au plaufond* is better. You will understand.

EDIE: Yeah, I've heard the name.

I'd heard the rumors, too. Legend had it Punaise was once an advisor to royalty. Or no, not true, that before porn she was a rural shepherdess who finally got tired of horny country boys who kept dicking the inventory.

LIMO DRIVER: I am to say that an overture of employment is soon to be tendered by a Mister Vogel, that my Mistress will hear his call this day at twenty minutes after noon, all this and also that she desires your presence. It is amenable?

EDIE: Lead on.

Another rumor said she was a pure untried maiden when she came on the scene. Or another, that she was already up there in years when she started her career, but was so well-preserved she could have passed for a debutante who wore SPF twelve thousand, survived on green tea and grass-fed fetusburgers, and slept in a pickle jar that sat inside a hyperbaric chamber guarded by revived Aztec mummies.

(The Limo Driver opens her door for her, slams it behind her, and grabs the wheel. He enters traffic and flashes the Cabbie his middle digit, the partition between them gliding downward.)

Or that she was born male, got romantic with a scalpel, and post-op she starred in films as a lady before she left the industry. Or, she left and then she had the surgery, and she was now named Murray, or Curly Joe, or Pinky Ring Pete from Pomona.

Driver: My name is Busu Mweisi. In Mozambique, I dubbed myself Nero, for *Bacio Nero*, the Black Kiss, you know. And it is the Italian, not our local Portuguese. A language of aggressors! I can of course speak it, though I will not, but we speak Swahili there, and I have more than a small English. My town is a port town, not a dusty *kijiji*, for we are east coast Africa. You heard they discovered the first tools at Oldavai Gorge? Not too far, eight hundred kilometers. My people are of that lineage. When the savanna dried up and the desert swelled up and puffed out the aboriginal Man to the four corners of the earth, we held fast. We are not Bantu, those latecomers, those upstarts. We were *there*. And you?

EDIE: (intrigued in spite of herself) Uh, I barely knew my own father.

BUSU: Yes, my employer said you come from low stock. She knows much, but she's a nasty thing. She's an ugly spider, and the world is her web, and something about you has made the fur twitch on her shaggy body. Might she seek a new lover?

EDIE: *Moi?*

BUSU: She has said you prefer the touch of a woman. You have ever felt the touch of a man?

EDIE: Periodically.

BUSU: It is that in your private life, your preference is women?

EDIE: Like they say, I experimented, and the experiment was a success.

BUSU: I will not press. I should add, however, that it is my habit to claim a kiss in exchange for a proffer, and later I will claim a kiss, nothing more, from you.

EDIE: I think the exhaust fumes are getting to you.

BUSU: No matter. Foreordination brooks no arguments.

(Edie shrugs and looks out the window, NARRATING in her own voice, but in a drier, more detached cadence:)

EDIE: The glass partition sighs upward, and she is alone with her thoughts. They cruise through familiar precincts and less so, the vast residences and their faux Spanish architectures gleaming in moneyed splendor under the bright yellow sun.

E, dressed for comfort and not in service to fashion, in jeans and a thin cotton blouse, light makeup and sneakers, is self-aware. She pulls out her compact, a coin slipping with it from her pocket, and opens it. Before she can take up her lipstick, the partition descends. "This you cannot bring with you. Please?" Busu lifts a hand from the wheel, not turning, in a politely imperative gesture.

She hesitates; the hand beckons. He explains that part of his duty as major domo is to prepare her for her prospective audience, and that she must relinquish not just her accessories, but "those simple frocks."

His courteous deportment is outlandish, reassuringly so. She passes him the compact. "Your shoes," she wears no stockings, "give me them."

Off come her sneakers, bouncing on the front passenger seat, each rapping on some unseen commodity. She curls her toes on the cold, fresh-shampooed carpeting and shivers in unaccustomed pleasure.

"Your slacks, if you would be so kind."

E does not feel so kind, not at all. Scanning the road, he fumbles and retrieves from the passenger side a white box tied in a purple ribbon and bow. She accepts it, pulls the ribbon apart, tilts the lid, and reveals two white slippers and a white hooded robe, cinched at the waist by a white belt, the cultish device of a supplicant.

To what?

Curiosity outweighs caution. She slides her back upward until her bottom hovers inches above the car seat. After a brief wrestling bout with her jeans, she settles into the embrace of the cushion, which exhales with her as the two supple surfaces unite.

Not waiting to be prompted, E undoes the buttons on her blouse. She peeps through the near window on her right: no pedestrians on the pale white-tiled walkways there. To the left: no automobiles close by. She discards the blouse. Her flesh is greeted by currents of cool air and the smooth expensive material behind her.

The last elements of decorum, her bra and panties, linger.

E sits quite tall, declining to be abashed at this charade, and stares at the rearview mirror in her most challenging style. Busu does not rise to the bait, his attention remains on the road. They coast through stations of palm trees, filed in perfect symmetry along the immaculate boulevards, their shadows sweeping past the limousine in dark waves. Then a sharp turn of the steering wheel.

"We have arrived," he says.

A gate swings open, guided by invisible intelligences, and they speed down a winding avenue, greenery everywhere, sculpted into strange attitudes animalistic and manlike. He slows to a halt by a decadent manor in Spanish Colonial accents.

Twisting, he extends an arm over the headrest and brandishes a Swiss Army Knife. "Seventeen functions! Marvelous. Here is one," a pair of clippers snicks out, "A brassiere remover." He snips the band that links the cups, her breasts droop a bit.

Silent, she tosses the useless apparel away, anticipating the finishing touch. It does not come. Instead, in a rare curtsy toward gallantry, Busu inclines his gaze and lets her shed her panties and throw the white robe over her shoulders. She dons the slippers.

"Now you are outfitted for your adventure. That door, you see? Rap twice and go in. It is not locked, it is a comity. You will be met within, go with them and do as they indicate. You are not to speak without permission. No, I cannot accompany you," he opens his door and hers, "perhaps later. Remember that you *are* an adventuress, one who dares anything to advance herself. *À bientôt,*" he tips his cap.

E wends her way up the walk, ascends steps guarded by a trio of vicious curs struck in stone, hefts the brass knocker twice, enters into the presence of a pretty young Girl draped in identical vestments, a slender blonde with a catbird smile, who puts a finger to her lips, escorts her to an expansive and elegant bedchamber, disrobes her, bathes her assiduously, dresses her in white, brushes her hair, and compelling her to lie down, darkens her eyes and rouges her mouth and cheeks.

As the eyeliner is penciled, E glimpses a woman in black weeds, gray maned, her face a cataract of wrinkles, floating by the bedroom and gazing within, her pale eyes glittering, and flourishing her head in approval...

CHAPTER 9

(Cut to Interior, Friday Noon. A Bedroom in Baroque design. Edie lies on the bed, the Girl hovering, penciling. She shoos her away.)

EDIE: (undertone) *Quit it, I'm gorgeous, good job.* (she sits up)

(The Girl retires to an inconspicuous area, assuming a contemplative, pietistic posture. The Woman drifts noiselessly through the doorway, wafts onto a chair at Edie's bedside, and flares her black sleeves, reaching her arms for an embrace.)

EDIE: We should...oh...okay... (recipient of bruising hug) Wow, you must really be hitting the gym. (she gasps) Hey, squeeze me any harder and our spines'll fuse! (she is relinquished) You're Punaise?

PUNAISE: (barest trace of a French accent, in a husky contralto) How dost do? Pray pardon if I trouble thy Repose, but I perceived thro' the Door of thy Cell, that thou hadst taken the Surplice.

EDIE: Eh?

PUNAISE: (indicating) Thy Cloathing, my Dear.

EDIE: Oh, yeah. Um, yeah.

PUNAISE: Child, thou art a Treasure. Somewhat of thy Aspect makes me sensible of that other Place—

EDIE: I realize it's before my time, but how long ago *was* the Golden Age?

PUNAISE: Fret not. Give me a Kiss, *ma Baguette*, and we'll speak on diverse Things. (she receives a peck, and frowns) Another, a la Florentine!

EDIE: What's that?

PUNAISE: I'll shew thee. (jaws agape, red tongue a-wiggle)

EDIE: Blah. (shrugs) Screw it. In for a penny. (they French kiss)

Don't worry, not gonna, nah, no chance. Fine wine and all, I get it, but wooing the Gray Ghost here would be the exact opposite of robbing the cradle. Which would be, um...grave robbing, I guess. Besides, I was afraid if I did grab some part of her, there was a distinct possibility it might come off in my hand.

(They separate.)

PUNAISE: Ah! Lard! The Kisses of that Mouth are a Wonder! My Body is in a Fire! (she beckons the Girl, who approaches) Enough of these Toyings. This Creature, my Mignonne, is a tolerable Mignonne, I own it. She is not excellently favoured as art thou, but she possesses a miraculous Physick. Go, Girl, and fetch out that Essence. (Mignonne departs) As thou, my unfledged Mignonne, may also, and full as savoury. (she grins, showing her lengthy yellow canines)

EDIE: Wait, is she Mignonne, or am I Mignonne? What's a Mignonne?

PUNAISE: Everything in its Season. (hesitates) Thou disputest with One, a Director in our Community.

EDIE: How'd you know?

PUNAISE: I am a recluse Soul, and thus have placed my principal Diversion in Knowledge of Intrigues, to every minute Particular. O disembarrass thy self, my budding Heart, my very Spirit, and be a Devote to my Confessor.

EDIE: Okay, you got me, I confess. That's why I'm here?

(Mignonne reenters carrying a tray bearing an ornate mirror, a shallow bowl of aqua vita and another bowl in the shape of a skullcap, a crimson liquid pooled in its crown. She bows and offers them to Punaise: her sleeve falls to expose a bandaged forearm.)

PUNAISE: (to Edie, as she secures the tribute and arranges the tray in her lap) I perceive thy Inquietude. Do not put thy self in Pain. Shall I paint thee a little Picture? (she fusses at her collar and withdraws a lace handkerchief, dips it in the scarlet fluid, and, mirror up, dabs at the edges of her lips, speaking in a desultory vein) "She was the most beautiful Creature... who was no ways culpable before but in some little Indiscretions... these were no more than petty Fooleries, which, notwithstanding, were sufficient to give a Handle to a jealous Person who had it in his Power to ill-treat... (blotting her forehead) ...an old Director superlatively ignorant... she took up almost all his Time, there was Scarce any Respite for any Body else... he told her that it was upon the Informations he had received of her ill Conduct that he came thither... under a Necessity to inflict on her an exemplary Punishment... (swabs her cheeks with the red substance) ...she took a quite contrary Method to what she ought to have followed: She imagined that he... had no other Design but to judge by her Weakness of what she was capable... upon this ill Foundation she answered him... with only Coldness, and Words scarce so much as indifferent... (daubs her crow's feet) ...He proceeded then against her... she cried, thundered, and threatened every Body but to no Purpose... (dips her lace in the bowl) ...At last... she put in Practice a very pleasant Stratagem. She called all... together... to the end, that... they might comfort each *other* from time to time... and... in such a manner, that he... could not disengage himself from this Trap. I could not see him in this Condition without bursting out into a loud Laugh... (she rubs her jowls with the carmine) ...I will not tell you what Method he took... but thou shalt only understand that he acquitted himself so well, that... she fell into a very great Weakness, but it was a very amorous one, which the Fury of her Passion had caused, and made this young Thing taste such a Pleasure which ravished her to the very Skies... (swipes at the wattles on her neck) ...recovered from this Syncope, her... Eyes were opened, and reflecting on what she had done and on the little Virtue she had received... she knew that she had been in an Error." (Punaise concludes by wetting a clean section of the handkerchief in the water and wiping her features, jaw and neck)

EDIE: Right. I got about two thirds, there.

PUNAISE: Hast thou not penetrated into the Sense of my Relation? Alas!

EDIE: Nope. You lost me at the bakery.

(She hesitates and peers at her. Rising, she goes to a window and pulls the curtains, letting in some daylight.)

EDIE: No way.

Yes, way. Either it was a trick of the light, or the guck on her skin had tightened it, but suddenly it was smoother and more toned, and she looked some four decades younger. By which I mean, she looked to be approximately nine hundred and sixty years old.

(Punaise beckons; Edie inches to the bed and sits.)

PUNAISE: I purpose thee a Wager, for my Diversion and thy Enlightenment. By thy Doings, this Man I spoke of is at present out of the Society. I have it in my Compass to deliver him. In ten Minutes he will call, desiring my Assistance; 'ere then, my Servant will set thee a Riddle. Answer rightly, and I shall not yield.

EDIE: What if I get it wrong?

PUNAISE: Thou agreest to abide here a Month's time, and attend me in my Pleasure.

EDIE: (frowning at Mignonne) How long has she been here?

PUNAISE: Near a Month. Tomorrow the Moon waxeth.

EDIE: The girl before her? And before her?

PUNAISE: A Month.

EDIE: Uh-huh. Did they walk out, or were they carried out?

PUNAISE: This is a trifling Distinction. Come, *ma Puce, ma petite Bichette*, satisfy me of thy Word: vouchsafe me to remain. (she rings a bell)

Riddle me this: did I aspire to be the only Maybelline Lady who had to nick an artery to seal the deal? Howsoever—and you didn't know this about me due to my shy and humble nature—but try sticking a brainteaser under my snout and watch me howl, thrash on the linoleum, maul the upholstery, and violently transform into a pussy-fanged, queen bitch, cryptozoic puzzle princess. Crosswords, anagrams, logic problems, used to be I'd practically bury myself under them to kill time while my directors were setting up the next scene. Later I read mysteries, too, but I stopped because it's almost always the guy who's not particularly important to the plot, so why does he keep blundering in, chapter after chapter? Speaking of whom...

(Busu enters the bedroom.)

BUSU: (to Punaise) What do you want, dreadful old reptile?

PUNAISE: (looking at Edie, who nods Yes) That's well. (to Busu) Truce, thou impudent Rascal. Relate to us with Civility one of the Histories we talked of. Which will it be, think'st 'ou? (she taps her chin) Here is the Catalogue:

White Wine in a Warm Vessel, a Curious Piece.
The Curvaceous Convent.
The Man of Many Parts, with Figures.
The Martyrdom of Saint Mookie. A Gallant Piece.
Too Long to be a Bunion.
The Prioress and her Poodle, very curious.

BUSU: My people were telling tales a thousand years before the Devil clawed you out of his rectum, you swollen beetle. I will tell her a story of my own.

PUNAISE: *Mais, plus de Sexe, et moins de Poésie.*

BUSU: *Chut!*

(Edie NARRATES, knotting her vocal cords into an approximation of Busu's sepulchral timbre:)

EDIE: In the decades intruding upon the two great Wars, there lived a Southern Creole named Lucien, of eminent family, reared in luxury and a natural dignitary of the salon, the opium den, the boudoir and the battlefield. He had opened all the shutters of his being to Fortune's weathers. He grasped at any pursuit, not out of fear of death; he had done much, risked much, and reckoned himself Death's stalwart. But his primary rôle was one who gathered experiences and built himself large out of their embers.

By his early forties he had used up his passions. A pall slumped over his world, his intelligence glanced on its presence and darkened. He was jaded, disinterested. The campaigner in him recommended a retreat: he cast his mind to New Orleans, his birthplace, and his twenty years' absence. He had no home, and no living family. Nevertheless, he wondered if he might find a ray there to shine on the malignant cells in his disposition.

Hiring an automobile to transport him, sailing the crest of the Causeway Bridge, he rolled his window to breathe the aroma bred by the Pontchartrain waters. Then the car descended into the ferment of the city and he was crushed to see not the brilliant diorama he recalled from his youth, but what seemed a lusterless hell that could never fire the wound in his soul.

At a loss, he lingered on. He wandered. He gave his days to drink. A wealthy man, he stole. He came from privilege; he lodged in dives. But he always dressed and perfumed befitting his station. He sifted through the dregs of the citizenry in his careless way, tempting fate, awaiting the knife in the back. His bulk and air of disregard shielded him.

One night he drank outside a club whose habitué sometimes amused him. They saw him in turn as the tall, minatory brown man whose coat was always black, whose cuffs and collar were always white, whom nobody dared pester without leave. After a time, he called the boy and said, "Who is that terror by the railing? The old man who spies at me?"

The waiter said he was of no account. "Sir, he sketches you, and he asks for money. Shall I eject him?"

Lucien swirled his glass. The venerable miscreant, seventy if he was a day, hook-nosed and hunched in his spattered pea coat, ended his remarks to the waitress or hostess at his elbow and sent her away, his rheumy blue eyes, so far apart they were birdlike, one by each temple, roaming the clientele.

The Creole drained his cognac and sat at the man's table. The old pensioner simpered and spun his pad. He said, "You saw how I included you in my sphere. Well! Everything is in an artist's sphere. And you assert the right of a confidante." He tapped the pad with his charcoal. Lucien said it was a favorable likeness, but the carriage was too genial and the mouth too jolly. "But I realize them as they wish to be, as they may yet be," he shook his head.

Lucien chose not to be offended. He ordered a second glass. Bored, he elected to be drawn into the rogue's intrigues. This villain? He was no danger, he was too old for his sins to be a danger to anybody but himself. The two conversed, they drank, summoned memories, told lies. Warmed by the brandy, the cheery bloom of lilac in the air, and the live jazz wheeling out of the club's windows, a fellow feeling sprang up between them.

After half an hour he threw a bill on the pad and stood. His wizened friend exclaimed, "Permit me to introduce myself! I am L'Ombre." Lucien gave his name. "You're an agreeable sort. I propose to demonstrate to you a prodigy, a spectacle you've not seen before. Will you join me at my studio?" He remitted Lucien's bill into his vest. "On my honor, I will sell you nothing."

Lucien engaged a taxi. The studio was a healthy distance, as his genie, collecting souls for his book, had just completed his nightly circuit. Neither spoke. In the darkness of the cab Lucien heard music from passing clubs, and watched the parade of streetwalkers flying their colors in a burlesque of womanhood, a pantomime sensuality, exaggerating the struts and poses of femininity to expand their radius of influence. He remained aloof. Not the most accomplished, the most distinguished of whores could have tempted him, anymore.

They stopped at L'Ombre's squat, a disused building on a char-black side street, and flicking their lighters they entered the stair and ascended to the third level. Lucien's comrade pried a door and switched on the lamp. They stepped past a big, graceless, sturdy generator and a palette of bottled beverages. In the uncertain illumination he saw a surprisingly clean, neatly kept lodging. L'Ombre had the whole floor, three narrow bedrooms behind closed doors and the rangy studio, where he had knocked down a wall to grant more space to perform his petit and grand guignols, to create art, to palter, to haggle commissions from patrons. Paintings tilted on every spare article, or lay heaped aimlessly. Yet more dried on a balcony.

By the balcony and a timeworn chaise, crouched a strapping many-legged apparatus. Six wooden limbs of equal dimension sprouted from a central nexus, jointed, guyed by cords and pulleys, ending at six easels with blank canvasses. Each limb bore a heavily articulated jointed wooden hand, and each hand clasped a charcoal pencil.

The old man fluttered into the hub of his enchanted nest, inserting his own hand in a leather glove from which wires led into the pulley system. Before the glove was another blank canvas. As he hummed and sketched, his six servants responded with admirable poise, in perfect concert. "There," he cried, "Exact copies, and not a copyist in sight!"

Lucien complimented him on his cleverness. In truth, he thought it a ridiculous conceit, a puppet show, a hobby horse for an overgrown child. One objection he did advance aloud. "Where is the original?" "Why, the nearest canvas, of course." He referred to that beneath his leather glove. "And when you remove it, and sketch on the air? You have copies, L'Ombre. Of what?" "Of..." the artist scratched his chin, "...of each other?"

Lucien laughed.

His elder pouted a moment, decamping from his wooden soldiers, the storm passed, and he took Lucien in with a heightened respect. "You've some wit up there. Splendid. And you've lived, I like a man who's lived. And you're well set up, if I may say. My friend, I have a proposition to put to you. A daughter I wish to get rid of.

"No, don't look for the door," he added. "Hear me out. You can always refuse."

His project was as follows. He had in fact two girls he was honored to call stepdaughters, twin sisters, prominent courtesans, who paid for his necessities and shared his digs. Their names were Mélanie and Cécile. They preferred to labor on alternate days, visiting clients in Mélanie's name, and leaving the Sabbath to other kinds of good works. The men they saw were all unawares of their deception, so alike were they.

The lack of concern for their personal nuances had begun to incite them to so high a degree, that Cécile now tired of the life, and was prepared to reform herself into a wealthy man's wife.

Their honorary stepfather proposed to install Lucien in the first of the three bedrooms for the night. Out of the second would come Mélanie. The two would *tête-à-tête* for a space, she would depart, and Cécile would likewise appear from her room. In the morning, if he was pleased and had pleased in return, they would chew on a light meal and a weighty discourse, after which Lucien would identify Cécile without prompting, based on her address and his prior knowledge of her idiosyncrasies, her lover's quirks. (L'Ombre would excuse himself if the Creole became properly diffident.)

Having eulogized her charms to the lady's satisfaction, he might claim her. "Only if you want her, *naturellement!*"

"*Bien sûr*," Lucien said.

He endured a tremor of curiosity. It was late, one berth was as good as the next, and he could dismiss the girls if they were too cheap or too diseased. If not, a *bouillotte* or two to heat his bed should be quite restful. At breakfast he would put on his politest manner and guess wrong or register ignorance, as he was not and could never be a companionable man. He consented, said his goodnight, performed his ablutions, and readied himself for emprise.

In his room he found a lamp shining on the nightstand. Undistinguished, unframed paintings littered the walls in semi-darkness, and on a corner table before three mirrors, tubes and pats of maquillage shone dully, two minute phials of scent glistened. A gentleman's vest lay slung on a chair by the table. A thick, stuporous, fruity tang swam in the air. By the bed was another balcony, shielded from the remnants of the street noise, whatever activity might present at two o'clock in the morning, by three layers of blankets hung from an iron rod. He pulled away a ponderous velvet coverlet, took off the last of his clothing, bustled under the sheets and let his mind drift until the door opened to admit Mélanie.

Had he fallen asleep, unknowing, and dreamed? He had never seen a vision this exquisite. Her hair was a shimmering blonde and fell in ingenuous tangles to her shoulders. The face was kittenish, a meld of innocence and mischief, with animated, wide-set aquamarine eyes and an amiable satirical smile which slashed without cutting, offering a swift intimacy. Her perfect beauty was leavened by the detail of a crooked nose, and though small of stature, the lines of her body were a woman's, richly provocative, but nothing cumbrous or even earthly: she was a nymph, a composite of mist and light. The floorboards declined to sound a note at her passage.

He sat up on the mattress and kissed her wrists, together, and the pads of her fingers, singly. He hesitated to do more. He was so aroused on the instant, that he feared he might lose his mettle and be unmanned before she could make her secrets known to him.

Mélanie guided Lucien into the bed and, overshadowing him, covered his eyes as if to say, *Touch. No more.* He kept them closed. He felt her mouth on him, felt how she gloried in his strength and his virility. He petted her breasts, and they quivered and slipped away, nocturnal creatures. She straddled his legs. Taking charge of his great rigid stave, she dandled it on her palm, kissed it in fond affection. *"Si beau!"* she murmured. He rose on a forearm to watch, however she had reached the lamp and extinguished it. All around him was black. He ran his hand down her lower back, her buttocks, prospecting to her vulva, tracing the contour of her sex, feeling it contract. She devoured him as if breaking a fast, ravening, and though the room was stuffy, he shivered. He envisioned nixes in the trenches of oceans, every surface nerve alert to the water's disquisition. He slid his thumb in her damp sex.

A jet of delight shot from her lips to his manhood, and a spark jumped within him. She was too expert, too greedy. The Creole, a virtuoso at holding his will intact in such circumstances, was overthrown by the expanse of his pleasure, and a fountain spouted out of him as he groaned his extremis and his disappointment. He sank backward.

Five minutes? Fewer? And he had given nothing in recompense. He heard a low-pitched chuckle, a pattering, the door flashed open and shut, he was alone. Mélanie.

Mélanie. He desired her still, despising her harlot's trick of giving and withholding in one and the same breath, making a game of man's weakness. But lying there, he knew her trap had no teeth. Because soon would come...*Cécile.*

The Creole switched on the lamp and stared up at the ceiling a quarter hour while his vigor mounted. He could cheat. He could mar her face, this one, so he could place her in the morning.

No. He would never stoop to a coward's subterfuge.

He became impatient. "Cécile," he said aloud.

The twin came in, naked like her other self, roughly currycombing her yellow hair from her brow. She was identical in all ways to her sister but for the scapegrace touch of vermilion-tattooed labia, of new-minted currency he supposed. She laid the ivory comb on the table in the corner and joined him without a sound.

Lucien attempted to be forceful. Sitting up, he caught at her when she approached and towed her to the bed. Cécile smirked in acknowledgement, bowed, bit his wrist hard enough to draw blood and as she danced by, wrenched the lamp cord from its socket. Darkness settled on his eyes. She clambered back on top of him and with a dusky grin, glued her lips to his. He tasted the tart, plummy wine: "Côt!" she snarled. He smiled. *No wonder she wishes to play.*

Cécile set about consuming him, plucking at his flesh, an immense carrion bird, translating the pains into pleasure by the bedeviling action of her fist inside his thighs. She clawed him. She meant to injure him with her passion, to shatter him in pieces and remake him as something less than before. This he welcomed with a most equable nonchalance. He cupped his hands under her ass and lifted her in the air, planted her foursquare on his swollen penis, and dropped her with a thump. She sighed. Arching her body, she tightened her grip on him and rolled her bottom as he seized and mauled her breasts. The nectar flowed out of her. She responded to violence? He could be violent. He slapped her rump, threw her underneath him and stabbed into her. "Harder. Again," she whispered. And now that he had loosened the stays of her nature, he sought to rip them free, to destroy her, destroy himself. "No!" He slid out and clutched his staff, tapping at her entrance, killing her of need for him. He felt her grasp at him in small chaotic blindisms. He waited for her to beg, trembling. Then he thrust deep in the well of her womb with a vengeance, obsessively, until the tides of pleasure and agony distilled into an ecstasy he had never tasted before, and rent him to shreds.

He collapsed onto the damp bedsheets. The bedroom door flashed and shut. Outside, through the curtained balcony, a bell tolled. Ten minutes had passed.

Later, he roused and marched onto the balcony, where he saw L'Ombre had left him half a bottle of acceptable Malbec, on a ledge. He sat in the little chair beside and sipped it, thinking, "What was that? Best or worst? Two quick fucks, or a connection I won't easily rid myself of?"

He thought, "Both. All three." He cursed the old man. He contemplated maneuvers. He drank, he spoke in his mind to departed enemies, men he had slain, in the tenderest terms. He wanted to live.

He crawled into bed and slept ten hours.

Shortly after noon he rejoined L'Ombre at his seven canvasses. He suffered the man to compliment him and pet him like a new relation. They agreed to split the difference between breakfast and lunch, his host serving coffee or beer, hot sausages or cold mutton. Lucien chose the mutton and a hot coffee.

"My friend, you've had your promenade. My daughters tell me they are satisfied, and I trust you were no less so. Now I shall call them in, and you will determine which is Cécile!"

"Old goat," the Creole replied. "No. Tonight we will try again. But next time, with..."

With what?

PUNAISE: (interrupting) Thou dissembled at the Countenances of the Girls. In that Account, they were Blackamoors.

BUSU: I tailored my story. When a poet is inspired by exquisite loveliness (he simpers at Edie), he must allow it to shine through his art.

EDIE: (standing) You win. (she rises on tiptoes and kisses Busu on the cheek)

PUNAISE: Mark me! (Edie looks at her) Dost yield?

EDIE: That was a side bet. (she sits)

PUNAISE: Resolve me, an' it please thee.

(Punaise signals Mignonne, who retrieves a black and silver candlestick phone from an end table and transfers it to Busu. It rings at once. He picks up.)

BUSU: A moment, Sir.

(Punaise dips her thumb in the crimson liquor, plunges it into her mouth, gulps, and licks it clean. Her cheeks fill with healthy color, her gray hair glimmers with golden strands: she appears fortyish at most. She accepts the phone.)

PUNAISE: (musical soprano) Charlie-boy. What up?

(Charlie's voice squawks from the receiver.)

PUNAISE: (nodding) Gimme a sec, snookums. Gotta check my schedule.

(She covers the mouthpiece and glances expectantly at Edie.)

EDIE: (to Busu) "With all three women." You said the Creole's second visitor got *back* on top of him, hinting it was the same sister each time, but that was a red herring just for me, 'cause how could it have been if number two was tatted up and her sis wasn't? which indicated the visitor, both times, was someone else (the first left when the door opened, she didn't, she left with the second), and also you said Mélanie would come out of her room to join him and, likewise, Cécile would come out of hers, so the room, the one Lucien was in, must be L'Ombre's, but why were there feminine things there? and this was Lucien's initial clue; and you mentioned the person who visited him tasted of Côt, but Malbec and Côt are two different names for the same wine, implying the third woman was on the balcony, laying low waiting for the light to dim and tipping the bottle there in between their trysts, and this was Lucien's second clue; and why was the room drenched in perfume, when the phials of fragrance were described as minute, suggesting the occupant didn't use a lot of scent? well it was perfumed that much to disguise the jasmine aroma Lucien had noticed earlier, his final clue, worn by L'Ombre's ally from the club: not a waitress, but his companion and probably a "working girl," who swapped places with the sisters in the dark, because he decided on his plan when he saw Lucien, and there was no time for his accomplice to bathe and change, she had no idea when they'd arrive, so she had to get right over there; and as for his "stepdaughters," they no doubt really were his daughters, their descriptions match his, and weren't prostitutes, or even very practiced, and he knew wealthy Lucien with his sophistication could only be enticed by a worldly woman...

(oxygen-starved gasp)

...so they did a switcheroo.

BUSU: Tolstoy said it. Every virgin is comparable, but every lady of experience is experienced in her own way.

EDIE: Whatever. And they lived happily ever after. That is, they lived happily after Lucien threw L'Ombre off the balcony for being a conniving two-faced pile of shit scumbag.

BUSU: *Adieu tout le monde!*

EDIE: And. L'Ombre's contraption is an extension of the artist, like a paintbrush is, so the separate pencils in it are like the separate bristles in a brush. All of the canvasses together are the original.

BUSU: My little blonde Basquiat! (he salaams)

(Punaise scowls. She returns the phone to Busu, who clasps the receiver and holds the mouthpiece at arm's length toward her, winking at Edie.)

PUNAISE: FUCK OFF! (Busu claps the mouthpiece on its hook.)

(Cut to black.)

(Fade In on Interior, Mid-Afternoon on Friday, a hag-ridden and woebegone Charlie in his Office, gingerly massaging the jagged contusion above his check, and slumped in gloomy near-defeat on his desk. The telephone buzzes. He punches the speakerphone button.)

CHARLIE: Yeah, Pie-Rite, Vogel.

SECRETARY'S NASAL VOICE: This is the office of Jose Marcos-Escolano-Ortiz-Mayo-Nebres-Maroto-Sanchez-Gonzalez.

CHARLIE: (under his breath) *Fuck.*

SECRETARY'S VOICE: —the Third. Forwarding a telephone call from Las Vegas.

CHARLIE: (normal volume) Put 'm on.

SECRETARY: One moment.

PAPI TORO'S gravel-strewn, latin-inflected VOICE: Vogel. Where the fuck are you?

CHARLIE: Mister Gonzalez, Sir. How you doing?

PAPI: Please, Charlie. Call me Papi Toro. How many times do I have to say? Only the District Attorney calls me Mister Gonzalez. (pause) You got the mattress I sent?

CHARLIE: Did I ever, Sir, uh, Papi. Thanks a lot.

PAPI: I christened it *"La Pitón Gigante."* I have one myself. I find it's like sleeping on a cloud...a cloud made of newborn babies...babies whose throats have been cut, so I can sleep on them.

CHARLIE: That's an evocative image.

PAPI: I'm considering using it in my ads. Charlie, I'm phoning because I don't see you at the show, and moreso because some rumors have come my way concerning problems with your talent. In a word, shrinkage.

CHARLIE: (weakly joshing) Never say "shrinkage" to a porn guy, Papi.

PAPI: *Basta*, Vogel! What's up?

CHARLIE: Ah, I had to dropkick a few strays to the street, is all. Part of the cutting back, what you instructed me. Pruning the garden of weeds.

PAPI: Plenty of talent left, yeah? The Expo started yesterday, I couldn't get you on your office phone or your cell. Where were you? And more important, them? I'm holding the fort here, we got a booth, a table, we got art, posters, we still need girls-girls-girls to push my sale through. Nobody's going to buy after just looking at you or me, *feo*.

CHARLIE: If they do, and can tear their eyes from my rugged male beauty, I'll have a metric ton of Grade A trim on deck, I assure you. Be there tomorrow. I'm wrapping up some last minute details.

PAPI: Okay. I'm checking in, right?

CHARLIE: Right.

PAPI: Be ready. Be prepared.

CHARLIE: Like a boy scout with a boner, I'm doubly prepared!

PAPI: Pleasant speaking to you. And enjoy the mattress.

CHARLIE: I'm talking in my sleep at this very moment, Papi.

PAPI: And *cabrón*, DO NOT FUCK IT UP! (a loud click)

CHARLIE: (meditative pause) I need wattage, and I need it now. (his face assumes a steely mien) It's time to unleash the succubus!

(Fade Out.)

CHAPTER 10

(Slow Fade In.)

(Interior, the "Spirits on Rox" Bar. Late Afternoon Friday. A thirtyish Man wearing a football jersey, blue jeans, and a hundred dollar haircut commiserates with the Bartender as Edie wanders in.)

BARTENDER: (to Edie) Would you like your usual Bloody Mary?

EDIE: Would you like me to staple your eyelids to the ceiling fan?

BARTENDER: No.

EDIE: Vodka. Hold the plasma. (she sits)

MAN: (speaking as much to his Sad Romantic Pilgrimage, as to the Barman) ...pissed at me? She said I "don't understand how women think." Here's a notion. You don't wanna be with a guy who doesn't "get" women, arrange to die a spinster, 'cause no guy to date has doped them out. Why not hate on all men?

EDIE'S THOUGHTS, heard in voiceover: *Don't tempt me.*

MAN: How about if women stick to their own? There. Done. Women with women. Who knows the plumbing better than the pipe?

EDIE: *Huh?*

MAN: Yeah, you go be with each other, all of y'all, and don't worry your silly heads that in a couple decades the whole race will be extinct!

EDIE: *Sounds like a plan.* (her beverage arrives) Thanks.

MAN: ...apprentice, if that, and yet I'm on her "Things to Do" list under the "Screw Them, and Then Screw Them" column, which okay I'm not saying I haven't been where she's at and done what she's doing, but c'mon, Busby? Frickin' Busby? And what am I, am I essentially the guy who females see as a walking talking punch card for free meals and crack-in-the-ceiling fucks until they sleaze through the floor studs to the next—

EDIE: Hey.

MAN: (looks) Hey.

EDIE: Hey. Can I say three words to you?

MAN: Three?

EDIE: Three words. May I?

MAN: Yeah.

EDIE: (clears her throat, waits a beat, digs a knuckle into the corner of her eye) Waa, Waa, Waa.

MAN: (forced grin) You're suggesting I've regressed into a childlike state.

EDIE: Mmm, pre-embryonic. You're one of the poor little wiggly fellas who didn't quite reach the egg.

MAN: I'm a spermatozoon! (waves)

EDIE: (tips her glass) Good luck with those twenty-three chromosomes. (drinks)

MAN: Thank you, but if it's a question of DNA, it's quality, not quantity, isn't it?

EDIE: Is that what you tell 'em in the sack?

MAN: (laughs in spite of himself) I'm pretty nifty when you get to know me. I'm a fun guy.

EDIE: You're an amusement park in the sheets.

MAN: I am.

EDIE: Because every lady who rides you has to vomit afterwards?

MAN: (another amiable laugh) Don't spare my feelings, please!

EDIE: (taking his measure) Still and all. You look relatively spankable. I wouldn't kick you out of bed for eating crackers.

MAN: You—

EDIE: "Crackers" is my nickname for my vagina.

(Caught off guard, he starts to speak, stops, grabs his whiskey, downs it, summons up his courage, and turns to her again. She's gone. He surveys the crowded bar and the Bartender, who responds with a "shit happens" shrug.)

(Cut to Interior, the Bar's Entrance. The door swings, and Charlie walks in. He inspects the patrons, the bar, the tables, spots someone and walks in their direction, unaware that an expectant Ed Tragos has oozed into the Shot and is following him.)

(Cut to Interior, a Table by the opposite wall. Edie bides her time there, fingers drumming. After a moment, Charlie enters the Frame and snatching up a chair, aligns himself tidily across from her. Ed dives into a chair behind her, and flicking his pad, clicks his pen.)

EDIE: Charlie. You wished to converse with me? (she sees his damaged cheek) Somebody forgot to duck.

CHARLIE: Huh. (he cases his surroundings) Classy place, your hangout. Spiffy. I could visualize dippin' my beak here, drownin' my sorrows at the end of a long day.

EDIE: I bet you've had a few of those, this week.

CHARLIE: Sorrows? Long days? You'd think so. I'm doing fine, though, Ariel. Appreciate your concern.

EDIE: It's *EDIE!*

(A plump young schlubby guy, comprised mostly of chicken fat, frizzy hair and spectacles, reeking of pork rinds and bong pipe aromatherapy, gravitates to the table and interrupts her.)

FAN: Hey, I recognize you, don't I?

EDIE: (staring at Charlie) Can't say.

FAN: Aren't you Ariel Caliban?

EDIE: Nuh-uh.

FAN: Yes you are! I've seen you. Ariel, that's your name.

EDIE: (looks at him in sudden recognition) Hi, Mom!

FAN: Me?

EDIE: (pleasant smile) Well, as far as I can recall, my mother gave me my name, not some limp dick barfly.

EX- FAN: Fuck you too! (he stalks off)

CHARLIE: Whoa. Guy sounded like a paying customer. You don't crap on the consumers.

EDIE: I shifted his frame of reference. Tweaked his reality.

CHARLIE: The way you've been "tweaking" mine, the past several days?

EDIE: Bingo.

CHARLIE: See, that's what I've observed about you, *Ariel*. You labor under the delusion everybody oughta live by your rules. You're in hardcore, but yet guys shouldn't connect the face with the name? You leave my employ, therefore every heifer in my stable should leave? And not least, *Ariel*, no Viagra on the set? Unbelievable. Most girls bless the day. What they want, the guy should get it up, get his nut, and get lost. You, you gotta have standards. This is porn! Who in porn has standards? Only you.

EDIE: Let it all out, man.

CHARLIE: To sum up, after due consideration, can you intuit what your problem is?

EDIE: Yeah. (fine-tuning his necktie) My home planet has a red sun. (she pats his shirt)

CHARLIE: Oh, now you're Supergirl?

EDIE: (folding her arms) Fuck Supergirl, and fuck Superboy and his dog, too. I'm your worst nightmare. I'm Super*man*, with a vadge and an attitude.

CHARLIE: No, you're approximately human. But there's what I'm in allusion to. My implication to a T. It's how you logicalize. Always struggling to outfox the universe.

EDIE: Finished? Or do you intend to drop another selection of pearls?

CHARLIE: (weighing his options) I've unburdened myself.

EDIE: (she regards him) No, Charlie, I can't change the universe. But I can change my universe. "Leanna" and "Kit" and the rest, they believe they can put their faces and everything else onscreen, and paper it over with a pseudonym. I don't. "Ariel Caliban" isn't my name, you blockhead, it's my description: a pure spirit among the brute beasts. And don't ever think that means I'm ashamed to use my sex to open a door, make a buck, hook a man, or straighten out a crooked world. You go on dealing your little place cards labeling who I am and what I do, buddy. That's your reality. I've got mine, and here's the scoop: I'm Ariel until they yell "Cut," and then I'm me, 'cause I'm the one who gets to choose.

CHARLIE: (clapping) Beautifully enunciated! And, so what? I'm talking about a pain-in-the-ass performer, you're treatin' the bar to a rendition of the "Marseillaise." It ain't germane. (he sees someone appear behind Edie's shoulder, Out of Shot, and grins) And also, too bad, too, 'cause it's moot. I've mooted it. It's done. I did it.

EDIE: (studies him) Did what?

CHARLIE: What all do I truly require? For Vegas, a hot carcass for the new buyers to slobber on, and some arm candy later at the *MEH* award show. For a week or two after, someone to aim a camera at. Doesn't have to be reliable, or stable, or even from our spacetime dimension. She just has to be *there*. You and I know you can't do this forever. There's no long game here. I got me some breathing room, gumdrop.

EDIE: What'd you do?

CHARLIE: Ariel, my love— (to the person behind Edie) *You're hired, you're hired, get in here*— (Edie twists: a Lilliputian, cursive-figured woman in scarified clothing and a shocking pink Mohawk, her wildly intense glare drilling craters through them, enters the Frame and joins them at their table) Indulge me to introduce my newest acquisition. The ubiquitously feared and regaled Banshie Phoenix.

BANSHIE: (to Edie) Hi. (leering at her breasts) How much did *those* cost?

CHARLIE: (to Banshie) Shush. (to Edie) And cookie-puss, I defy you to seduce, finesse, manipulate, or otherwise wield a sliver of influence over this runaway caboose.

BANSHIE: (sliding her posterior to and fro) This chair is sticky. Why is every chair I sit in sticky?

CHARLIE: (pushing out of his own chair) LAX at the crack o' midnight, Bansh.' (to Edie) And Hey. Drinks are on me.

EDIE: Goodbye.

CHARLIE: Give ya an extra thousand smackaroos if you'll swallow, heh-heh. I'm kiddin'!

EDIE: Goodbye.

CHARLIE: You girls play nice, now. (waving) Ta-ta. (he gets up to go)

(Ed galumphs toward the table with Charlie in his crosshairs. Before he can make contact, he's stalled by the Man from the bar.)

MAN: Nope. I saw her first, bud.

ED: Unhand me, sir. I have pressing business!

MAN: Losers weepers, asshole.

(Charlie exits. The two men continue to argue beneath Edie's and Banshie's conversation.)

BANSHIE: Uck. (glances at Edie) What. A. Kuh-Reep!

I know, I know, Charlie. But c'mon, how fucked up could she be? Right off the bat, she recognized your consummate vileness.

BANSHIE: Truth is, I'm way past the booze-slash-pills-slash-powder thing these days. Not refined behavior at all. Trying to be more one-with-nature. I'm part Cherokee, you know.

EDIE: (whisking an invisible pot with her pinky) *Maque choux.*

BANSHIE: Gesundheit. Not to subjugate the psyche to the flesh, understand? Is my new...thing. I'm like the dudes who, who spin around and around until they see Buddha or Yoda or somebody.

EDIE: Dervishes.

BANSHIE: Or they swat their butts with thorny branches.

EDIE: Flagellants.

BANSHIE: Or they squat there and don't eat anything for, like, a whole year, and they're so skinny they float away.

EDIE: All right, ya got me. Yogis?

BANSHIE: And I thought, what if, what if not to be outside of the otherness, the elsewhere, but inside of the outsideness of it.

EDIE: You interest me, strangely.

Okay, pretty fucked up. I did try to shine a light on the gaping maw of crazy that was "Banshie-babble", though: I sat there and struggled to figure out each of her references...

(Banshie rambles on Out of Shot, speaking at lightning speed. Edie is in Medium Close Up, inscrutable, the Camera Zooming in tighter and tighter. Her musings crawl along the bottom of the Screen, chyron-esque, as footnotes.)

BANSHIE: And the trick is in flipping the "off" switch on the positronic meat robot[1], or else information flows nonstop, not only TV-radio-computers-satellites but signals from planet Boson in the Leptoquark system[2], re-encoding the Selectrical ball which is our brains[3], which is onions that you peel and there's all kinds of layers like also a Russian doll[4], except you can't eat the doll and you can't give an onion to a Russian kid for Christmas, although you can give a lump of coal, it's just old dinosaurs[5], and categorically if you can fit a dinosaur in a sock you can fit the cosmos, the entire cosmos, between your ears, and the same action of spontaneous combustion[6] in the reptile stem would recreate from the singularity of racial memory a mutual synchronistic simultaneous through-line across the time space continuum[7], like in a black hole but skinnier because immaterial, or dark matter where we end up anyway[8], the mass of which, the mass is what came before. Examples? Alexander and Caesar. Napoleon. Krotus and Lee Kuan[9].

1. Science fiction. Robots have "positronic brains."
2. No such planet. No such system.

3. Wait, wait, hold on. Old IBM Selectric typewriters had golf ball thingies with letters on them.

4. Russian nesting dolls. Good. Good. Big doll, smaller inside, et cetera.

5. Dinosaur to fossil equals carbon. Easy one.

6. Dinosaurs did not spontaneously combust. Death by asteroid.

7. Getting tired. Hard to concentrate. Must close eyes.

8. Second wind. Feel better. Dark matter is everyone who ever lived and died?

9. Examples of people who lived and died, but two are from future...how could...or wait, they're from "Star Trek" reruns—

EDIE NARRATES: Fortunately her last remark shook me out of it, and I did what I always do when someone barfs a "Star Trek" reference. I said,

EDIE: Check, please!

...and searched for the Exit sign.

EDIE: (rising) I walked here. Got a car? (Banshie nods) Let's go.

(The Bartender approaches as Banshie rises. Edie unsnaps her pocketbook.)

BARTENDER: It's covered.

EDIE: Change for a ten. Quarters. (to Banshie) We might be on the road a while.

(The Bartender vanishes with her bill. Ed jitterbugs past Edie's beau and parkours into her line of sight.)

MAN: (to Edie) You can do better!

ED: (ignoring him) We meet again, Madam.

(Edie stares a canyon through him)

ED: Should I call you Eden, or Ariel? Or perhaps Ouida?

(No response.)

ED: I wonder, if you can't even settle on who you are, who's to say you exist at all?

(She socks him in the arm.)

MAN: Ha!

ED: All right, you exist, you exist! (rubs his arm) But it would appear, lady, that your curriculum vitae has lately developed a downward momentum, an impetus, if you will, cascading down the declivity of your vocation in its soon to be most abject phase.

EDIE: What-the-fuck? Are-you-talking-about?

ED: I am offering a litany of bad acts from a bad apple who insults her fans, assaults her colleagues, and does her damnedest to ruin her studio. An account you'll read in due time, courtesy of *Wangler Magazine*. They'll eat it up, which is your misfortune. It's practically a done deal. And if my ascendancy is to be built upon your fall from grace, pardon me if I sleep very well, thank you.

EDIE: You're going to jumpstart an opportunity by climbing on my still warm corpse. Poor, sorry Ed.

MAN: That is sad. Have some self-respect, dude.

ED: Before I bid you farewell, Madam, before I show you my back, I ask the eternal question: "Any comment?"

EDIE: Yeah, come to think of it. (the Bartender returns with her roll of quarters) How's this? It's a nothing story if I'm at Pie-Rite and Charlie calls bullshit, and you blew your chance with him 'cause he just left, and he never answers phone calls from strangers, and the Pie-Rite offices are an armed camp which you'll never get into, and you're no reporter, and you won't find him in Vegas unless *he* finds *her* there, and that's not going to happen because I won't let it, and please enjoy viewing another five hundred cumshot videos by Monday.

(She grips the roll of coins in her fist and biffs him in the nose.)

MAN: Mommy!

EDIE: Now if you still want to "show me your back," I'd be happy to kick you in the ass, too. No? (she links arms with Banshie) It's Girls' Night Out, fucker. Don't wait up. (they ditch a psychically fuzzy Ed and march to the exit)

MAN: (assisting him to a nearby chair, stanching his nosebleed with a cocktail napkin) Okay, I'm not too proud to say this. I've never been so turned on in my life!

(Cut to Interior, Friday Late Afternoon, Edie in Close Up. As the Camera Pulls Back, we discover she's in a Car in the passenger seat, Banshie at the wheel, both staring ahead in grim determination. Banshie continues her string of observations, inaudible under the Narration and the noise of the car engine running at high velocity. Not once during their discussion does she look at Edie.)

But I wasn't with Pie-Rite, meaning I was on borrowed time unless I could ensure that I was your sole option before the weekend ended. How to do it? And prior to that, I had to chaperone my new bestie, which was a full time job in itself. Of course I'd heard of Banshie Phoenix. The terrified screams of countless producers, directors and stars had reached me. Let's see, mobbed-up boyfriends, doubled-down substance abuse, and a side order of fruitcake? For Banshie, life was a New York pizza, and she wanted one with everything. And lotsa sausages...

BANSHIE: (talking, endlessly meandering stubbornly loquacious blabfest) ...would be freer—

EDIE: You suppose you could slow down a bit? Somewhere down around Mach One or Mach Two?

BANSHIE: (puzzled) What's your name?

EDIE: It's Edie, remember? (glances out the window) Was that a photon we passed?

BANSHIE: You smell like, (considers) Marcelle!

EDIE: Marcelle. Right. Is she the person who signed your release papers?

And though most adult performers spend the occasional night in Bugtown, Banshie evidently owned a timeshare *there.*

BANSHIE: (sounding slightly repentant, somewhat vexed) Go on, BET me I can't sit in the saucer.

EDIE: (baffled) What saucer? There is no saucer. (she looks at her) Banshie? Um, where are we going?

BANSHIE: You'll see. (she spins the wheel, to a screech of tires)

(Cut to Exterior, the Courtyard outside a bureaucratic building in Late Afternoon, a women's political rally in progress. Boards held aloft read "Surf the Third Wave Here!" and "Sex-Positive, Gender Negative!" Banshie and Edie cool their heels at the edge of the enthusiastic slogan-chanting crowd watching a firebrand female speaker, poised on top of the wall of a stone fountain decorated with granite statues of cherubs, stabbing the air and delivering violent imprecations. Banshie is fascinated by something to do with the statuary: the Camera Cuts Back and Forth between her in Close Up, and the cherubs. Speaker and crowd noise are muted by Edie's Narration.)

My problem was, I had to do anything necessary to keep her from LAX, and Las Vegas, that weekend. To manage it, I'd have to go wherever Banshie went, and do whatever Banshie did, all the while nudging her in any direction but *the airport. So when she spotted a group of protestors and wandered by, I trotted along.*

SPEAKER: And their trick? Information. Television, computers. Systematically encoding our brains like we're robots, like dolls!

EDIE: (in Close Up) I'm impressed you're interested, Banshie.

SPEAKER: We've got to show more pride in ourselves!

EDIE: Can't we save it for another time?

SPEAKER: Maybe this reasoning fit the age of the dinosaurs. Not we here today!

EDIE: Banshie?

(She turns to her.)

SPEAKER: Call us envious? Of men? What's there to envy?

(Cut to Wider Shot: nobody is next to Edie.)

SPEAKER: Men, whose same actions are now revealed to be unacceptable and immaterial!

(Edie cranes her neck, searching.)

SPEAKER: What does it matter, you ask? Given where we end up anyway? Let me tender some examples.

(Edie sees Banshie, at the fore of the group of onlookers, clambering unbidden onto the fountain wall to stand by the Speaker, who starts in surprise.)

BANSHIE: (in ringing tones, to the crowd) That's-Not-All! (she repeats the phrase several times, until the crowd echoes it)

SPEAKER: Okay. Outstanding! If one of you wishes to add to the discourse, declare yourself! Sister, speak your truth!

BANSHIE: (refers them to the thin streams of water issuing from the cherub statues) You-Have-To-Pee! (she repeats the phrase several times as well—the crowd does not echo it)

SPEAKER: *What?*

(Edie, making for the fountain, lunges up and tugs at the cuff of Banshie's pant leg.)

BANSHIE: (swaggering) I'll bet I can piss on the tablecloth in front of the masses! (she stabs into the air, mimicking the Speaker's gesture)

SPEAKER: (hands on hips, unamused) I'm not joking. Get down. Go home.

BANSHIE: (chanting) Pee-On-Me! (spying Edie, she jumps to the pavement) Pee-On-My-Cunt! (casting an arm athwart Edie's shoulders) Pee-In-The-Air All-The-Way To-My-Cunt!

(At the mention of this word, the mob charges at them as one, rumbling and glaring at the two with looks advertising the likelihood of bloodshed.)

EDIE: (dilapidating under Banshie's arm) Uh, she's been unwell of late...

BANSHIE: (waving blithely at the Speaker) When she spots us going at it (jerks her thumb at Edie), she'll *have* to wee-wee!

EDIE: (breaking loose, she herds her to the curb) In the car! We can "go at it" in the car!

(Dissolve to Interior, the moving Car. Banshie is driving and talking, Edie silent. Peeking at her from the corners of her eyes, Edie pulls on her seatbelt in a deliberate slow motion movement and clicks it in place with studied insouciance.)

Yeah. But there were signs in her behavior, I thought, suggesting that the chick had imprinted on me, and having played

*a few farmer's daughters in my career, I pondered: if I could hold
her head to solid ground and draw a straight line from there to,
well, to anywhere but you, Charlie, I might yet mesmerize her out
of your clutches—*

(Accompanied by a thump and a yowl, a stray cat goes flying
up the hood and the windshield, to oblivious reaction from
Banshie. Edie leans into her seat, wall-eyed.)

—or not...

(Dissolve to Exterior, Friday Evening, the car seen in Medium
Shot, a seedy industrial part of town visible in the Background.
Banshie slams on the brakes.)

Even still, maybe there was a method to her madness after all.

(She speaks to a street person wearing a tinfoil cap, who spray
cleans her window and gives her directions.)

*I could tell she was searching for something specific. Possibly
her marbles. And soon she'd obtained directions from the local
gentry...*

(With an avaricious smile, he extends his paw for a gratuity.
She nabs the bottle, spritzes his cap, low-fives him and zooms
away.)

*...stiffed him, attended to his hygiene, pressed the flesh, and hit
the gas. And a couple of kitty corpses later, we'd arrived at what I*

suspected must be one of those warehouse dance club party spaces.

(Dissolve to Interior, a Warehouse. Edie and Banshie patrol past shelves bristling with firearms: pistols, shotguns, automatic weapons. Banshie selects a lighter weapon, giving it an expert appraisal. She studies Edie's troubled demeanor.)

BANSHIE: What?

EDIE: We're in the Sam's Club of killing machines, that's what! You told me we were "going to a shindig"!

BANSHIE: (picking up and inspecting a bigger weapon) So?

EDIE: So how about we go home and paint each other's toenails?

BANSHIE: (snickers and pats Edie's arm) What an idea!

(She hefts a shotgun, breaks it, and nudges Edie, indicating she should follow suit. Edie, in spite of herself, dangles a revolver from two fingers. The pounding of footsteps follows straightaway.)

EDIE: (alarmed) Banshie, do the owners of these guns know we're here?

BANSHIE: (mystified) I have to sit on the plate naked where everybody can see!

EDIE: There is no plate, and nobody else is... Uh-oh.

(Two men skid around shelving, wielding Uzis.)

BANSHIE: (covering her mouth and muttering) *They smell like jizm.*

EDIE: Like trouble, more like. What did you get us into? Banshie?

BANSHIE: (to Edie, in full bellow) Since the winner sets the policy, I'M RIPPING OFF YOUR PANTS IN VIEW OF THE ENTIRE ROOM!

(The men catch sight of them, and shouting their wrath in a foreign tongue, fire in their direction.)

EDIE: Run, damn it! (she drops her pistol, throws Banshie's gun on the shelf and yanks her Out of Shot)

BANSHIE: (as she recedes) Wait. The Cardinal is who, again?

(Exterior, the Warehouse, Friday Evening. They run outside, trailed by the two men, who remain in the Frame, emptying their weapons at them.)

(Interior, the Car, the two cheek by jowl as before, racing through traffic with the howl of a police car siren growing in volume behind them. A yelp is heard, and another cat sails up their windshield.)

BANSHIE: (to Edie, glaring at the rearview mirror in disdain) Make believe you didn't see.

EDIE: You know, what if we stop?

BANSHIE: I want them to go.

EDIE: I doubt they're going anywhere.

(Exterior, the city Street. The police cruiser stalking them slews into a parked car, loses control and crashes.)

(Interior, the Car.)

EDIE: Crap. Look what you did!

BANSHIE: So what?

EDIE: So get us out of here before the whole cavalry shows up!

BANSHIE: (explaining as if to an infant) I can only towel off in "the church."

(She abandons the steering wheel to etch air quotes.)

EDIE: I don't see any— (twisting sideways, she captures Banshie's hands and wrestles them onto the wheel) —see any church— (the speeding car dips into a pothole and Edie's skull strikes the windshield, knocking her senseless.)

(Cut to Black.)

(Fade In.)

(Interior, Saturday Noon. An Auto Body Shop, ill-lit, tools and gear glimmering. Edie, unconscious, her forehead gashed at the hairline, a round bruise trickling a short line of blood, is seen in a Close Up, which Pulls Back as she wakes to find that she's been chained from the ceiling by her shackled wrists.)

BANSHIE'S VOICE: (muttering repeatedly from Out of Shot) Rack and ruin...

EDIE: Wh...Where am I? (she squints at the sound)

(Banshie materializes. She's wearing a welder's helmet, and carrying a live blowtorch. She recites her words with clinical detachment, as a doctor might speak to a patient.)

BANSHIE: Be still, please.

EDIE: (wild-eyed) You're not going to hurt me, Banshie.

BANSHIE: (waving the flame by Edie's forehead and her wound) It'll dry.

EDIE: My cut? I'm sure it has already. Banshie, I'm your pal, right? Your partner in crime?

BANSHIE: (waving the blowtorch fore and aft) See the eye?

EDIE: The *flame*? I see it.

BANSHIE: It's an egg.

EDIE: Okay, but the egg is a very hot egg!

BANSHIE: Want to play with it. (she sways the flame inches from Edie's face)

EDIE: No! (she passes out)

(Cut to Black.)

(Fade In.)

(Interior, the Body Shop, Saturday Night. Edie sags in a chair, a model of slothful tranquility, unconscious, no longer in chains, and half-undressed. She comes to, sees Banshie is nowhere in evidence. Camera Follows as quietly, carefully, she puts on her top, locates a door, enters a Stairwell, ascends gray concrete steps past whitewashed concrete walls under a bare light bulb, and steals outside by another door.)

(Exterior, Night, Minutes before Dawn. Edie, in the act of exiting the doorway, finds herself on a twilit Rooftop. As she shuts the door, Banshie is heard yards away.)

BANSHIE: (at the roof's edge, glowering over her shoulder at Edie) Well, Padre? What are you doing there in your shed? You're tossing off, too, aren't you?

EDIE: Careful, Banshie. I'm not certain how high up..."tossing off"?

BANSHIE: Padre, I haven't told you my greatest sin. (she surveys the precipice in a dignified fashion)

EDIE: I, um...

BANSHIE: (twirling, she looks down her nose at her) My greatest sin, Padre, is that I'm talking and tossing off at the same instant.

EDIE: You mean you're going to jump? (she creeps forward, near enough to touch her)

BANSHIE: If you doubt it, I'll show you.

(BANSHIE grabs Edie's arm and, hauling her close, launches them off the roof, Edie screaming, Banshie laughing uproariously.)

(Exterior, the Street below. Tall stacks of abandoned cardboard boxes lie on the sidewalk by a scattering of trashcans. Edie and Banshie land in the empty stacks with surprising lightness. Edie scrambles free and stares upward, scowling.)

EDIE: (vast annoyance) A two story building? Seriously?

BANSHIE: (lying prone, her chin nestled on a box, gazing up at Edie in palpable devotion) Don't you ever again toss off without me.

EDIE: (unable to control her anger) Sure, crazy lady. The next time I plummet to my death, you'll be on my speed dial!

(Close Up on Banshie, mooning at her, to slow Fade Out.)

CHAPTER 11

Afterward, I found out most of a day had passed in the hours I'd been unconscious. So that was our Big Thunder Mountain Ride on Friday night, me in my one-woman chain gang on Saturday, and Saturday night on, and off, the roof. My luck, the solitary microscopic lobe of Banshie's gray matter that continued to operate happened to contain her conscience. She seemed to feel bad about putting me through the wringer, and asked her BFF (me) to see her off at LAX early Sunday. I convinced her to hang until flight time at a hotel by the airport, and meanwhile I sneaked a peek at a black book I'd glimpsed sticking out of her rear pocket, placed some calls, and arranged a "fais do-do," as they say back home...

(Slow Fade In.)

(Interior, Sunday Morning, a nondescript Room in an Airport Hotel. Throughout the scene, the roar of planes can be heard periodically, departing or landing. Banshie sits on the lone king bed, polishing off an enormous breakfast. Edie, a small bandage on her forehead, stands at the door holding the handle. Someone in the corridor is rapping a regular "shave-and-a-haircut-two-bits" rhythm.)

BANSHIE: (appetite glutted, she swipes her jaw) Let's let bygones be bygones, Marcelle. Yesterday was plain wrong, but we can be friends.

EDIE: Promise?

BANSHIE: I swear we won't touch you anymore.

EDIE: Who's "we"? You, and your other huggable personalities? (she opens the door)

(A Clown, in full getup, battered porkpie hat, red wig and makeup, waits in the Hall.)

EDIE: Wild guess. You're not from Room Service.

CLOWN: I dunno, Cooties, you called me. Banshie's acquaintance. Remember?

EDIE: The address book. (she lifts one of the large, fluffy green cloth buttons running down the front of his garb) You're Mister "Big Balls"? Imagine my disappointment.

CLOWN: (chuckles) She's a caution, ain't she? (he strolls in, shadowed by a heretofore unnoticed Little Person) By the way, the Geek sends his regrets, he's under the weather. (he peers around theatrically, stage whispers from behind his hand) Chicken pocks! (honks his horn in her ear)

(Banshie bounces at the sight of him, clapping and squealing.)

CLOWN: (sashaying to her) Phoenix, my baby with the rabies, wipe the foam off yer chops and gimme a kiss!

EDIE: (speaking to his back) Are all those phone numbers going to be from the circus?

CLOWN: Circus? What circus? (he collapses in Banshie's arms, followed by his four-foot colleague, who bounds onto the mattress beside her and dithers with her blouse)

BANSHIE: (brushing at him) You're out of your tiny mind. I'm not doing it in a bed the way matrons do! Now, with Marcelle...

EDIE: No, you guys indulge. I'm good.

(Before she can swing the door, she's jostled by a Lady with a heavy growth of beard, who enters without a word and joins the team. Foreplay ensues, at the nucleus of which is Banshie, who begins by reaching into the Clown's baggy pants to her armpit, fishing.)

BANSHIE: Sir Edmund, gimme! Yank it loose!

CLOWN: You want it, Toodles, you got it. (he drops his trousers to his ankles, expertly. His oversize shoes and top remain.)

(Edie pushes the door closed. It's pushed in again by an unshaven Pinhead wearing a saffron muumuu with red polka dots, the tuft of hair on the crown of his head tied in a dainty bow.)

PINHEAD: Are we having fun yet? (he draws a bee-line to the bed)

EDIE: (to herself) Sometimes, you don't even ask. (she shuts the door)

BANSHIE: (welcoming the new arrival) Idiot! (she sees Edie pushing at the door handle as the Clown and the Little Person pick at her garments) We swore not to touch you, Marcelle, why are you deserting us?

EDIE: You kidding? I wouldn't miss this for the *world*. (she leaves the entranceway)

BANSHIE: (trying to be helpful, directs the Clown's attention to Edie) You could wallop her in the face with your ejaculate...

CLOWN: (squints at Edie) I could do that.

EDIE: Rain check!

CLOWN: She don't play, schmookie. She gets off watching. (he fiddles with her breast through her shirt) Let's titillate her.

BANSHIE: (pensive) Milk is for pussies, isn't it?

CLOWN: (he doffs his hat, hooking it on a bedpost) Couldn't-a said it better myself!

You can bet I decided to punt, Charlie. By now I'd realized the ever present danger in living Banshie's habitual weekend, alongside Banshie's habitual playmates, is that some morning you're liable to wake up in a tubful of ice with one more scar and one less kidney.

(The Bearded Lady removes Banshie's shoes and socks.)

Incidentally, not being an aficionado of Screecher Features, this was the first time I'd gotten a gander at Banshie in the buff.

(The Pinhead pulls down Banshie's jeans and panties.)

Turns out she had all the stock pornstar whoop-de's. Big hair. Big makeup. Nerf ball boobies. Soul patch snatch. And so many piercings, she looked like she'd scored last place in a nail gun fight.

(The Little Person slips off Banshie's blouse, exhibiting much body art.)

You want a girl with plenty of tattoos? The people in her tattoos had tattoos.

(Her retinue divest themselves of their clothes, with Banshie's assistance.)

Bumper to bumper, this lowrider had seen more customizing than a Tijuana Chevy.

(They gangbang her, in an increasing fervor.)

And all packed into an economy-sized chassis. To get a sense of scale, picture a hamster; then Banshie; then a slightly larger hamster.

(Sex proceeds, through a series of Dissolves, with occasional Shots of the clock radio on the bed stand.)

Someone once told me her nickname on the set used to be "Squirt." Although in our line of work, that might have nothing to do with her height...

(A flea springs out of the Lady's beard.)

EDIE: Eww!

(She NARRATES in a helium squeak:)

EDIE: Friend, you may wonder how the power of locution be within the province of such as I. Verily, I am but a humble insect. Howbeit, whilst supping at a healthy serving of mankind's puissance during my career, I claimed for myself another share of Man's condition, and became a thinking, as well as a feeling creature. Know therefore that I am acknowledged by my own to be a signal votary in the wider community of bloodsuckers, not merely by the breadth of my expression, but also by my field of employment. A gourmet in a nation of gourmands, having married high-flown tastes to my flighty peregrinations, I seek the stickiest of fleshpots: I am a connoisseur of orgies. And espying a *pas de cinq* in process of being enacted therewith, I quitted my perch in the pileous eaves and, posthaste, endeavoured to disport amongst the players.

Understand that my exercise was strictly emblematic of my type, the subtlest of surgeries, leaving my patients none the wiser.

Weaving my antennae in the air, and applying my several senses to all aspects of the two ladies on display, I beheld a veritable cross traffic of curled extremities, plump thighs, wagging breasts. Where each sat, out peeped a slitted eye, the first adit finespun and peach-like, the second splashy and robust.

I settled upon the coltish calf muscle of the young sprite called Banshie, whose tender offices appeared central to the covenant, and whose blood, I can attest, had warmed to a ready pitch. Sipping at the delightful fare, and gesticulating my vibrissae in little ecstasies, I remarked the microcephalic chamberlain to our right, who recommended to my charming companion the nearby Dwarf.

'Frig him. He's keen,' said he.

The gentle Banshie was willing enough. As she grasped the surprising long limb of his member, flexing its shaft and worrying her palm on the purple bulb at its end, he was chided by my erstwhile perambulatrix, the Bearded Lady. 'You are presumptuous, Sir Dwarf,' said she, herself, like the rest, altogether *dishabille*.

'There,' the simple Pinhead said, ignoring her, 'There's his bell tower. And two fat clappers beneath!' Allowing that the whole form of Man bulks extensive from a flea's vantage, I had to concur. By way of comparison with its two fellows, it certainly was a whopping big foreleg.

The disproportionate person of the Dwarf began waving about his barbarous instrument, his dowser's rod, lilting at the two watering holes, the Clown, a dedicated voluptuary of the noblest order, looking on in appreciation, when of a sudden Banshie snatched it out of the air and laid it at her silken inlet. Her heels wended skyward; the incautious Dwarf, advancing on the gate, soon surrendered his charge with a wizardly flow of semen as could have drowned her lower quarters. 'It's from his gumballs!' the Pinhead cried, stamping his feet.

The Bearded Lady shifted her interest to the Clown, arranging her aspect to best advantage and encouraging her most savoury morsel to wink merrily in his direction. Requiring no further stimulus, he nodded his enormous genitals in her face and made as if to lunge, whilst she and the Pinhead together fingered the place where Banshie of late had been well irrigated by the Dwarf. The Clown penetrated the Lady's mouth, gripped her ears, and sought to lift her bodily by the soft palate, diving in with such brio that her vision blackened, her two comrades crowing their praise.

Discomfited, and my cells singing in concert with hers, so great was my deliquium that when Banshie's errant hand grazed at my current residence, all my six legs lost their purchase, I toppled in a swoon and, rescued by instinct alone, rebounded to dry dock atop the Pinhead's ear. His unwholesome blood, however, I disdained to sample.

Moan chased after moan, and Banshie, arching her back, briefly extended her freehold into the rural seat, making the

Bearded Lady fairly prance; the Clown, spying her readiness, withdrew from above and set up down below, waylaying her with a ferocious vivacity. 'Assassin! You dispatch me!' she sighed.

These agreeable indulgences carried on for some time under the vigilant regard of the Dwarf and his co-partisan, the Pinhead, inciting them to newer and greater delectations. The Dwarf leaned his huge bully stick in Banshie's face, inviting her inspection, which she gave with every sign of approval; his abettor filled her to bursting with his staff, barreling down the slender passage.

The aforesaid engagements, accompanied by the odd squall or snarl, occupied the succeeding minutes, when the Pinhead hallooed his orgasm and a prodigious quantity of semen spun into her entrails. The Dwarf, urged to completion, mopped Banshie's tongue once, twice, and sluiced her gums with a monstrous hot discharge which billowed her cheeks.

At sight of this the Clown redoubled his efforts, attacking the Lady's particulars until the gathering sleekness there expedited them to the moment of truth. Grimacing, he slid out and drove on in earnest, splashing her womb with the wondrous magnitude of his release, her orbs rolling in their hollows. 'Heavens, what bliss!' he whispered to his coterie. Their glances met, and his eye flew to the admiring Banshie, who in a flash spread her loins and bade him enter.

Beside them the Bearded Lady fell away, an arid, nerveless spectre, and was forgotten. Nerveless she may have been, bloodless she was not. I sprang to the crook of her arm and dipped into the flushed skin there. In candour, so meagre and wraithlike ran the stuff in her veins, I half expected to swallow it all in one gulp.

The three remaining worthies set about courting Banshie, the Pinhead and the Dwarf nestling their pricks in her lush mouth, their motions advancing quickly from civil to criminal, and the new-fortified Clown arguing his suit in her private docket.

'See her draw his very knackers into her,' declared the Pinhead.

'Faith! How she clings to me. Magic!' said the Clown.

'Have a care! She'll make you spend,' the Dwarf warned.

But her ungentle frigging of the two men's lances as they jousted at her lips, had brought one to the brink. The Dwarf himself swore an oath, and her cheek glistened with his own spend.

Tiring of their devotions, I resolved to hurry the tale to its denouement. I leapt onto the other of her viceroys' swaying testicles, niggled my sharpest mouthparts therein, and with a *cri de coeur* the Pinhead gasped and, concluding his part in the engagement, let his member shower a storm of semen on her smiling mouth. At last, sailing his vessel up and down the straits of her sex, the Clown felt the delirium tremens seize him, shrieked, and poured into her a veritable tidal wave of spume, as Banshie went with him into the full embrace of paradise.

Thus it was, that knitting about from warp to weft, I saw where once was a dash of hurtling bodies, now abided a sad welter of boneless, sallow layabouts, and with a dismissive hop

I heeded the prescription writ by scholars of every stamp, stripe and species: I sought out more sanguine shores...

(Dissolve to Hotel Room, Friday, an hour later. Edie, epoxied to an easy chair, legs stretched, susses out a newspaper crossword puzzle.)

EDIE: What's a nine letter word for "Valley separating Los Angeles and San Bernardino"?

CLOWN: (reaching his apogee) *Cucamonga!*

EDIE: (writing) Thanks.

Now the original plan was to fix Banshie's sights on anything not involving airplanes. But considering she had the attention span of a Mexican jumping bean crossed with a Peruvian coca leaf, Plan B was to try to run down her disgracefully huge life force until she couldn't see to pee...

(After their prolonged period of incendiary sexual abandon, the energy of the participants has flagged. Except for Banshie.)

...But that was easier said than done...

(Edie discards her newspaper and, rising, starts toward the john. Everyone on or off of the bed lies in various crumpled heaps—except for Banshie.)

BANSHIE: (spotting her) Stay out! There's a naked man in there!

EDIE: No, there isn't— (noting her alarm) I'll go in and tell the nasty naked man to go away.

(She enters the bathroom, shutting the door. The moment she's gone, Banshie punches at the Clown. He lugs his torso up.)

BANSHIE: Sir Edmund, you'll do whatever I ask, right?

CLOWN: (blinking at her) Whazzat?

BANSHIE: Bang me in my ass.

CLOWN: That teeny *tuchus*? Ah, I guess if I can fit in one of those clown cars—

BANSHIE: Until it's steaming hot.

CLOWN: That's the only way I do, baby-kins. (inhales) Now bump your booty over here, and we'll take a trip up Clown Alley.

BANSHIE: (positioning on elbows and knees) I'll open up!

CLOWN: You do that.

(Edie returns as the Clown goes in for seconds. She sits, spellbound in admiration.)

Gotta say, I was impressed by the additional half hour that followed. From now on, as far as I'm concerned, carny sex is the way to go.

(Sex continues, more ferocious than the previous free-for-all but witnessed more briefly, through Dissolves punctuated by glimpses of the clock's display. The Clown gasps his final lusty effort and wilts to a thread, as worn out as the others. Edie claps opera-style.)

EDIE: Felicitations, my candy-colored friend. Excelsior!

CLOWN: (raising his arm) Nuhhh... (it falls again)

(Edie rises, strolls to the bed, sizes up the two spent occupants, and inspects the readout on the alarm clock.)

EDIE: (to herself) Eleven am. Eden Gann, get ready to ditch this scene and hit the slots. (she hikes a plane ticket from her jeans, and peruses it, lullabying Banshie) *"Fais do do, Banshie ma petite sœur"*—

(Banshie heaves bolt upright. She smiles and shoots Edie a libidinous look.)

EDIE: (veering away) Yiy! How are you not comatose?

(Banshie crooks a forefinger at her.)

Yiy, indeed. I'm afraid I'd wandered too close to the swirling vortex of soul-consuming sexual chaos referred to in physics as

"The Banshie Zone." Submitted for your approval: she was weary, not whipped; eleven in the morning left time enough for her to catch a plane, and the interest of your prospective buyers, in Vegas; and clearly, Vogel, if I intended to defeat you, I was personally going to have to smoke this little girl's butt right down to the filter tip. Well, the great ones do not bow before Fortune's challenges, and so...

EDIE: (deep breath) Precious, where have you been all my life?

(She shoves the anesthetized Clown off her end of the bed, folds back the sheets near Banshie, and shucks her top.)

BANSHIE: (ogling her breasts) I'd prefer them here. On a plate.

EDIE: Of *course* you would. (she kicks off her shoes)

BANSHIE: Raw testes, egg-shaped gonads, white as pearls and pink like blood. Like eyeballs.

EDIE: I *know.* (she wiggles out of her pants)

BANSHIE: Egg whites are the white of an eye, and the yellow is the pupil. Eggs and eyes are the same shape.

EDIE: That's *very* true. (she jettisons her panties)

BANSHIE: And my ass cheeks are shelled eggs, hard boiled. And my poots stink like gunpowder, and my piss shoots like gunfire.

EDIE: *Sigh.* (she gets in the bed)

BANSHIE: Promise next time we're outside, you'll throw eggs at the sun and blast them to bits with your pistol.

EDIE: Lookin' forward to it! (she bends toward her)

(Fiercely debauched and completely exhausting sex ensues, Edie matching Banshie stroke for stroke to the point of ruin, ending with the participants unconscious. Edie NARRATES, offering a play-by-play in Banshie's wired, antic vocalise:)

EDIE: As Marcelle converged, Banshie caught sight of a fleeting, tentative twitching movement beneath her pillow. She lifted a corner. Like a performer taking a curtain call, a red sphere scudded into the ditches made by the wrinkled bed linen and spun to a perfect landing at her hipbone.
  "Why, hello!" she said. "Are you an egg, or an eye?"
  "Neither," the ball said. "I'm Sir Edmund's nose."
  "Pleased to meet you," she said.
  She picked it up, letting its warmth bloom across the flat of her hand. An electric current, a fizzing network of spider veins, blossomed hotly from her palm to her wrist to her knuckles, to the tips of her fingernails. "Wow, it feels like scratching the worst ever itch," she said.

"And that's just your hand," Edmund's rubber nose said through its shadowy nose hole. "May I?"

Banshie lay down, put the nose in the dint of her navel. "You most certainly may!"

Watching the ceiling, she felt the rubber ball careening through her ribcage, past her solar plexus to her sternum, where it stopped and harrumphed in embarrassment.

"You might have to help me here," it muttered.

"Oh gosh yes. Sorry."

Banshie rescued the nose from the well between her breasts, fixing it by its opening atop her left nipple. She detected a gentle and then a more desperate nursing there. "Okay?"

The nose hummed away at its task, paying her no mind.

She saw Marcelle lying propped up. "So this is—this is what we're doing," Marcelle said.

Banshie started to reply, when a narrow blue-green flame speared her left boob, a wonderful sharp spritzy sensation like a garden hose full of orgasms saturated her titflesh, it hopped to the right boob too, and she said "Ooh ooh oh hrumpf ugga ugga," as it geysered up above her excited yob-goblets into a fireworks display of cummingness, stars and stripes included. "Brrr. Good good GOOD."

"...I could come back later," Marcelle suggested.

The nose rolled sideways and through its damp recess said, "We can all go. Want to? Let's us all go."

"Go? Go where?" Shivering, Banshie held it up and peered at the dark circumspect pupil.

"You'll see. Hold on." She squeezed Marcelle's hand. "Now, push me onto your nose, hard, harder than Fourth Year Chemistry. Push!" and Banshie stuck on the red ball, grinding it, pushing, her nose slipped in, and still she pushed, her head narrowed and disappeared within, the opening clenched on her neck and skittered southward, yoking her shoulders, she wriggled like cramming her whole body into Young Miss jeans, and gripping Marcelle she was unceremoniously evaporated and sucked in entire and the momentum took Marcelle too, both annihilated falling through a timeless black void until they coalesced, two raindrops puddling, onto the steps of a grand ethereal temple.

"Okay," Banshie said. "That was a first."

"Wh-where's the hotel?" her confederate said.

Banshie frowned. "What you're saying makes no sense, Marcelle." She inhaled the scented air. "Gun oil. Waffle irons, aluminum crutches. Genetically modified tomatoes."

Marcelle, sitting near her, sniffed and pointed. Banshie saw a half-naked man with distinguished pectorals and insouciant abdominal muscles waiting not two yards away, his white robe parted, his stiff snickerdoodle seeking the heavens. He was totally golden, hair of gold and skin, too.

"You. Yeah, you. Wanna tell us where in fuck we are?" Marcelle said.

The luminary pointed and they saw they were on a ledge of a tall mountain, the far-flung landscape swaying under an ocean of creeping mist. He pointed up, and they blinked at the summit, its pinnacle hazy inside an immense pale cock-mushroomy cumulous cloud.

"I am called by some the Eggtimer," he said. "It is my given responsibility to maintain the separation betwixt the twin poles of the male and the female climax. For men, a good ten minutes in, twenty tops. For women? Sometime this week. Maybe next."

Marcelle said, "And that's what you do for a living? Proud of yourself?"

"Well, I..."

"When you were a kid you said, 'I'm gonna grow up to be the Eggtimer and screw with people's sex lives?'"

"Okay now, that's a gross oversimplification!"

"Why are we here?" Banshie said, rising.

"Each hundredth century," he said, mustering his dignity, "I must re-un-synchronize the timing of the female pleasure point. To reaffirm the verity that sex for man and woman is in its essence a generative act, and Mankind should no more look to it for other gratifications than would a worm or a wildebeest."

"Ugh," said Marcelle. "Sick, sick fuck."

"And you need us to what?" Banshie said, when he left them and strode to the foot of the steps, to a lustrous figurine, an eidolon of himself wrought in bronze, retrieved an hourglass the size of a Vietnamese pot-bellied pig from where it sat parked behind it, beckoned, and she and Marcelle bounced off the steps onto the crisp grass heaving their southern extremities their fingers jangling their pussypurses thrashing squirming Banshie groping for Marcelle's cherry orchard gasping Ooh-ooh-ooh Marcelle likewise while their host held out the hourglass.

"For a quarter hour, you will endure a nonstop sequence of orgasms whose progression will be neither arithmetical nor geometrical, but exponential, until you have ascended to a level of bliss so exalted that I may recalibrate—"

"Woof! Done," Banshie said, sitting up. "The best in a month. What's next?"

"I, um..." the Eggtimer fumbled with his clock, "You are atypically orgasmic. But now that your aptitude has 'bottomed out,' as it were, I can exploit the recovery phase by returning you to this state, on my own schedule." He tapped the hourglass until every grain of sand was collected in one end. As he did, Marcelle, scrambling up the scales of her separate ecstasy, remarked, "Ghruhh...gning-ningh-uh-uuhm!"

Banshie said, "I am a bit numb down there. You should pitch in, this time." She gestured at the area between his thighs.

"It is not permitted. It seldom ends well. I commend to your attention Zeus and Semele, Eos and Tithonus...um...Poseidon and...uh...and...Med—" Banshie had parted her legs and begun jimmying her crotch. "Uh...I can, however, bespeak my salutations to the day, thusly," he chivvied his delighted cocklebar, upending the hourglass.

"*Meow*. That's it," she said, splooshing her finger into herself, checking for signs of life.

His man-slab was long, thick as a Christmas ham and golden as the rest of him. Gilded veins climbed the shaft, and his two enormous jelly babies jumped in their candy bags at each stroke.

She licked her lips. "Yeah, you love it, don't you? Give it to me, hang me from your bindle stick and take me around the world, sextramp." His smoky yellow eyes brightened. He took an involuntary step forward and away, his rhythmic handywork unfazed.

Lying beside them, Marcelle gnashed her teeth and bodyhopped in place, spanking her red ryder with the heel of her hand, hissing through bared teeth and farting shamelessly.

Meanwhile, small spectral pleasures flickered inside of Banshie's fringe benefit. "C'mon, fisty fucker, pummel my muff with that big red boxing glove of a dickhead." She saw his ballsack tighten. "Yeah, caramelize my love onions, I want your honey glaze. I want to feel the pitter-patter of little spermy feet on my mamelukes."

Groaning "UUURGGH! NYMPHAWN AI KALON OROS TODE NAIETAOUSI URRFFHH!" the Eggtimer drained his expense account at her from two yards' distance. She felt a piquant yawning sensation in her bush baby.

"Aah! aah! Aah! We're back!" she yelled, kicking at the grass. She leaped up. "Fugga-me more, more, now!" She snatched at his downcast Doric column. "Now now now!"

He reeled backward, shocked by her vehemence. "Perhaps we might snuggle for a few minutes?" he stammered. "A brief refractory period is expected?"

He circled Marcelle's spasming form, putting her in the way as Banshie dived at his robe. Her trixie had developed a serious case of empty nest syndrome. She panted, "Don't you know I'm your hot sticky quim queen, and you're my beautiful golden fuckwand magician," they danced around Marcelle, "and my vault craves a hundred gold bars in it, a million, my Fort Knox pussy wants a whole US gold standard supply of dicky bars in it?"

She started again for him, when a steely grip closed on her ankle and sent her toppling into Marcelle's embrace. Nerveless and unaware, her eyes enameled over, Marcelle shifted and scrunched her ladybird on Banshie's. Scissoring hard, she sank her canines in her friend's calf muscle and the blood in Banshie's veins whooshed to her clit, towing her comprehension along with it, and she was wrenched headlong into Marcelle's mounting orgasmic delirium:

The temple and its occupant were gone. They stood, wallowing side by side in a rising ocean of she-spunk, arm in arm, in their solitary golden half-eggshells. They stared at each other, speechless.

The steaming breakers carried them nearer to the massive cocksummit she'd seen moments before, nestled in its clouds. It was exposed. Lesser hills bulged from its base, two scrotumous grab bags, and dwindled beneath the foamy tide.

Spiraling, they saw the mountain was furrowed by a network of passes where portmanteau creatures with feline bodies and mannish heads and torsos ceased their activities, tracked the eggcrafts' progress, raised their cupid bows, launched fleshy missiles their way, and were plunged under the warm sea swell and drowned.

They travelled upward to the bulbous crown. It had begun expelling its precum gasses, the atmosphere smelled of chlorine and oiled leather and musk, it swarmed up into Banshie's womb and a thousand tiny fires from the earth's center touched her own.

"OooOOOH. Oof!" The desiccated air seemed to dilate her vitals, levitating her above her eggship, though she detected it against her feet. "God oh god yes! I'm very close, so close."

The penile mountain head convulsed as their eggshells skidded onto its gnarled, ridged crest. A narrow eyelet by the peak examined them.

Banshie pulled herself and Marcelle to their knees, groveling on the coarse stone, and said, "Mister giant hungry rock candy monster Walter Wanger, are you going to give us double decimal dick service? Spew it, we love your lurid lovely spew, we love to eat it and drink it and live in it and die, we love—" The mountain thundered, staggering them, falling in a single eggshell entwined, the eyelet pulsed once, and twice and thrice, and shot a blinding stew of lava and knotty debris at the darkened sky, raining down on the jizziferal ocean surface. Wherever droplets landed, the surface boiled and loosed dovelike shapes, flapping indignant wings and fluttering about them, and Banshie clasped Marcelle in the bottom of the craft and mewed, "Ooh bad baby bad baby hold me you devil baby, make my pussy squeal," she ground their privates and rotated her hips, "Everything everything I want it your juices your womb titties legs brains think your thoughts wear your skin be all the way in you yes YES!" tightening her labial lip lock, the doves scattering and rushing off to evince them winged and singular, she and Marcelle, borne skyward, wafted by the heat of their sexmaking, their limbs extended, the eggshells and the sea's rough play far below, their perfect wings thrusting them toward Heaven's high as deep inside Banshie the final option nuclear big bang exploding calamitous climax shroomed and she cracked shattering in an infinity of pieces not to be mended she *was One yes they were One a new light flared she became the light and the light sputtered, sputtered and dimmed, and...*

(Fade Out.)

CHAPTER 12

(Fade In.)

(Interior, Monday Morning. The hotel room's Bathroom. An exhausted Edie lies fast asleep in the bathtub, shivering: the tub is filled to the top with ice water. From Off Screen we hear the splash of the washroom's sink faucet gushing. She wakes with a start.)

EDIE: (Staring at the ice water in dismay) No-no-no-no. NO!!

(She jolts up, touching her waist, craning and patting, probing her kidney area for indications of recent surgery. She finds no wound.)

EDIE: Whew.

(To the sound of someone humming a jaunty air, Camera reveals the Clown on the reverse side of the closed shower curtain as Edie slides it to. He's standing in front of the running sink fixing his makeup, too absorbed in his business to mark her presence.)

EDIE: Hey Zeebo. Did you put me on ice?

CLOWN: (without turning) After you collapsed yesterday you looked feverish, so, yeah. You're welcome.

EDIE: Asshole. (stepping from the tub, she snaps up a towel)

CLOWN: (now he scowls at her, in sublime wroth) That's right, abuse the gentle harlequin. All *we* do is bring merriment to young and old, and what do we get in return? The high-hand treatment. A clown is a saint in greasepaint, but I suppose such is our sole reward for being a friend to mankind. *Bupkis!*

EDIE: (moves forward until she is inches from him) Ass. Hole.

(She sweeps by, bulldozing him out of her way, and enters the sunlit Bedroom. Symptoms of the previous day's convulsions are everywhere: displaced paintings, overturned furniture, scattered bed linen, orphaned articles of clothing. The window is shut, the room tranquil, Sunday's visitors gone. Behind her the Clown is framed by the washroom door, and before her lies Banshie, naked, sprawled face up on the mattress, unmoving. Clutching her towel to her chest, Edie strides to the bed and shakes her experimentally. There's no response.)

EDIE: Wake up, you.

(She shakes her more violently. Banshie's forearm flops off the edge of the bed and her knuckles strike the carpet with terrible finality.)

EDIE: Fuck me. (she pokes the corpse) Fuck me! I killed her. I'm a murderer. (she sees the Clown by the washroom, arms crossed, observing) I fucked her to death!

CLOWN: Eh. (blasé) Happens.

EDIE: Help me get rid of the evidence, or I'll kill you too!

CLOWN: Relax, she'll be fine. Her heart isn't beating, that's all.

EDIE: Wasn't there a dumpster below our window?

CLOWN: She does this all the time. Some yoga shit. Recharges her battery after a wicked night.

EDIE: What?

CLOWN: She'll come out of it. Sleeping Beauty. Put your lips to hers, it never fails.

(Skeptical, she bends and plants a smooch.)

EDIE: Nothing.

CLOWN: *Ahem.* Your nether lips.

(Edie grimaces in disgust, hurls away her towel, straddles Banshie's head, and subsides downward. After a moment, Banshie's eyelids drift open. She gasps and squints at her in glassy discombobulation. Relieved, Edie climbs off the bed.)

CLOWN: She'll be kinda loopy, though, for a while.

EDIE: How can you tell?

CLOWN: She—

EDIE: Never mind. Help me get her cleaned up and dressed, or I'll still kill you.

(They jerk her upright and transfer her from station to station like a lobotomy case, in Montage, as Narration resumes.)

There it was, Vogel. Scientific proof solid of two facts.

(Sticking her under the shower.)

Fact A, that girlfriend here didn't get her name by accident; and Fact B, that she was determined to be the immovable object and the unstoppable force, occupying the identical universe, and sadly the universe in question happened to be my own.

(Blow drying her hair.)

All week long I'd been bossing people's lives, and here was somebody else doing the same thing, but to Death itself. How could I compete with the living dead?

(Brushing her Mohawk.)

And the Expo was in the past, alongside my chance to be rehired. And anyway, another few days like this, and they'd be trying the Kiss of Life on me. And Banshie was a much better kisser than I am.

(Brushing her teeth, too.)

BANSHIE: (drooling suds) *Blas Begas...*

EDIE: Shhh.

So you had me beat. And worse, I couldn't leave Banshie alone in her fragile condition with a guy who wore size thirty-seven shoes. And she didn't carry ID, and she couldn't yet string two words together to tell me what the address was of the home for the criminally insane that she'd escaped from.

(Slipping her into her clothes.)

The only remaining choice was to deposit her at your *office door, remove my biohazard suit, and say, "Mazel Tov. You two deserve one another. Now be careful not to land on my foot when* you both *drop dead."*

(Edie fixes her and Banshie's makeup and puts on a fresh bandage. They guide her out of the hotel room, Edie slamming the door before the Clown can depart with them, leaving him mouthing silent obscenities.)

But karma had other plans, as it turned out...

(Dissolve to: Interior, Late Monday Morning, the Hallway outside Charlie's Office door. Papi Toro, an enormous, expensively accoutered but unsavory individual, rages at the sealed entrance, jiggling the knob and banging the glass. Ed, his nose the color and dimension of a festive Christmas tree bauble, stands in attendance beside him.)

ED: Many thanks, as I was saying, for your gracious invitation. My gratitude will surely be reflected in the quite laudatory *MEH* profile to come. I promise you'll be delighted. Are you certain Charles Vogel is in there?

PAPI: Where's the key I got from security?

ED: Left trouser pocket. About my story.

PAPI: We'll get there.

ED: I haven't given you the background information.

(Papi plunges two dirigible-tonnage fingers in his slacks, a key ring jangles loose.)

PAPI: Want to play, Vogel? We'll play. First hide and seek, then human piñata!

(Edie and Banshie approach. Banshie, dazed, lurks in a doorway; Edie lounges on the wall near Charlie's office, fists in pockets. She watches with a baleful expression. Papi finds and inserts the key, and sees her.)

PAPI: *Pinche cabrón!*

(Ed, seeing her too, covers his nose and slaloms behind Papi.)

EDIE: Who're you?

(Papi offers her a lethal glare, scrapes the key out and towers over her.)

PAPI: Who am I? *Chinga tu madre*, I'm the black fucking hole at the center of the galaxy, who am I. Papi Toro Gonzalez! I own this business! You work here, you work for me. And there's gonna be some goddamn blood-nasty business to befall, I tell you, when I track down our pal Mister Vogel. Who am I? Who the fuck are you?

EDIE: Shemales. We're taking the studio in a new direction.

PAPI: Get the fuck out. You're no guy. If you're a guy, prove it. Show me your cock.

EDIE: Sorry, I left it in my other pants.

(Charlie enters the hall on his way to his office, freezing when he and Papi lock eyes.)

PAPI: Vogel! Who's this creamsicle with the smart lip and the busted head? The Unknown Soldier?

CHARLIE: (drawing closer, hand outstretched) Papi, my friend...

PAPI: Look at the beat-ass three of you. If somebody is passing out ugly sticks, where does the line start?

CHARLIE: Papi, my good friend, I was about to call you!

PAPI: Mister Gonzalez to you. You got plenty of "Grade A trim" for Vegas, you lying *puto?* I was *in* Vegas, and where were you? You see? (raises his huge meat hook, the thumb poking heavenward) See my thumb? I haven't seen it myself for days, because it was up my ass while I waited for you to arrive. Soon it's going to be up your ass, "my good friend."

CHARLIE: Mister Gonzalez, Sir—

PAPI: Egg on my face, no girls and no sale!

CHARLIE: It grieves me you should believe I—

PAPI: Too late for that, *mijo.* You're on my dance card today. First, I'm going to cut off your *nalgas,* boil them down to a paste, and make you brush your teeth with *nalga*-paste. Then I'm going to dip you in molten wax, fill the wax mold with dung beetles, and promote Dung Beetle Charlie to the head of the studio. And finally, I'm going to strangle your mother, sell her body to science, use the money to buy a sewing machine, use the machine to sew patches on my elbows, and use my elbows to beat your brains out!

CHARLIE: Really, resorting to mothers is so unnecessary. I'm sure this is a misunderstanding?

PAPI: Because I should have been at the Bizarro World Las Vegas, you were hiding somewhere else on the map? "Us do opposite of all earthly things?" Prepare to be pounced upon, *ese!* (he pounds toward him, the walls shaking, plaster falling)

ED: (exposed, he whips out his notepad, writing) "The week's events culminating in their natural conclusion, as Toro and Vogel enact their Waltz of Death."

CHARLIE: What! Who's this?

ED: (writing) "...the hulking behemoth flung himself at the quivering wretch with homicidal abandon..."

CHARLIE: Shut up! Don't give him ideas!

PAPI: I've got an idea you'd like me to play Whack-A-Mole with your vital organs, *pendejo!* (he hurtles onward)

CHARLIE: (flailing) I'm a bleeder!

ED: "A broken man, bawling his death hymn."

EDIE: (inspecting her fingernails) He's right, actually. It is a simple misunderstanding.

PAPI: You don't mix in this, girlie. I'll spread you on a fucking cracker. (he clenches Charlie by the shirt front)

EDIE: To be frank, I guess you could say it's my fault. (peers upward) Right, Charlie? I was supposed to call Papi.

CHARLIE: (latching on in desperation) Uh, right. Right. 'Cause of the thing.

EDIE: Right. The thing where you were going to create a separate adult expo, in Atlantic City (Charlie's old back yard, he's got people there), to attract the East Coast trade that doesn't always go to Vegas. The small-to-medium companies and distributors, who tend to get lost in the bigger companies' headlights.

CHARLIE: Precisely! But the, watcha call, the logistics...

EDIE: Weren't particularized.

CHARLIE: ...the logistics were non-particularized!

EDIE: Did we burn the midnight oil or what, Charles?

ED: No. No. Not having it. When exactly did inspiration strike?

CHARLIE: (ignoring him) It was a last minute brainstorm that's definitely coming together, Papi.

PAPI: (to Edie) What happened to the New York expo, the, uh, the "East Coast Video Show"?

CHARLIE: (to Edie's inquisitive glance) Relocated to Baltimore a couple years ago as the "Home Entertainment Retail Expo." Went tits up, anyways.

EDIE: That's right, they were relocated to another town and given a different name, but it didn't save them. They still met with an untimely demise.

PAPI: Yeah?

EDIE: You can probably relate.

ED: (to Papi) Explore to the bedrock of your common sense, Sir. This is nothing but the biteless bark of a woman who—

EDIE: It's a major stop-the-presses story. Tragos, here, is going to write the exclusive for *MEH*.

ED: Exclusive nonsense!

PAPI: (continuing to hold Charlie up like a ragdoll) Us running the show behind the scenes, with other studios involved?

CHARLIE: Yeah, a big-fish-small-pond deal. Among the smaller outfits, we're a bigger fish.

PAPI: We're a bigger fish, with no guppies. You think I'm unaware your girls are in the wind? Word travels.

ED: (to Edie) I already have a story, much thanks to you.

PAPI: And what I heard, one of your hires has been taking a wrecking ball to my organization! Ariel Gann...Eden...

EDIE: Yeah, that was me. Eden Gann. Hi.

PAPI: (squinty reconnoiter) How do your panties fit, all the brass inside 'em?

EDIE: Empty rumors, you said it yourself. Would I be here at Pie-Rite, with Charlie, if that craziness was true? Please.

PAPI: Sensible. And the missing girls?

EDIE: We let 'em go. Clearing the decks, right, Charlie?

CHARLIE: (to Papi) Going for fresh faces, man. It's the lifeblood of the industry! (Papi relinquishes him. He smooths the front of his shirt.)

EDIE: Not all new faces, you understand. You also need the familiar. That's why Mister Vogel has asked me to stay on and have my own line where I introduce these new girls, and I'll be *the* face of the studio.

CHARLIE: Eh...

EDIE: I mean, how could I ever leave my Charlie? You couldn't *drag* me away.

CHARLIE: Yeah.

EDIE: Just *try* getting rid of me. I *dare* you.

CHARLIE: You're loyalty moves me. I could honestly cry.

PAPI: Touching, but how are you bringing in the other studios?

EDIE: The logistics he mentioned? It happens Charlie's number two man is no longer with us, so I've accepted his offer, his very generous offer, to play a more prominent role within the company.

CHARLIE: What! I, uh, you know, no assurances. Papi might not be on board with that.

PAPI: You, be quiet. You, continue talking.

ED: No. (waves his arms) Gentlemen, both feet in the real world, if you please. Allow me to guide you through the transactions of the last seven days, whereby hangs a tale which should shed the most pellucid of lights onto the proceedings.

EDIE: Sure, Ed. Why don't you tell Papi Toro about the article you're pushing *Wangler* to publish? And what it'll do for his business?

ED: (considering Papi, and dwindling several inches into his clothes) Well...heh...

EDIE: Or we could go on with the exclusive we were discussing?

ED: (rallying) Exclusive, yes, by all means!

PAPI: Other studios. Bringing them in how?

EDIE: Oh, that's why I brought Banshie here. She's worked for everybody. She knows the studio chiefs. Intimately.

BANSHIE: Bhurji...

PAPI: (rotating on his axis, to look at where she stands tick-tocking from side to side) Banshie? Phoenix? How did I fail to recognize you? You're my favorite porn star! (his gaze doesn't leave her for the balance of the scene)

BANSHIE: Blehh...

EDIE: She's a bit under the weather. Jet lag, maybe. Charlie, why don't you and Ed toddle off like loyal little soldiers, and Ed can call *MEH* to arrange a more congenial interview time (you can expect to talk to one particular friend of mine, too, Ed, and I'm certain she'll have lots to say to you), and you, Charlie, can make some phone calls in there, and I'll make introductions out here?

CHARLIE: I—

EDIE: Scoot.

ED: But—

EDIE: Scoot.

ED: (plodding off) They never spoke to H.L. Mencken this way...

CHARLIE: (glum resignation) Fine, whatever.

EDIE: (as he fumbles for his keys) We'll wait. (he unlocks the door) Almost there. (he retires into his office) And he's gone.

(to Papi) I'm snapping a mental Polaroid. I want to remember what kismet looks like. How in a classic love song, the verse and chorus lead to each other again and again as if they were meant to be?

PAPI: I'm tone deaf.

EDIE: Or, a delicious meal and a...horizontal wine tasting? A perfect pairing of two distinctive ingredients.

PAPI: Irritable bowel syndrome.

EDIE: Or, um, when they discover a decapitated corpse and later the head turns up in someone's refrigerator, and they have to stitch it back on?

PAPI: Now you're making sense!

EDIE: That could be the two of you. Body parts about to be stuck together.

PAPI: Miss Phoenix, may I buy you a cup of coffee?

BANSHIE: Coffee?

EDIE: Coffee, Banshie. *It's a stimulant.*

BANSHIE: Oh. Okay!

PAPI: (presenting his bicep) Might I attempt to escort you? (they depart)

EDIE: (snorting in disdain) Men!

(Whistling a country waltz, she grips the doorknob and we Dissolve to the Opening Scene of the two in Charlie's Office.)

CHAPTER 13

EDIE: And that, Charles, is how I spent my winter vacation.

CHARLIE: Well played, Gann.

EDIE: Mm-hmm.

CHARLIE: I would describe you as satanic, except Satan is the Prince of Lies, so he presumably has acting talent.

EDIE: (laughs) Yeah, my talents lie elsewhere.

CHARLIE: But are you positive you're gonna be able to reel in those studios?

EDIE: Hmmm. Will I be able to manipulate a studio boss into giving me what I want? Gosh, let me think.

CHARLIE: Good point. (pauses) Here it is: I surrender. You win. Satisfied? You're rehired.

EDIE: Me and Shelly both.

CHARLIE: Yeah okay, both on the payroll. (picks up a pen) Any bad habits I should know about?

EDIE: Uh, yes. (wracked with guilt) Ever since I lived among the cannibals of Melanesia a few years ago, I've developed an appetite for human flesh.

CHARLIE: (unperturbed) Shame on you! (he scribbles something)

EDIE: That my signing bonus?

CHARLIE: What else? Do I write ten thousand dollar checks to the Red Cross? (continues scribbling) Friggin' starving widows and orphans...they can each select one of my butt cakes and chow down!

EDIE: You ought to be more laid back, lover.

CHARLIE: Awright, okay, I can admit it. You were a worthy adversary. Doesn't diminish me in any way. Who said, "You can judge a man by the caliber of his enemies"?

EDIE: Samuel Colt?

CHARLIE: Could be Oscar Wilde.

EDIE: You read too much, Vogel.

CHARLIE: (smiles) As the little boy said, "Can I keep doing it until I need glasses?"

EDIE: Uh-huh...you're going to try charming me right out of my socks, aren't you, pookie?

CHARLIE: Socks are a good start. (puts down his pen) I calculated, all we've been through of late, the exchange of fisticuffs is at an end, we've showered and toweled each other off...

EDIE: Wow.

CHARLIE: Now is the time for some make-up sex.

EDIE: Yeah. That is not happening. Nothing personal, but I'd rather gouge out my uterus with a melon baller.

CHARLIE: (invoking the Muse of poetry) John Keats: "I met a lady in the meads full beautiful, a faery's child."

EDIE: I'm not fucking you, Charlie.

CHARLIE: "Her hair was long, her foot was light, and her eyes were wild."

EDIE: Not fucking you, Charlie.

CHARLIE: "She took me to her elfin grot."

EDIE: I am not f— "grot?"

CHARLIE: Grot!

EDIE: I'm afraid I'm currently subletting my "grot."

CHARLIE: Stay with me on this. Since you haven't used it for a week, I propose to scrape the barnacles off yer snizz with my dingus.

EDIE: Hmmm. My "snizz" doesn't really appreciate nautical references.

CHARLIE: How about this? What if I have here a portrait of your dog, with a gun to its noggin? (holds imaginary photo, raises imaginary gun) To wit: screw me, or I'll shoot the pooch?

EDIE: Do me a favor? Shoot the damn dog.

CHARLIE: (drops the imaginary photo in dismay) No kidding? Shoot your doggie?

EDIE: You are aware I don't own a dog, right? (rises)

CHARLIE: But hypothetically, though.

EDIE: Shoot the hypothetical dog. (she reaches, picks up the check)

CHARLIE: You'd let me shoot Fluffy, or was it Muffy?

EDIE: (she walks to the door) Shoot Muffy, Charlie. Shoot her in the belly. Make her suffer.

CHARLIE: Correct me if I'm mistaken, but I'm beginning to suspect there's only a remote possibility of action, here.

EDIE: (opening the door) See you on set tomorrow.

CHARLIE: Awright, Edie love. Tomorrow it is.

(Edie whirls in the doorway)

EDIE: Why Charlie, don't you remember? The name's Ariel. Ariel Caliban! (exits)

(Charlie sighs. Reclining and knitting his fingers behind his neck, he falls into a daydream. Accompanied by his voiceover NARRATION, we witness his sex fantasy:)

CHARLIE: The door creaked open, readmitting Arielle. She had changed to a short black dress, tailored to meet the curves of her figure, demur yet somehow daringly immodest. She eased into a chair. Charlie approached her and bending, lifted her skirt.

"Are you mad? No! Anybody might walk in!"

He crouched, and touching her hips, organized her body in direct opposition to him in her seat. Arielle breathed a murmur, low and undulant. She was suddenly, vividly alive. She allowed her legs to drift apart, watching him sit on the edge of his desk.

"I see you made yourself indelicate for me, beneath your clothing."

"Yes..."

"Well?"

Her resolve slipping, Arielle grasped the hem of her skirt, and drew it up the length of her thighs.

"Continue."

She squirmed, in a moment's indecision: the silence of the outside hallway gave assent. She slid the material to her waist, attending how the cool office air stirred her naked sex.

Charlie's eyes were heavy-lidded, his consideration almost devout, but his diction was clinical. "The remainder."

She straightened in her chair. She must keep nothing from him; she wanted to know his pleasures as an intimate would. Fumbling behind, she tugged at the zipper, and the fabric fell from her shoulders. "I have lovely shoulders, too," she thought, "Smooth, and flawless. And my breasts and my backside, all of me, a fine sapling, not yet marred by age or the elements. And my nipples are young buds, and my pussy is petals folded." She coaxed the dress down along her arms, awkward, unwilling to stand. Charlie's gaze had her rooted to the spot.

The rustle of the material as it slid under her and draped to the floor, and his odd, distended breath, were all the sound she heard. She saw the effect of her beauty in his eyes, how they reflected arousal and amusement back to her in equal measure. She closed her own eyes and shook her hair, shameless, expectant. She longed for his approval, and cared nothing for the rest.

When she extended her legs and looked up, a sleeper waking, she found him upright, rubbing his palms. She understood then that he was extraordinary. He was glorious. "An Adonis," she thought. "An Apollo." She could sing paeans to his manhood, could serve him in rites sacred and profane. She stared at the powerful swelling below his midsection, at the adroitness with which he swung himself in her face, jutting toward her in his trousers.

"I shall take you now," he said. "You will surrender to me as no man has caused you to surrender. You'll be mine to the soul, and for all time. Do you agree?"

Arielle felt she had entered upon a demesne with its own law and language, and feared a rash comeback might put her at hazard. But she conceded that she could, would, only say Yes.

"Use me as you will!"

He unbuttoned his trousers. She guided out his prick.

"Suck."

Instantly she was on her knees. She took the large well-sculpted glans in her mouth and without further ceremony, sucked it into her throat. She held him there precious seconds, rapt, before leaning away and grasping the shaft. As her head nodded, she heard him speak.

"You didn't hesitate because you knew you could do no wrong. There is no wrong in so-called Vice, in yielding to real pleasure."

Arielle removed him. "What is real pleasure? Isn't all pleasure real?" She resumed her ministrations.

"Nonsense. Every saint, and sinner, recognizes that true ecstasy is had by submitting to One greater than oneself. The commonalty live in shadow pleasures, endured by those unwilling to stare at the Sun and be blinded."

"Bfft—" Arielle removed his penis, "But, aren't there genuine and terrible vices, to be avoided?" She began sucking again.

"Pleasure and pain," Charlie said, "are two facets of the selfsame coin, and Vice alone encompasses both. To make do with one is to inhabit a partial existence, and so to be an incomplete person. In the future, Vice will assume its rightful place at the Crown of Creation."

Arielle shifted to his testicles, trying their weight on her tongue and deliberating. She said, "And am I to be impelled at this future religion without a say in the matter?" She laved the dome of his manhood, applying herself in particular to the slit, and moaning, swallowed him until her nose bumped his stomach.

"Yes," he said. "You must accept that the religion of pleasing me is no different than any other: you are acting out your destiny, and the will to resist is an illusion. A cosmic joke, at which gods like myself laugh!"

Though she craved the taste of his salty release, she halted and said, "What of virtue? Is there no use for virtue?"

She bent, sliding him between her lips. In a benediction from above, he cupped her chin and tilted it upward. "Beauty is the paramount virtue. That which is beautiful urges us into its orbit and beyond, where all else is the black folly of modesty, of false virtue, surmounted by the shining lights of countless wanton acts. Beauty is the spell and the spur."

Arielle stood, ashamed of her ignorance. She ached to learn more, to be deceived no longer. She envied Charlie's clarity.

"Am I beautiful?" she asked.

"Eh. You'll do," he said.

"Take me!" she whispered.

He cleared a space on his desk, stepped out of his clothes, and sweeping her in his arms, laid her on the bare, chill surface. Arielle raised her knees. She fondled her breasts, their tips actively expressing her eagerness. As he settled on top of her, he gathered her again in his arms, showering her with kisses.

She lusted for him and, in parallel, was overwhelmed. Apprehending and brushing aside her disquiet, he at once pushed into her. She believed he was too rough, she was not ready, she had succeeded in convincing herself that this was the source of her distress when he pierced her inmost quarter, and she knew that she hungered to be overwhelmed, indeed she must have it.

A scraping of feet on cobblestones. Hands clasped under long sleeves.

She melted where he was, more with each stroke, her warmth swelling to grip him. Her breath stopped.

The priest scourges the penitent's body.

She was present and yet lost in a reverie of exotic locales. She sensed a pressure behind her eyes and a lucid heat on her closed eyelids as if she lay swooning on beach rock, balmy silky water rushing past her in wave after wave.

Infante and infanta, twins joined at the hip.

Featureless onlookers thronged around them, to incite, to participate. She felt invaded in every part by callused hands, gross genitals, yellow teeth. She wept, her head thrown back, Charlie thrusting at her in a fury.

At the spinning center, Mars sextiles the Querent's moon.

Slipping into orgasm, she cried, "Come in my face! Oh, swear you'll come all over my face! Come on me, please! I want it, I love it so much!" and he pulled out and sent his seed flying in endless ropes onto her cheeks and her lips, in her hair and inside her mouth. She seized his penis and plunged it into her throat, urging him to completion.

Satisfied, he relaxed beside her.

They lay quiet for some time, staring at the ceiling. Then she sighed, "Oh, my dearest. You've made me a virgin, and taken my innocence once more. You're my first and last. There can never be another. From this moment on, I'll do anything, anything you wish. Command me!"

(Dissolve to Charlie in his Office, performing handstands in his lap, his computer blocking the viewer's eye line below his waist. His injured face has miraculously healed.)

CHARLIE: And you see now, Arielle, how the act of total submission to my smallest desire will make you, uh... uh... (torso rigid, he finishes himself out of sight) ah... aah... aaargh!... aaah... aaah... umm...

(Moira walks in the open door and freezes, a picture of disgust. She lurches into a lone shelf on the wall, toppling several items: books of erotic fiction, classical mythology, comic books, a history of Southern Louisiana, and a stack of loose DVDs, which scatter on the floor in broken shards.)

MOIRA: Hey!

(He glances up at her, panting.)

CHARLIE: ahhh... ahhhhhhhhhhhhhh.........

MOIRA: (...)

CHARLIE: ahhhhhhhhhhhhhhhhhhhhhhhhhhhhhhhhhhh. (deflates into his chair)

MOIRA: (gritted incisors) I-NEED-A-NEW-JOB!

(Grinning, he blows her a kiss.)

CHARLIE: *Cuca-monga!*

(Fade Out.)

AFTERCLAP!
(ABOUT THE AUTHOR)

Colwen Kirst... is a babe crying out in the wilderness.

's lips say no, but his eyes say yes.

ate his twin while in the womb,

just for the extra elbow room.

has shaved three seconds off his time.

looks longingly at the Primordial Slime.

speaks in rhyming four beat couplets.

strums strumpets. sexes sextuplets.

says, Give another chance to klezmer?

mixes business with pleasure; trademarks "bleasnure."

found Heaven too touristy. didn't stay.

needs a few more minutes of sleep, okay?

has mastered the Xuán Jī Bù stance.

struggles to do it while wearing Spanx.

won the popular vote, damn the luck.

gives somewhat less than a solitary fuck.

always sleeps with one eye open.
wants a hit of that shit you be smokin'.
rules his roost, but bows to fashion.
insists the "bleasnure" thing will catch on.
doesn't feel the least bit guilty.
overuses the Spanish tilde... Lo sieñto, I'll start agaiñ. Colweñ
Kirst...
gets you, he really does.
bestrides our planet like a colossus.
is tuned to his own personal bandwidth.
will gut you for the price of a corned beef sandwich.
heard the angels sing, in a vision.
advised them to work on their "Spread Mouth" position.
(that last one was for choirmasters only.
any mystery why I'm lonely?)
went to India with Mother Teresa.
left in an hour, to party in Ibiza.
hails our robot overlords:
"Hey, Klaatu barada nikto, Gort!"
suffers from terrible synesthesia.
thinks your voice sounds very fuchsia.
still believes in Santa Claus.
knows nothing about a quadruple homicide. Nothing. Why
would you think he does?
might be mankind's finest specimen.
understands his rights as they have been read to him.
is thought "the Greatest Bard of the Age."
has reached the bottom of this page.

CRAVEN, UNSEEMLY ASS-LATHERING BIT

Hi!

Publishing is a jungle. Reviews are machetes. If you're so inclined, leave an honest one. Don't worry, I have unshakeable confidence in your superb taste in literature; you read this book, didn't you?

--CK

1
2
3
4
5
6
7
8
9